THE FORSAKEN CHILDREN

CHILDREN

THE BRITISH HOME CHILDREN

NAOMI FINLEY

Copyright © 2020 Huntson Press Inc.
Copyright © 2021 Huntson Press Inc.

Huntson Press

Inc

All rights reserved. Without limiting the rights under copyright reserved above, no part of this publication may be reproduced, stored in or introduced into retrieval system, or transmitted, in any form, or by any means (electronic, mechanical, photocopying, recording, or otherwise) without the prior written permission of both the copyright owner and the above publisher of this book.

This is a work of fiction. Names, characters, places, brands, media, and incidents are either the products of the author's imagination or are used fictitiously. The author acknowledges the trademarked status and trademark owners of various products referenced in this work of fiction, which have been used without permission. The publication / use of these trademarks is not authorized, associated with, or sponsored by the trademark owners.

ISBN: 978-1-989165-34-8

Cover designer: Victoria Cooper Art
Website: www.facebook.com / VictoriaCooperArt

Editor: Scripta Word Services
Website: scripta-word-services.com

NAOMI FINLEY

THE BRITISH HOME CHILDREN

PREQUEL

THE BRITISH HOME CHILDREN

PREQUEL

LIVERPOOL-1921

CROUCHED BEHIND THE GRAVESTONE, SPYING ON THE GRIEVING FAMILY as they lowered the casket into the hole. A shadow swooped overhead, and the cemetery's guardian cawed. I elevated my gaze, and my heart lurched into my throat as the well-fed raven plunged straight at me. I ducked, avoiding its talons. Lifting my head, I scowled at the creature as it landed on the peak of a white marble mausoleum. Squeezing my eyes tight, I tried to regulate the rapid thumping in my chest, only to jump when the church bells struck three o'clock, sending the spirits of the dead scurrying over my flesh.

Blimey! Gnawing on my lip, I glanced from the Wolseley car parked on the roadway back to the funeral. The large-bellied priest's voice droned on, harmonizing with the soft weeping of a woman. In the deep shadows of afternoon the gravedigger waited, looking bored. After the deceased's loved ones left he would leave the grave exposed, walk to the alder tree that appeared to have existed since the beginning of time, and settle in to eat a hearty meal before his snores would disturb the peace of the cemetery.

Guilt swirled in my belly at what I planned to do, but I swiftly suppressed it.

Some days back, my six-year-old brother, William, had fallen ill. Mum's toil in the workhouse paid little. We required every coin to keep food in our bellies and shelter over our heads, leaving no extra for medicine.

Hunger knocked a constant reminder on my ribs. Two or three days had passed since I'd eaten. I'd lied to Mum that hunger had overcome me and I'd devoured my fill of the scraps the kitchen wench had tossed into the street on the way back, because there'd been scarcely enough to feed William and Mum. If she had known, she'd have insisted I eat hers, even though stress and malnourishment had hollowed dark circles under her once sparkling blue eyes and her cheeks were sunken. I felt her bones when she hugged me.

The priest fell silent. He and the family shared a few murmured words before he turned and hurried back to the majestic stone church perched on the hillside, its stained glass windows gleaming in the sunlight. For a moment I stood mesmerized. In my fifteen years I'd found little beauty in my harsh existence, but I often paused when passing through the graveyard to listen to the choir and admire the splendor and the colors.

A year ago, in the dead of winter, I'd hidden behind a wheelbarrow piled high with firewood as a gang of vandals pelted rocks at a side window and shattered the glass. Rage had boiled in my chest, and I'd considered delivering a good tongue-lashing to their leader, Brock Everly. He was around my age, but although I wanted to knock his block off, at barely five feet compared to his nearly six feet, I was no match. The plonker and I had been at odds for years, ever since he and his gang had encroached on my territory.

Brock had an irritating way about him. His cheeky grin was reflected in his honey-brown eyes, and if you weren't careful, you could get caught off guard when you rested there for a spell, which agitated me all the more. His cleverness could be your undoing. Like me, he relied on his wit and skills to take a stab at life. I preferred solitude. I snuck in, then vanished before anyone was the wiser. He led a gang of misfits. I figured the fool did possess a heart, the way he looked out for them. That didn't alter the fact that there wasn't room for two of us in my district. The area had been mine long before his scamps had shown up. I'd set him straight one day and thought we'd reached an understanding, but it seemed he had forgotten—a fact I planned to reacquaint him with the next time our paths crossed.

After the priest had run the scamps off he'd waddled back inside, and I stepped from behind the shed and strode to the window. I stared up at the dark hole where a stained glass dove had once been. Heart heavy, I bent and retrieved a shard of glass from the grass and regarded it with awe before tucking it inside my satchel. Hearing the weighted footfalls of the priest, I had fled.

The car's engine roared to life. I shook off the memory and all thoughts of Brock Everly, returning my focus to the task at hand.

The gravedigger moved to the grave, lifted his shovel, and threw several shovelfuls of dirt into the hole. My throat tightened with each toss of dirt. He looked over his shoulder at the church for signs of the priest, then to the roadway and the distant car, then dropped the shovel and strode to the alder tree. He lowered himself to the ground and dug through his sack, removing a package wrapped in brown paper. He peeled back the wrapper and I gulped, my stomach clenching with hunger. Raising the sandwich to his mouth, he took a huge bite. I moaned softly, salivating. Time ticked slowly by, and my legs cramped and tingled with pins and needles while I waited for him to finish. After what seemed an eternity, he slumped back against the tree, and minutes later, loud snores rose from his slack mouth.

I took a gander around to ensure I wouldn't be spotted before standing and dashing forward, only to land flat on my face, my legs betraying me. I cursed and rolled over to sit up and give my lower limbs a good rub before trying again. This time my legs didn't fail me, and I darted to the open grave.

Peering at the coffin, a shudder coursed over me, but without hesitation I retrieved the metal spike from my satchel and eased myself over the side of the grave. Using the spike like a piton, I made my descent, and dropped the last couple of feet, landing on the coffin with a soft thump. The casket was smaller than usual; the deceased man or woman must be of smaller stature. Crouching, I listened for approaching footsteps, but hearing none, I started prying the coffin lid open with the spike.

I knew how wrong it was to do what I was doing. My heart hammered in my chest and my eyes filled with tears, but I brushed them away with the back of my hand. William and Mum needed me. Just this one time and never again, I told myself.

After a few minutes' effort, the lid gave way and I caught my breath. I peered up at the blue sky and wondered if the ghost of the person within would haunt me for the rest of my days. Pushing the thought from my mind, I stepped into the narrow space between the casket and the earth wall. I squeezed my eyes shut. Then, without further delay, I pulled open the lid and opened my eyes. I gasped—a young child lay within. *Oh, bloody hell!* The wee lad wasn't much older than my brother. My lip quivered as I stood grappling with myself. Tears burned my eyes. Dishonoring a grown person, I may have been able to live with myself, but a child…well, it didn't sit right.

I was moving to lower the lid when sunlight glinted on the golden elephant clutched in the child's hands. I hesitated. An image of my brother's pale face appeared in my mind's eye, and I heard his cries. "I'll burn for this." I gritted my teeth, reached out, and pried the toy from the dead hands. "Forgive me," I whispered as the trinket came free. I dropped the treasure into my satchel and lowered the lid.

With the help of the spike, I climbed out of the hole. When

my feet stood above ground, I regarded the coffin. I made the sign of the cross, as I'd witnessed the priest do, and muttered another apology. I turned to leave.

A hand snatched the collar of my oversized long coat and whirled me around. The toes of my boots brushed the grass as I dangled before the gravedigger.

"You rapscallions don't have respect for the living or the dead. Grave robbing is a crime, and I'll see to it you pay for your greed."

"Please, sir. It's my little brother—'e's real sick."

"I won't hear it. 'Tis the same excuse I've heard time and again." His spittle speckled my face, and I regarded the remnants of lettuce hanging in his wiry black beard.

"But it's true," I said, tears echoing in my voice. "My mum works 'ard, but it ain't enough."

"Keep the pleading for the bizzies."

No! Panic surged, and I clawed at his arms. Without medicine, William would die, but unlike the child, he would be cremated and buried in a mass grave without markers.

"Feisty little lass, ain't you?"

I hung still. My strength was inadequate against the gravedigger's grip, and no amount of wit would release me either.

A flash behind him captured my attention, and before I could figure out what was happening, he let out a wail, and he let go of me. I collapsed to the ground in a heap. He whirled around to fend off his attacker. I caught sight of Brock, his keen eyes pinned on the gravedigger and his fists ready.

I gulped.

"Hazel, run," he said, ducking the bloke's swing.

I scrambled to get to my feet. "But—"

"Now!"

Without further protest I turned and ran, darting around

headstones until I reached the tree line. Only then did I pause to look back, and my throat squeezed at the sight of the gravedigger towering over Brock, splayed out on the grass. A wail lodged in my throat and a heap of guilt plunged into my belly, but again my thoughts turned to my little brother, and with one last gander, I turned on my heel and faded from sight.

———⟡———

I charged down the alley, with the butcher close behind. Mud splashed into my shoes and squished between my toes.

"Thief! Stop her."

Heart thrashing against my ribcage, I pumped my legs faster while tightly clutching the opening of my satchel, cringing with each squawk from the panicked hen inside. "Quiet, you bloody 'en," I said, as though she would listen. If I managed to shake off the butcher, the bird would give me away, and I didn't intend to fall into the bobbies' hands.

An image of Brock's dirty face and warm brown eyes flashed into my mind, but I gave it the boot and darted down a trash-filled alley before swerving to duck through an open doorway.

"Pardon me," I said to the family within, who didn't appear any better off than mine.

They gawked at me, and the reedy woman pointed at the back door.

I bolted back into the maze of Liverpool's slums.

Realizing the butcher's cries had faded, I glanced over my shoulder without slowing, but I didn't stop until stitches cramped my side and forced me to pause to catch my breath. In the shadows of a crumbly flat I gripped my side, breath heaving. The hen clucked her protest as I opened my bag to ensure I hadn't lost the medicine in the chase.

I'd paid a price that should see the doctor rot in a cell for abusing his practice by cheating Britain's impoverished. Back when my family had a proper home in London, after the war had returned my dad a stranger and a shadow of his former self, he had visited a doctor to tend the gangrene devouring his leg and his frail mind. The doc had taken care of him, all right. I bit down hard at the injustice. He had turned my dad into an addict, and only months after we'd moved to Liverpool, he had taken to the docks and streets, begging for coin. We never saw a shilling. Incapable of making the rent, Mum, William, and I found ourselves out on the streets. Some months later, a friend brought the news of Dad's murder. Someone found him in an alley, and a witness claimed that the culprit had stabbed him to death for a mere shilling.

I didn't think of him, as the pain was too much to bear. I stocked fond memories of our life before the war, times when Dad's dark eyes sparkled as he reminisced about how he'd captured the bonny lass from Ireland. Mum called out for him in her sleep, and I sometimes caught her daydreaming with a pensive smile on her thin, colorless lips.

"Life is too bloody 'ard." I choked back tears, kicking at a pebble and sending it bouncing off a stoop. I turned the corner and trudged to the dark, dilapidated shack we called home. The rifts in the plank wall did little to keep out winter's frigid wind, or summer's heat, or the stench of the decaying dead nearby. The bedroom fire grate doubled as a cooking hearth and, most days, it was inadequate for both that and warmth.

At the threshold, I pulled back the tarp covering the door as William broke into a coughing fit. I raced to the pallet made of blankets in the far corner of the shack and dropped to my knees. "William, it's me, 'azel." I rolled his small form over. Sweat drenched his clothing and pooled in the hollows around his large brown eyes, so like my dad's. I touched his hot forehead. The fever wreaking havoc on him continued its rage.

"You've been gone so—" He coughed and winced, gripping at his chest. "It 'urts real bad." His tears mingled with the sweat.

I removed the brown glass bottle from my bag. "I know. I've brought you medicine. You will be back to your old self in no time." I unstopped the bottle and lifted his head to place the bottle against his lips. "Just a small sip." Mistrust of the doctor's prescribed dose reduced the amount I would allow him. "That's a good lad." Relief rushed over me as he swallowed, but as another coughing spell erupted, I reached for the tin cup of boiled water I had tried to get him to drink hours earlier. Then, I hadn't been able to get him to wake. "'Ere, you must drink and keep the medicine down."

He managed a small sip.

"I've brought food to make broth," I said, and as though opposing my statement, the hen pecked at the side of the satchel and let out a soft cluck.

I tried to get William to take another sip, but he was too weak; he collapsed back against the pallet. "I can't." His whisper was more a croak. Misery shone on his pale face, and worry strummed in my chest.

"That is all right. A bit weary, you are. Nuffing a good rest won't cure. Lie back now." I poured some of the water onto a cloth and mopped his forehead and limbs. "I'll start the broth, and once you…" My voice drifted when I noticed his closed eyes. I lifted his small hand and kissed his fingers, his face a blur beyond my tears.

Pushing to my feet, I walked to the table made from wooden crates, set my bag down, and removed the hen. Holding her by the feet, I strode out the back door, grabbing the ax on my way outside.

Hours later, Mum returned filthy and weary from the workhouse, but she forced a smile and walked straight to William, who rested peacefully, thanks to medicine and a little food in his belly. She kissed his cheek before lowering herself to sit on the floor. Leaning back against the wall, she closed her eyes.

"Mum?" I stood with a bowl of watery meat stew I'd made from the hen and the last potato.

Her eyes fluttered open, and she peered up at me. "Please forgive me, luv. I guess I'm a bit weary today." She tried to pull herself up.

"No," I said a bit too loud, stilling her in mid-movement. "Please, don't get up." I knelt and held out the bowl.

Her small smile revealed gray and yellow-stained teeth, and the trembling fingers she lifted to pluck a feather from my hair were reddened from years at the workhouse. She peered into the bowl I handed her, and her brow furrowed. "How'd you come by this meat?"

"A kind bloke gave me an extra shilling for the flowers." I offered her my best smile.

Lying came easy for me. Most times I tried to stay close to the truth, but I wasn't opposed to doing what needed doing when life required it. Survival came to those who could outrun and outsmart those around them. The way I looked at it, if I stayed a jump or two ahead of people, I could never lose. Nights I lay awake, pondering on different scenarios and how I'd handle them if they arose. I suppose I spent too much time thinking about how I'd outwit Brock if I caught him trespassing. My skills with a slingshot could put any boy to shame. Now, though, as the thought surfaced, my heart felt heavy. Had I been wrong about him? He'd risked getting nabbed by coming to my rescue.

The deep channel between Mum's eyes deepened. "What is it, luv?"

"Nuffing. You bes' eat up." I squared my shoulders, displacing the melancholy dancing on my soul.

"Bless ya, luv. Don't rightfully know what I'd do without ya." The spoon rattled against her teeth as she took a bite. Closing her eyes, she moaned, and her face softened with a peaceful expression. A single tear cascaded over her cheek and disappeared into her unkempt tresses. "Saints be praised," she whispered.

Pride swelled in my chest. For tonight, at least, we would eat. I figured the sin of stealing the hen would be far less troublesome to her than robbing the dead. Glancing at my brother, whose chest rose and fell in deep sleep, I offered silent gratitude for the treasure I'd taken so he might yet live. That secret I would never reveal to anyone. So help me, God.

After ladling myself some stew, making sure not to take too much, I settled on the dirt floor next to Mum. We ate in silence, both lost in the luxury that warmed our bellies.

———◇◆◇———

Three days later, William's fever had broken and I was seated on the pallet with him cradled in my arms when Mum returned home early from her shift. One glance at her grimace told me something grave had happened.

I plucked the shard of stained glass from the broken church window from his small pile of treasures and handed it to him. "Stay 'ere; we shan't be long," I said. He bobbed his head but tossed a concerned look from me to Mum. "Ain't nuffing to worry 'bout." I cupped his cheek before pressing my lips against his blond curls.

Clambering to my feet, I walked to the back door without looking at Mum. Rolling back the tarp, I stepped out.

Outside, the pungent scent of decaying corpses that seeped

through the thin walls and tarpaulin doors of the shack became unbearable. I gagged, and bile burned in my throat. Across the alleyway, lying in sewage and puddles from last night's rain, an emaciated girl wept over her mother's body. It was only a matter of time before one of us joined the bodies lying in the streets and slumped on stoops. The chittering and squeaking of rats drew my attention to the rodents picking at a child's carcass. I stormed forward, sending the rats scurrying. A brazen raven dove in to have a go at the child who, upon further inspection, I recognized as Johnny, a boy but eight or nine years old. The harsh reality endured by Britain's poor did not discriminate for age. Last winter the cold had claimed his dad, leaving him an orphan. I had offered him a nibble from time to time, but any spare bits were rare. Life had seen an end to his misery, and I felt gratitude for that. Like so many, he was now food for the vermin, a sight that never became less jarring.

Mum joined me. "Did you know the lad?"

"Yes." I turned away, unable to stomach the sight.

Her footfalls stopped behind me. Too afraid to ask, I turned to face her and waited for her to divulge her reason for returning home early. The unemployment rates had soared, and Mum had been lucky to hold her job as long as she had.

"They let me go today. Said there ain't enough work."

The façade of strength I strove to maintain in her presence in hopes of easing her worry wavered. I stumbled back, and Mum grabbed my arm to keep me from toppling over. "But 'ow will we pay Mr. Milton the rent?"

I had returned one afternoon with William and paused at the sound of a man grunting. In the gap between the tarp and the wall, I'd seen Mum with her skirt raised and Mr. Milton's trousers around his ankles. Tears streamed down her face—and mine—that day. I'd witnessed my fair share of whores in darkened corners and understood what had happened between them. We had gotten behind in the rent after Mum fell ill with influenza last Christmas. The shelter the shack provided was barely worth a shilling, and certainly not the price she had paid to keep a roof over our heads. No matter how I tried, I couldn't pluck the memory from my mind. She had sold herself once, and I wouldn't stand by and allow it again.

She gripped my shoulder. "I'll find—"

"Well, there ya are," a voice boomed, and Mum and I spun to find Mr. Milton darkening the threshold. He looked down an oddly broad nose with unruly black curls jutting from the nostrils. The bloke had the face of a mule and teeth to match. "Word has reached my ears that you were let go today." He flashed a god-awful smile that made me cringe. "I won't take no excuse for collecting payment. Unless you are looking to wager up something more satisfying." His eyes raked me from head to toe.

"Leave off." Mum waved a hand in dismissal. Nostrils flaring, she marched to him and stood inches from his chest.

Glee radiated from his face as he peered down at her. "If you'd been a tad more lively when I had a go at ya, perhaps I'd consider giving you a break on the rent."

"I said, leave off." She bounced on her toes and jabbed him in the chest.

He threw his head back and laughed before pinning her wrist behind her back. "We will see who has the last say."

Leaning down, I plucked a rock from the ground. Squinting at my target, I took aim and with one swift movement, I launched it at his forehead. It found its mark. He wailed and lifted fingers to the gash gushing blood down his face.

"You're a proper meff, ain't ya?" He darted toward me, and I stepped back as Mum put out her foot. He stumbled and went down, hitting the ground hard.

I lunged for a broken board and landed a blow on the back of his head as he tried to rise. In my panic, I delivered another, followed by another until he lay sprawled in the mud, unmoving.

Mum glanced at the wretched neighbors who had gathered to gawk from Mr. Milton to us. She rushed to my side, removed the plank from my hands, and threw it into the alley. Then she knelt beside him and held the back of her hand above his mouth. Fear swept over her face, and she mumbled a few inaudible words before looking up with a big smile. "He yet lives," she said loud enough for all to hear, her smile never slipping.

She rose and gripped my arm and dragged me back inside.

"Ouch, Mum, you're 'urting me."

"Sorry, luv, but we'd best be gone before he wakes." She cast a worried glance back the way we'd come.

"What is it, Mummy? I 'eard noises." William stood, weak and trembling, a few steps from the pallet.

"Quick, Hazel, gather what you can," Mum said, then turned to William. "Nothing, pet. You be a good lad and do as your mummy says, all right?"

Grabbing my satchel, I shoved in a slab of stale bread and the blade. From the lone shelf, I gathered the flower Mum had worn in her hair on her wedding day. William's treasures, the last of his medicine, and the drab coat Mum and I shared followed. I glanced around for something else to shove inside, but there was nothing.

"Come, luv." Mum wrapped a coat much too warm for the weather around William's thin shoulders before hoisting him into her arms. Though he was thin, she staggered under his weight but caught her balance.

The look in her blue eyes was one I'd witnessed there before. The night Dad had returned home, changed. I recognized the look—clear, indisputable fear. Confused, I gawked at the back door, where Mr. Milton lay just beyond.

"Hazel, we must go now!" She darted past me.

I gulped and charged after her.

That day we walked to what seemed the ends of the Earth. Mum kept an eye over her shoulder and tensed at every sound. The strength she found to trudge into parts of Liverpool I'd never journeyed to before stumped even William. He, too, eyed her inquisitively as her bizarre behavior that had started in the shack continued. Surely Mr. Milton had a concussion, and wouldn't feel up to following us.

Over the next week we found refuge in doorways, stables, and gullies, and scrounged up any morsel of food.

The morning Mum stirred me from sleep, the stars still twinkled overhead. My clothes clung to my body from the downpour that had us huddling together until exhaustion had pulled me into a frightful sleep filled with Mr. Milton.

"Is it Mr. Milton?" I quickly sat up, my gaze scouring our surroundings.

"Shh," Mum hissed. "No, I believe there's no need to worry about him. There's something I must do." A shadow of guilt raced over her face. "I need you and William to stay here until I return. I'll be gone a few hours."

Leaning in, she kissed my brow before standing and clambering up the ravine. At the top, she paused, pain and heartache haunting her face. I frowned, but before I could call up to her, she turned and disappeared.

I worried if she would return, but then rebuked myself with a reminder of what I knew about Mum and the sacrifices she'd made to provide for us.

As the day wore on, we found ways to entertain ourselves.

We skipped rocks in the river, watched the seagulls, and picked out animal patterns in the clouds. But as night fell, anxiety picked at me. William had fallen asleep, and I lay close against his body, finding comfort in his nearness. Most days, it had been just him and me, and I wondered what either of us would ever do without the other. My heart hammered a little faster at the thought. Blinking off tears, I played with one of his curls, as I often did to make him fall asleep at night, and softly sang his favorite lullaby.

Sleep, my child, and peace attend thee,
All through the night
Guardian angels God will send thee,
All through the night
Soft the drowsy hours are creeping,
Hill and dale in slumber sleeping
I my loved ones' watch am keeping,
All through the night.

Mum returned with eyes red-rimmed from crying, and defeat slumped her shoulders.

"Mum?" I swallowed hard as she lay down beside me.

"Hush, luv. Sleep," she whispered.

I feigned the breathing of sleep. For a long time she shook, and her silent tears dampened my hair. I lay still until my body ached, permitting her the solace I had found in William's closeness some hours ago. Embracing the warmth of their bodies, I fell asleep dreaming of a place where hunger and cold didn't exist.

The next morning, she awoke us at dawn. "Come, children, we must go." Hollowness hauled at her voice. "Gather your things."

"Where are we going now?" William sat up and rubbed the sleep from his eyes. Always a happy lad, he never complained, and possessed a tenderness not compatible with the world.

"You will know soon enough. Let's be on our way," she said with a foreign bluntness.

He slipped a hand in hers and started the climb out of the ravine.

Again, we walked, and old blisters on my feet from ill-fitting shoes reopened and new ones formed. The seam on my left shoe gave way, and the front flap slapped happily as we trudged on toward uncertainty. Mum had indulged William with answers to his constant questions, but her mind seemed to scarcely focus on us. Soon William's energy depleted, and he grew weary, and Mum looked ready to fall at any moment.

"I can't go a step farther." William's face was sweaty and red from exhaustion. He perched on the bench outside a tall building with a sign I couldn't read.

William had never been to school, and of the years I had attended, I recalled liking the place at first, but as the months had dragged on, I yearned for the freedom that existed outside the schoolhouse's brick walls. However, when our lives had changed for the worse, I wished I could go back to that time, which seemed like a lifetime ago. I heaved a sigh and pushed unpleasant thoughts from my mind.

"It's not much farther," Mum said without looking at us. She had been avoiding my gaze the whole journey, and the time or two that our eyes had met, she dropped her head, and her lip quivered. I'd tried to swallow the panic gripping my throat, but it was no use.

What was she up to? And why did I feel our lives were about to change yet again?

But doing what I always did, I sought to calm her fretting and turned to my brother. "Fancy a piggyback?"

William's eyes widened, and a smile flashed on his face. "You ain't too tired?"

"What malarkey do you gibber? Why, I got legs of steel." I slapped my legs and bestowed upon him a first-class smile.

"No 'ill is too 'igh and no road too long. 'Urry up now, or the ride may take off without you." I knelt as he wrapped his arms around my neck, and I bit back the gasp as I pushed upright and he wrapped his legs around my waist. So small, yet so heavy. I gritted my teeth and glanced at Mum, who stood observing us with tears pooling in her eyes. "Shall we?" I arched a brow.

She lifted a dirty hand, brushed away the tears, and nodded.

The apprehension I'd been feeling all day sank deep into the pit of my stomach, but as she turned and continued down the street I attempted to reach God.

I know you ain't paid no mind to Mum's words or mine, but somefing is coming. I feel it in me bones. I don't know what it may be. But this one time, do you reckon you could lend me an ear? I waited for a sign from Him, but when He didn't answer I dropped the notion of asking a favor. Perhaps God was just another folklore or fable people made up to keep people believing in something.

Soon the city was behind us. About a mile into the country-side, we paused in view of a grand red brick house on a hilltop. A black wrought iron fence marked the home's perimeter, and we heard the squeals of children at play.

"What is this place?" I glanced at Mum.

"Our last hope." Mum swallowed hard. She stood peering at the place as though trying to find the courage to continue.

I gulped and looked back at the house.

"Can we play wif the other children?" William asked as I slid him to the ground.

Mum blinked and looked down at him, a sad smile playing on her lips as she cupped his curious face in her hands. "Yes, luv."

William grinned, let out a whoop, and hurried on ahead.

I stood trembling, my legs threatening to give out at any moment. "Mum, what 'ave you done?"

"It won't be for long. I'll be back."

"No." I turned to look at her, tears spilling over my cheeks as my reserve of strength evaporated.

"Hazel." She gripped my forearms. "I can't bear to see you and William suffer anymore. I've tried. God knows I have."

Suddenly indignant, I snapped, "Stop. 'E doesn't exist. If 'e did, we wouldn't be standing 'ere."

"I will find a new job. Once I have money, I'll return. They promised you will be cared for here."

"Is this an orphanage? We ain't orphans!" For the first time, I loathed her. How dare she abandon us! My belief in the goodwill of others had steered me wrong before…but my own mum? The devastation was too much to swallow.

Her hand slipped to her slender throat, and she looked bewildered. "What? Never. Do you think so poorly of me?"

"We want to stay together." I squared my shoulders and rooted my feet. "Together is how it should be. I will find work too. Please, Mum." My panic turned to heaving sobs.

She stepped forward and clasped the back of my neck, pulling my forehead to her lips. Her tears trickled down my nose. "Do not be cross with me. I wish it wasn't so. As much as I can't stand to see you go hungry another day, I can't imagine one night without you." She drew back, seized my chin, and forced me to look at her. The gleam of certainty in her eyes gave me some solace. "I will not abandon you. When I return we will leave Liverpool, and I know how you've always wanted to return to London. It should only be a few weeks, and then we will leave this hell hole once and for all. All right?"

I bobbed my head, but the tears never stopped.

"Good lass," she said.

"Mummy, 'azel, are you coming?" William's sweet voice called.

"Yes, pet." Mummy turned a beaming smile on him, but as

she glanced back at me the smile faded, replaced with sorrow. "I must ask you to be strong for you and your brother. Can you do that for me?"

Numb, I again bobbed my head. Strong? I was a master at feigning strength and courage, I thought sardonically. Even when I wanted someone to pick me up and carry me for a while.

"'Urry," William called again.

Mum slipped her arm around my waist, and together we walked to join my brother. At the gate Mum lifted the latch, and it swung open. I hesitated, giving the home a long gander before I proceeded up the pathway.

Inside, the stark white foyer and the eerie silence made me glance back at the door. Before I could escape, the click of heels on tiles announced the appearance of a stern-looking woman with the warmth of a brick wall. Mum and she exchanged words when she joined us, and she gestured and said with unsettling curtness, "Follow me."

As she led us down a window-lined hallway, I looked out at the children who'd been hidden by the front of the home. I decided they seemed happy enough. I turned my attention to the walls, naked of paintings or decorations, as empty of character as the woman we followed.

The hallway gave way to a large room where two lines of people stood waiting to speak to the women positioned behind desks. "Wait here, and when it's your turn, Miss Ainsworth will assist you." She nodded toward the chipper redhead sitting behind one of the desks. Without another word, she spun on her heel and clicked off.

The cheerfulness of the woman behind the desk drew my attention. She spoke to a woman dressed in a threadbare cotton dress and a thin blue sweater with more holes than not.

"You must know it is what's best. The opportunities are

endless. We have several receiving homes in Australia, across the British Isles, and as far as Canada. I know you want what's best for them." She looked to the little girl and older boy in chairs to my right.

The blonde child rocked on her knees and pressed her face against the windowpane, eyeing the children at play. "Look, Charlie, they got toys and everything."

The boy sat with a cap squeezed between his hands and never lifted his head to acknowledge her as tears plopped onto his dark trousers.

"They will receive an education," the woman continued in a cheerful tone that got under my skin.

I glanced at Mum, but she stood stoically peering straight ahead, so I looked to William, but he no longer stood between us.

"'Ello?" Hearing his bright voice, I twisted to find him standing before the little blonde girl.

She spun around in her chair and delivered him a delightful smile. "Oh, hello."

"What's your name?" William inched closer.

"Name's Alice Huckabee, and this is my big brother, Charlie."

William reached out and touched her arm, then snapped his hand back, as though she were a fragile doll that would break. She giggled and held out her arm for his inspection. "I'm a bit dirty, but Mummy says they will give us a proper bath 'ere."

William snuck a look at Charlie. Alice waved a hand. "Don't mind him none. He don't fancy baths. Says they're for girls."

William lifted his small fingers to stifle a giggle.

"Come, sit with me." She patted the chair next to her. William hoisted himself up. "What's your name?" She wiggled closer to him, as though starved of body and spirit.

"I'm William Winters. That me sister, 'azel, and Mummy." He pointed at each of us.

Although we stood second in line time moved slowly, and I tuned in and out of the conversations around me. The redhead continued to speak of foreign places. As she spoke, I pondered on the happiness Mum, William, and I could find in the lands of promise she crowed about, and for a moment, I almost believed her words. However, when our turn came, the woman looked from Mum to me and then back at Mum. "Is this your girl?"

"This is my Hazel." Mum beamed with pride.

"Perhaps she should have a seat until we discuss matters."

"Ain't nothing you can't say in front of her," Mum said, tipping up her chin.

The woman's brow dipped. "If you say so." She lowered her head and picked up a pencil. "Names and ages of the children."

"Hazel and William Winters. She is fifteen, and my boy is six."

The woman wrote in the ledger open before her.

"It is as I discussed with the headmistress yesterday. This is only for a short while. I will return for my children. You understand?" There was an unfamiliar harshness in Mum's voice.

The woman's hand paused, and she looked up at Mum. Her earlier upbeat demeanor vanished, and a hard glint appeared in her blue-green eyes. But, as quickly as it had gone, her gaiety returned. "Of course. It will be as you discussed with Miss King."

The stiffness in Mum's body relaxed, and she allowed a small smile.

"Now, I trust if you were here yesterday, you've already filled out all the paperwork."

"Yes, ma'am."

"Very good." She scraped back her chair and rose. "If you will excuse me, I will go and check that everything is in order."

The woman seemed too perfect, from her perfectly styled hair and her perfect yellow dress, not ruined by years of wear or the grime of the streets, to the way her curvy hips swung as she sashayed down the corridor. I decided I didn't like her—nuffing about her. A filthy rat, cloaked in yellow. I gritted my teeth. "Let us leave this place," I said to Mum. "I told you, I will find a job and prove to you we can make it work this time. I shan't let you down." Tears welled.

She stood stiff, but her eyes glistened with tears.

"Please, Mum."

"It's just for a while," she said, but I wondered if the reassurance was more for her than me.

After several moments, the woman returned with a forced smile that never passed her bright red lips. White teeth gleamed like the strand of pearls at her throat as she addressed us. "It appears everything is in order. Now, say your goodbyes. We will be closing our doors to outsiders for the day, and tea will commence shortly. If the children are to attend, they need to be bathed and clothed."

Mum turned to face me, smiling unsteadily, but her eyes shone with mounting panic. She strode to the chair and retrieved William, and without protest, he hurried to match her pace.

"Goodbye, Alice 'uck-a-bee," William called over his shoulder.

In the hallway, my feet froze as a woman in a white uniform strode toward us. However, it wasn't her that sent my heart into my throat, but the slumped shoulders and solemn expression on the clean face of the boy following her.

"Brock?" I clutched his arm as he passed.

His hair slicked back, he was dressed in new tan trousers, a crisp white linen shirt, and polished brown shoes. I'd never thought it possible for him to look so dapper.

He gasped and halted. "Bollocks!" he said, followed by a string of curses under his breath before his brown eyes, radiating sorrow, met mine. "You or me—I see getting caught or escaping didn't matter anyhow."

"They brought you 'ere?"

"After they let me rot in a cell for a week," he said. "Any chance you caught sight of the lads?" He referred to his gang.

"No." I wished I could tell him differently and somehow remove the heartache in his eyes.

He glanced at the window. "Little buggers counted on me, but I failed them."

It was my fault. Guilt ran rampant in me. "I'm sorry."

"Come along, lad. Miss King is waiting." The woman in white had paused at the end of the corridor.

Brock looked at the woman. "I'll be right there." He turned back. "Don't blame yourself. It was bound to happen sooner or later." He lifted a hand and gave my chin a gentle nudge. "Take care of yourself, Hazel."

I opened my mouth to respond, but all words left me and I stood like a gaping plonker. He smiled, and continued down the hall.

Nausea roiled in my stomach. Why had he looked so disheartened? The rat had said we would receive food, a place to sleep, an education, and a washing, amongst other luxuries I couldn't recall. But Brock had acted as though he still sat in a jail cell.

I glanced back the way I'd been headed, and with one final look in Brock's direction, I raced to catch up with my family.

They were waiting at the front double doors. Upon my arrival, Mum pulled me into an embrace and kissed my cheek. "I promise you," she whispered before stepping back.

My throat tightened, and my eyes burned, but I wouldn't allow any tears to fall.

"Mummy, are we leaving now? You said we could play." William's brown eyes searched her face in confusion.

"And you shall." Her brittle laughter sent chills rushing over me.

He frowned, looking around the foyer, then back to her. "Are you leaving?"

"Not for long. Just a short spell, and I'll be back."

"But I don't want you to leave." Tears pooled in his eyes.

She knelt before him and crushed him to her chest. "No tears, my boy. I'll come to get you as soon as I can." She regarded me over his blond curls, her blue eyes gleaming with tears.

I forced a smile. "Come now, William, it will be as Mum says. She will be back before you know it, and we will be together again." The lie rolled off my tongue, as they always did. True to his good nature, William promptly strode to my side and slipped a hand in mine.

Gratitude shone in Mum's eyes, and at that moment, I wanted to beg her yet again to take us with her, but she burst into tears and fled the building.

I wondered, over the years to come, had she always intended to leave us? Or had there been profound reasoning behind her decision?

THE FORSAKEN
CHILDREN

For the British Home Children and their families

PROLOGUE

Liverpool, 1921

COLLEEN HAD NEVER REVEALED TO HER DAUGHTER THE LIFE THAT had expired at her hands. After all, the swine deserved to die.

Now, the pressing urgency to put Liverpool behind them as a distant memory seized Colleen Winters's every thought. It was only a matter of time before the bobbies caught up with them, and she wouldn't see Hazel imprisoned for the death of their landlord. The lass had a whole life ahead of her.

She had left her children with the organization that arranged homes for British orphans with families throughout the British Commonwealth who were willing to adopt them and provide them with the means for a better life. It had been her only option—it offered food, shelter, and a hiding place. The day she had inquired about shelter for her children, the headmistress, Miss King, had scrutinized her over spectacles balancing on the tip of a narrow nose. After lengthy consideration, Miss King had claimed they wouldn't turn anyone in need away. She agreed to house Colleen's daughter and son for a few short weeks until she earned enough money to return to London. And now, at last, she had. Colleen had enough money to get them out of Liverpool that night.

At the landing outside the double glass-paned doors, she paused to catch her breath. The door behind her squeaked, and a weeping woman raced past her and hurried down the steps. She gawked after the woman, recalling her own distress a month or so prior.

"Can I help you?" a voice asked behind her.

She swung to regard the redhead who'd registered her children. "Aye; you may recall—"

"We deal with several faces every day. We can hardly recall everyone," the woman interrupted impatiently, a hard glint in her eyes.

"I understand," Colleen said, wanting to gather the children and be gone. "I've come to collect my children."

"Collect?" The woman's brows arched.

"That's right. Miss King agreed that your organization would shelter the children until I could earn some money. I understand I'm a bit late. I don't have much, but I'm willing to pay for the trouble." She forced a smile, trembling under the woman's scrutiny.

"What is your name?"

"Colleen Winters. My children are William and Hazel."

"I see. Wait here, and I will go and speak to Miss King."

"Would it be all right if I stepped inside, out of the sun?" The journey from the city to the countryside had left her ready to collapse. She glanced through the glass doors at the pitcher sitting on a stand inside the foyer. Her parched lips and throat begged for relief.

"I'm afraid that won't do. Stay here, and I will return." Before Colleen could protest, the redhead hurried back inside and disappeared down the hallway.

The sun stung her pale flesh, and time ticked slowly by. She sat on the steps, wringing her hands together. After a spell, she stood and went to the doors to peer inside for the woman. The foyer was empty, and the metal pitcher enticed her. Gripping the brass knob, she pulled open the door and crept inside. Lifting the pitcher from the stand, she filled a glass and gulped the water back, then lifted the pitcher again to replenish.

"What are you doing in here? I told you to wait outside."

Colleen's hand froze in mid motion. She set the pitcher down and swung around to face the redhead—and behold the scowling face of Miss King.

"I'm sorry, but you were gone so long. You see, I've made the journey here from the—"

Miss King put up a hand to silence her. "Follow me."

Colleen slipped past the other woman, who stood with her arms crossed, her face a mask of disapproval.

Inside her office, Miss King gestured to the chair in front of the desk before circling to seat herself. She peered across the desk at Colleen, who sat with her hands clasped tightly in the folds of her stained blue dress. "It saddens me to inform you that your children are no longer here," Miss King said.

"Not here? What do you mean?" Heart racing at the news, Colleen scooted to the edge of her chair.

"We expected you weeks ago. The agreement was a few weeks, and from the records, I can see it's been over a month. We aren't a boarding house."

"But if not here, where are they?" Tears collected in her throat.

"I suppose they are comfortable and enjoying the luxuries of their new homes."

"New homes? But—"

"Mrs. Winters, you are a widow without means to care for your children; it's our duty to help get children off the street."

"But orphans. My children aren't orphans."

"No, but you abandoned them and in the eyes of the government that makes them orphans. Don't you wish a better life for them, where—"

Colleen jumped to her feet. "Their life is with me. I'm their mother. No one will love them as I will." Limbs trembling, she pressed her palms against the desktop to steady herself before narrowing her eyes at Miss King. "Tell me where my children are. Tell me now!" Her voice resounded throughout the small office.

Miss King rose, towering over her. "Calm yourself, or I will have you removed without the answers you seek."

Colleen heaved a sigh, fighting back the tears. "Where are they?" Her voice hitched. "Please, I beg you, tell me."

"I suppose they would have landed in Canada by now."

A rift opened in her heart. Her voice barely a whisper, she said, "Canada?"

"That's right. The children will be awarded to new families."

"It can't be. I am their mother. I promised them. I..." The room spun, and Miss King and everything around her receded. Legs buckling, she plunged into a sea of darkness.

CHAPTER 1

The Atlantic Ocean, 1921

AM HAZEL WINTERS. A GIRL WITHOUT A HOME. A BURDENSOME BY-PRODUCT *of Britain's poverty.*

The evening meal roiled in my stomach as the vast ocean waves licked the ship carrying me and my six-year-old brother, William, and the other children, toward our new homes.

Weeks prior, hungry, homeless, and without hope, my mum had taken us to the organization that helped Britain's poor families and street urchins to achieve a better life. The lying rat with red hair, seated behind the desk, had smiled and crowed to another mum about the abundance of possibilities in a faraway land. Many nights, as I'd huddled with my brother and Mum trying to find warmth while my stomach burned and twisted with hunger, I had dreamed of such a place.

Before the war, we had a proper home in London. Although we had never known wealth, we had been happy. After Dad returned from the war as a haunted man and a stranger to us all he had moved us to Liverpool, but it was after his senseless murder that life became even more problematic.

At fifteen years of age, I understood Mum's struggle to ensure we didn't end up like the emaciated children whose corpses lay decaying in the alleys of Liverpool. But as Mum had walked down the front steps of the institute, I had an inkling that we'd never see her again.

If she had returned, it wouldn't have mattered; within days of our arrival, the organization placed my brother and me on a ship with other children headed to receiving homes in Toronto, Ontario.

"'Azel?" William's sleep-laced voice cracked beside me on our bunk. "We almost there?"

"Soon," I said. Silvery moonlight poured through the circular window and stretched across the cramped room we shared with four other girls. Miss Sinclair, our chaperone, had allowed William the security of staying with me, and I was grateful. I lifted his small fingers and traced them in the moonlight, soaking up every memory because, when we landed, I feared what would become of us.

"Will Mummy be waiting for us?"

"No." I swallowed hard. "But don't you worry none, 'cause she is finking of us, like we are 'er."

"'Ow will she find us all the way across the ocean?"

The innocence in his sweet voice gripped my chest, and thoughts I'd grappled with since our departure filled me with despair. The sea had swallowed up Liverpool and all hopes of our return to the safety of Mum's arms. All we had left in the world was each other.

I pulled him close, into the crook of my arm. "I reckon it'll be mighty 'ard."

He was quiet for a minute or two, then he said, "You ain't gonna leave me, right, 'azel? 'Cause I don't want to be alone."

"You shan't. Dad is watching over us."

"But I can't see 'im," he said.

"You don't need to. Just know 'e is." I stroked his hair.

His brown eyes pleaded with me. "You won't let no one take me from you?"

"You're tired. Close your eyes and try to fink of 'appy thoughts."

"I try to fink of Mummy. 'Er eyes and the sound of 'er 'eart against me ear. I'm afraid I will forget Mummy like I did Daddy."

Soon after Dad had left for the war, Mum found out she was pregnant. William never knew the man who'd walked through life with pride and devotion to his family. I recalled Dad's countless stories of the bonny lass from Ireland and my parents' courtship. And how his eyes sparkled when he swept Mum into his arms and broke out in dance while singing "Molly Malone." After releasing her, he would swing me around our small flat until, breathless, we'd collapse into a chair. I had resisted the memories of happy times because to think on them meant to recall all I'd lost. However, as the ship took us far from all we'd ever known, I clung to the mere glimpses in time. I bit down to stifle my sob and turned my head to hide the anguish twisting my heart.

"We must never forget where we came from," I said. "Sleep now. When you wake, I'll be right 'ere."

"Promise?"

"Promise," I said.

He rolled onto his side, and I scooped into the warmth of his body.

"Sing it, 'azel."

I hummed the Welsh lullaby Dad had sung to me.

Sleep, my child, and peace attend thee,
All through the night
Guardian angels God will send thee,
All through the night
Soft the drowsy hours are creeping,
Hill and dale in slumber sleeping
I my loved ones' watch am keeping,
All through the night.

Long after William's soft snores rose, worry chewed at me. What awaited us when our ship docked? I'd seen enough in my young life to understand the likelihood of William and I staying together was small. A kernel of anger wedged in my soul for Mum. She had abandoned us. Her choice to trust the people at the institute had cost me my family—the only valuable possession life had given me.

"Bollocks!" I scrubbed at the tears of defeat and fear streaming down my cheeks.

My thoughts drifted to Brock Everly and how he had risked himself to save me from the gravedigger, only to be nabbed himself instead. Our paths had crossed again at the institute. Then on the dreadful day when we stood in line on the docks in Liverpool. He had observed me over the other children's heads, and I'd expected to witness hatred but found only sorrow before he turned and boarded a ship headed for Australia.

Because of me, he sat on a ship heading somewhere far from home, away from the young gang of lads who had counted on him to survive. The knowledge of what my actions had cost them all sheathed me in a tomb of guilt from which I couldn't break free.

CHAPTER 2

S OME DAYS LATER, WE DOCKED. MISS SINCLAIR, AND THE OTHER workers assigned to guarantee the children from the emigration organizations reached our destination, herded everyone off the ship and onto the congested docks.

"All right, form a line," Miss Sinclair said. The lads' chaperone, Mr. Barnet, an unsmiling man with a pomaded black mustache, stood beside her, holding a bunch of strings from which dangled signs. "Mr. Barnet holds signs stating your name and age. You will wear these around your necks until you reach your new homes. Here is where we all must part. I will accompany the girls to their receiving home, and the lads will go with Mr. Barnet. An advertisement has already gone out in the newspapers, and we expect your new families to start arriving soon."

I stood numb and trembling as a staff member slipped the sign around my neck.

William tugged on my hand. "Our new family wants a girl and a lad, right?" His eyes shone bright with building anxiety.

Silent tears cascaded over my cheeks as my fears became a reality. "I don't know if we're gonna get the same family."

"But I want to be wif you." Tears streaked his cheeks, dirtied from the journey. "I'm skeered."

"Me too." I placed my arm around his shoulders. Beyond my swelling tears, Miss Sinclair's face faded. Around us, younger children whimpered while older siblings tried to calm them.

"Listen up!" Mr. Barnet's voice thundered, and we jumped. A hush fell over the children.

"You mustn't be sad. This new life is far better than the one you had in England. It will be hard, but you will not go hungry." Miss Sinclair smoothed back the dark tresses escaping her hat. I'd have considered her face pleasant if indignation at her disregard for the fear and heartache rippling through the children didn't consume me. "Lads, move to the left and follow Mr. Barnet. Miss Smith and I will see to the girls. Now let's not delay. Hustle."

William turned into my side and pulled at the fabric of my dress. "Please don't let them take me. You promised Mummy you'd take care of me."

His words struck me in the heart. A promise doomed from the start, I thought. I used the sleeve of my navy dress to blot my tears and lifted his chin. "Oh, bloody 'ell, William. I don't want to leave you any more than you do me. But we ain't in charge 'ere. I know you're skeered. Now, remember what I taught you?"

He nodded. "Me sister is 'azel Winters."

I repeated the endless questions I'd tried to drill into his memory during our voyage. "'Ow old am I?"

"Fifteen."

The urgency tightening my chest intensified. "Where did we come from?"

"England."

"Where in England?" I shook him a little too roughly, and he whimpered.

"Liverpool."

"What are our parents' names?"

"Colleen and Alfred Winters."

"Good lad," I said. "You mustn't forget."

He shook his head.

"Now, what do I always tell you?"

"That I'm stronger than I reckon," he said.

"And?"

His lip quivered. "Nuffing in life is too 'ard as long as we love each other."

"That's right. For now, we must live in each other's 'earts. You are my brother, and I love you, and no one can ever take that from us."

"Come, come, move along." Miss Sinclair nudged me forward.

"'Azel!" William wailed, and I felt his grip on my dress loosen. "No, I want me sister. Get your 'ands off of me."

My heart fractured. Anguish coursed through me, and I glanced over my shoulder as Mr. Barnet grabbed hold of William, who bucked with outstretched hands and pulled at the air as though trying to reel me back.

"Move." Miss Sinclair's hand guided me into the line.

The fear in my brother's pleas rooted my feet, and I turned to her. Her eyes widened with surprise at my determination. "'Ave you no mercy? Let me say goodbye," I said.

"Very well. Make it swift." She turned to steer the other girls.

I pushed through the others, and when I reached William, Mr. Barnet released him and he ran to me. He fell against me and squeezed my waist as sobs racked his tiny body. "I can't live wifout you. I ain't strong. I ain't..." His tears dampened my dress.

I peeled him off of me and bent until I was at eye level with him. "I want you to promise me somefing."

"Anyfing."

I pointed up at the heavens. "Take a gander at that sky up there."

He bobbed his head and arched back his neck.

"When you're 'appy or troubled, fink of me and know I will

be finking of you. During the day, look for my face amongst the clouds. At night, search for me amongst the stars, and I will do the same. Although the land may separate us, we will share the same big sky. Okay?" I looked at him, and he nodded. "I will find you. One day we will be together again. 'Old onto that. Promise me."

"I promise," he said.

Mr. Barnet stepped forward and put his hand on my brother's shoulder. There was no empathy in his dark eyes.

I dropped my small black suitcase with the few belongings the home in Liverpool had given to us all. Pulling William into my arms, I squeezed him with all my might, until I thought his frail body would break. "I love you," I whispered in his ear.

He fought back sobs. "I love you too."

I held his face between my hands and kissed each of his cheeks before I straightened.

Mr. Barnet directed William toward the line of lads exiting the docks, and he craned his neck to see me. Through blinding tears, I lifted a hand and waved, watching him go. *I will find you,* I breathed. After they had faded into the crowd, I dropped my hand to cover my heart before retrieving my suitcase and turning to catch up with the girls.

CHAPTER 3

A S WE ARRIVED AT A BROWNSTONE BUILDING WITH A WRAPAROUND porch I inhaled the air, not contaminated with the sewage and decay of Liverpool's slums but redolent with the scent of blooming summer flowers and fresh-cut grass. A willowy woman with a mass of freckles guided us up the stone walkway and past an oversized sign staked in the front yard. The brief education I'd received left me unable to read or write, but I studied the letters' arches and strokes, determined to fix them in my memory.

Inside, several women clad in black cotton dresses and white pinafores greeted us. They took our pictures and entered our names and details into a ledger. Then we were passed off to a middle-aged brunette woman with a hostile face. Unlike the other women, she wore white cotton gloves. At her side stood a blonde woman with her head lowered and hands clasped in front of her.

While the girls murmured amongst themselves, I inspected my surroundings, intent on capturing the place's layout. I mentally mapped the walnut staircase that rose to a landing, where a tall, lanky woman dressed in a high-neck cream blouse and dark skirt stood observing us with a hawk-like visage and an unreadable expression. She braced her hands on the railing, and a key dangling around her neck glimmered. I assumed by the looks of her that she was a person of importance. Pulling my gaze from the intensity of the woman, I plotted the front and interior doors and the windows on my mind's sketch before focusing on the wardens positioned in front of us.

The head warden glanced at the woman before turning her attention back to us. My heart leaped as her voice sliced through the foyer. "Silence!"

An immediate hush fell over the girls. A smaller girl of seven or so gripped her sister's hand and whimpered. The sister, not more than a year or two older, put an arm around her shoulders, never letting her eyes leave the warden. I envied them the security they had in each other, at least for the moment.

"That is Miss Keene, the 'eadmistress." The woman craned her neck and pointed a crooked index finger at the observer on the landing above. "My name is Miss Scott, and this is Miss Appleton." She gestured at the younger warden, who gave us a small smile and fluttered a wave. Miss Scott's face twitched as though she was irritated by Miss Appleton's gesture. "We are 'ere to answer any questions that may arise and to manage your needs. Now form a line, single file, and follow us."

She led us to a room where a hostile scent slapped me in the face and scorched my nose. White linens covered beds lining opposite walls. The polished floors and stark gray walls gave the room an emotionless aura, like all the happiness and warmth had been sucked out.

"You will stay wif us until your new families come to get you. Miss Appleton will see to your needs. Matters of greater importance will be 'andled by myself and, if need be, the 'eadmistress. We run a tight ship, and insubordination will not be tolerated. Understood?"

A chorus of "Yes, Miss Scott" rang out.

She squared her shoulders. "Good. It's getting late. Drop your fings, and Miss Appleton will take over from 'ere." She turned her all-seeing gaze on Miss Appleton, who seemed to cower under her intense demeanor. "I expect you to 'andle the girls accordingly and ensure a repeat of last week doesn't occur."

Miss Appleton kept her head bowed. "I will see it doesn't."

Miss Scott marched from the room, leaving Miss Appleton and us staring after her.

"Welcome, girls." Miss Appleton leveled a nervous but pleasant smile at us. "I hope you will find your stay with us satisfying." She had an accent unlike Miss Scott. Likely born and raised in Canada. She probably never endured a hard day in her life.

No one spoke. I stood eyeing her with curiosity. Why had the headmistress put a woman of meek demeanor in charge of us newcomers? She hardly seemed capable of dealing with Miss Scott, let alone a gang of guttersnipes. Everyone knew a fortress was only as strong as its weakest soldier.

Miss Appleton gulped under our inspection. "Find a place to put your suitcases down. Then follow me. First you will bathe and change into new clothing. After that you will go to the dining hall for your evening meal."

We did as instructed and hurried to follow her as she retreated down the black-and white-tiled hallway to the door at the far end. She gestured for us to enter. Inside the white-tiled room, staff stood waiting. Several metal appliances at about head height jutted out of the walls. Miss Appleton pointed to a bin to our right as we walked into the room. "Remove your clothes and put them in there. Then you're to shower. The staff are here to help the younger children."

Splattering drew my gaze to the metal appliances. They were spouting water. Although we'd become accustomed to bathing during our time at the home in Liverpool, we'd done so in clawfoot tubs. Each bath drawn had allowed for three girls to bathe before the water had turned murky. My heart beat faster, and I saw my nervousness reflected in the gawking faces of the others.

"Now, hurry along. Your evening meal will be served shortly, and Miss Keene detests tardiness. She will unleash her displeasure on us all." Miss Appleton stepped forward to assist the weeping child from earlier. The staff followed suit.

I unbuttoned my dress and let it slip to the floor before removing my undergarments. Trying and failing to cover myself, I walked to the first open spot and stepped beneath the water. As it splashed over me, its chill snatched my breath and rattled my teeth. When the water warmed, I backed into the waterfall and lifted my hands to stroke my fingers over my shorn blonde hair. Upon arrival at the institution in Liverpool, they had shaved our heads to rid us of lice, and after catching my reflection in a mirror, I'd marveled at how I could pass as either a boy or a girl. The hardship of life on the streets had stunted my growth, and my breasts had never blossomed. It was on the voyage that I first noticed the crimson dampness staining my undergarments.

Bathed and dressed, I walked with the other girls to the dining hall. Miss Scott and Miss Keene's unsmiling faces awaited us. When we were seated, metal plates holding mashed potatoes, peas, a slab of bread, and a single hunk of pallid gray meat were placed before us. Exhausted and famished from our journey, I dove in. While I ate, I eyed Miss Keene and noted the panicked glance Miss Scott threw in her direction. Moans of satisfaction rose from us as we scooped the mashed potatoes into our mouths. Gravy oozed between my fingers and down my face.

"Stop!" Miss Scott's face contorted with disgust. "Are you savages? You will use your utensils like civilized people, or you won't eat tonight or any other day."

A look of disapproval flitted over Miss Appleton's face, and she craned her neck to look at Miss Scott but promptly regressed to her previous submissive behavior. *Ain't got a lick of a backbone in her*, I stewed.

Hunched over my tray, I stared at the girl across from me, who sat gawking back. We straightened and lifted the napkins next to our plates and wiped our faces and fingers. Murmurs and the clatter of utensils striking plates filled the dining hall.

Miss Scott stood at the head of the long metal table with her gloved hands clasped in front of her. "When you're finished, you will go outside for fresh air until you're called in to prepare for bed. Lights go out at 7:30 sharp, and each day you will rise at 6:00 a.m. After breakfast, you will perform your chores and then join Mrs. Steward for your daily studies."

Studies? Well, at least one promise the redhead rat in the institute in Liverpool had made proved correct. Our new wardens intended to teach the "street savages" to learn. Although I'd never had much use for learning, I realized that learning to read and write might do me good if I intended to find my brother.

I spooned a mouthful of potatoes into my mouth. Blocking out the chattering around me, I decided I needed to concoct a new plan if I were to survive in this sham of a promised land.

CHAPTER 4

FTER DINNER I JOINED THE OTHERS IN THE BACKYARD ENCLOSED BY a black wrought iron fence. Small children raced around, caught up in a game, while other girls engaged in conversations. I moved away from them and strode to the fence to gaze at the empty fields that lay beyond. Thoughts of my brother and how scared he had to be feeling tugged at my heart, and tears brimmed in my eyes.

I tipped my head back to look at the sky and whispered a prayer. "I reckon, if you are up there, you might do me a favor. Would ya mind watching over me brother? And, if you ain't too busy, could you send 'im a family to love and care for 'im?" I crossed myself as I'd seen a priest at the boneyard do while I hid behind a gravestone to see what treasures the family intended to bury with the body. I gulped. I guess the guilt of what I took that day would follow me all my days. Don't get me wrong. I've done my fair share of thieving to survive. I warn't a saint, and no pearly gates would open for me, but taking from the grieving... well, it warn't right. I lowered my head, ashamed I'd asked a favor when I warn't fit to be heard.

"Do you think He is up there?" a squeaky voice said behind me.

I turned to find an auburn-haired girl with wire spectacles and jutting teeth. "What?"

"God." She squinted up at the sky. "Do you think He exists?"

I shrugged. "I reckon believing 'e does is better than feeling alone." Just weeks ago I had questioned His existence, but desperation gripped me.

She looked at me. She appeared to be around twelve years old. "I'm Lucy."

"I'm 'azel."

"I heard you mention a brother. Is he all you got?"

I wanted the solace of solitude. A moment to gather my thoughts. Was that so much to ask? I stifled the urge to turn away. "That's right. At the docks, they separated us."

She lowered her gaze. "That's what they do. I ain't seen me sisters since they went to their new family. They didn't want me. I've been here for months now, and not a single family has taken me. I heard the staff talking 'bout sending me back to England if someone doesn't choose me soon."

"Why did they take your sisters and not you?"

She lifted her dress to knee height to reveal the metal braces strapped to her legs. "Ain't much use to them, I guess." The emptiness in her words thickened my throat. "The young children have a better chance of being adopted into families that will raise them as their own, maybe even love them. But the older ones work their farms like mules."

"'Ow do you know this? They said we'd be adopted and given a proper education." *Whether we wanted one or not.*

She slapped her knees and belted out a laugh before shaking her head. Her mockery made me clench my jaw. "Played you for a proper meff, did they?"

As I narrowed my eyes at her, she sobered. "Don't worry none. They tricked a good many. When you've been here as long as I have, and you ain't got anything to do but walk the empty halls until a new shipment of guttersnipes or returns come, well...you hear things. Just last week, another girl was returned by a family."

"Returned?"

"Yeah, that's what I said. Here, if a family takes you and they don't take a liking to you, they can bring you back. Sort of like a library system. Borrowed and returned." She pointed to a reedy brunette hanging back in the shadows of an ancient tree with massive branches that stretched over the yard. "You see 'er? That's Clara, the girl that was recently returned. She said the missus put her up in a stall in the barn as though she were no better than the animals. Served meals to her there, too. Clara was in charge of cleaning and cooking meals, but the missus didn't like her none. Not from the day her husband brought her home. Said Clara was too pretty, and she didn't like the way her bloke looked at her."

I regarded the way Clara stood with her gaze flitting around the yard, as if she expected to be jumped at any moment.

"Her flesh is seared with the marks of the hot poker the missus punished her with if she spotted so much as a speck of food on the clean dishes," Lucy said.

Nerves fluttered in my chest. What if the homes awaiting us were filled with such horror? William's face flashed before me, and I felt physically ill. "Leave off." I lifted a hand to shoo her. "Go on. Skedaddle."

"I don't mean to frighten ya. But take my advice: you bes' toughen up if you expect to survive out there." She nudged her head at the open fields. "Besides, He ain't up there. I tried Him for many nights after they took me sisters and He ain't ever answered back."

My knees knocked as I turned away and gripped the knobs of the fence for support. *Please let it not be so.* I gulped back the rising tears as torturing thoughts of William suffering at the hands of his new family played in my head.

Gabby Lucy left me to go unleash her depressing words and advice on other unsuspecting newcomers. I spent the next hour conjuring up happy memories of times before the war.

"Oh, William." My body shook, and tears fell as I gave in to the fear and worry. How could I possibly find my brother? I didn't know where they'd taken him.

I braced as a gentle hand rested on my shoulder, and I glanced at the blue, red, and yellow paint staining the fingers.

"Please don't cry."

I spun to find Miss Appleton standing behind me. Compassion softened her countenance. "Care to tell me what troubles you so?"

Yeah—I didn't want to come here. The ember of heat that had smoldered in my chest since the day Mum had left us at the institution ignited. I scrubbed away my tears and peered at her. Although she seemed different from the rest of the wardens, I wouldn't trust her or any other who denied they were holding us against our will.

"I suppose I should expect you to consider me no different than them." She glanced at Miss Keene and Miss Scott, standing on the back porch, engaged in conversation. "They can be quite intimidating."

I saw what she was doing. Yes sir, saw right through her. Presenting herself as the good warden while keeping an ear and eye open for any information she could run back to the headmistress.

The evening breeze ruffled the locks of hair escaping the tight knot on top of her head. The same hairstyle pulled back the brows of all the staff. She attempted to smooth the wisps back into place, and catching me staring at the color staining her fingers, she held them out for my inspection. "In my free time I like to paint. It's an escape for me."

"What you escaping from?" I thought the question remained in my mind, but my lips parted in surprise when she replied.

She glanced at the house before her gaze turned to Miss Keene and Miss Scott. "This place."

"If you don't like it, you can leave. Some of us don't 'ave that choice."

She turned to look at me, her mouth unhinged at my boldness, and hurt flashed in her eyes. I swallowed hard, wishing I'd held my tongue, though I didn't know why—I didn't owe her a bloody thing.

"What is your name?" she asked.

"'Azel Winters.

"Everything isn't so clear-cut, Miss Winters." She walked to the fence and gripped the knobs as I'd done earlier. Taking a deep breath, she released it as a sigh. Curiosity pulled my feet forward, and as I stood beside her at the fence, she said, "You seem like a clever girl. I saw how you inspected every nook and cranny. You must know girls of your age will be the first to go." She sent me a sideways glance. "I don't mean to be blunt, but a sound mind is a necessity to survive. Set your mind so you may face what comes."

Why did I get the feeling she was warning me? Had Gabby Lucy been right? My heart thrashed as I peered at the fields speckled with wildflowers before returning her gaze. "If you care so much, why do you allow children to be enslaved?"

The coldness in my tone summoned a pained gaze from her. "That is fair." Eyes downcast, she picked at the paint on her nails. She turned to leave, but paused and touched my arm. "I don't allow it; I aim to stop it." She strode away, leaving me gawking after her.

Later, after Miss Scott had locked us in our room for the night, I considered Miss Appleton's words. I decided I would keep my eye on her. Something told me there was more to her than I'd thought.

CHAPTER 5

T HE NEXT MORNING, DRESSED IN NAVY BLUE UNIFORMS, WE GIRLS marched in a single file behind Miss Scott to the dining hall. Chatter and whispers rustled through the line. Miss Scott quelled the girls by coming to a sudden halt and sending each of us plowing into the person ahead. Protests arose.

Miss Scott peered down the line. "Let's keep it down, shall we?"

"Yes, Miss Scott." Our voices were loud in the corridor.

"Very well." She spun back around and continued marching at a uniform pace that reminded me of the soldiers patrolling the streets during the war.

Someone bumped me from behind, and I looked at Lucy as she motioned for the timid girl between us to skedaddle. The girl gawked like a simpleton, but seemingly aware of Lucy's seniority, she obeyed. I kept my eyes on the knot on top of Miss Scott's head, ignoring Lucy until her hot breath moistened my neck.

"Doesn't Miss Scott remind you of a giraffe?" she said.

"'Ow you reckon?" I continued my observation of the back of Miss Scott's head.

"Why, she has a neck much too long and ears that stick out like trumpets. I bet she can hear me even now." She lowered her voice. I glanced over my shoulder, and she flashed a crooked smile. "Did they nab you from the streets too?"

I ignored her. When breakfast finished, I planned to inquire about William's whereabouts, and Lucy's nattering put us at risk of punishment. I couldn't waste time. What if the receiving home shipped my brother off to somewhere else before I could find him? An invisible weight rested on my shoulders.

In front of us, a willowy girl tilted an ear to eavesdrop before craning her neck to look at us. "I got me a dad. We ain't got a lot, but we had each other. He probably thinks I'm dead in a gutter somewhere. Never got to say goodbye." Her lip quivered, and she turned away.

The ache of her grievance resonated, and I swallowed hard. "I'm sorry," I said, but she never acknowledged me.

"All right, 'ere we are." Miss Scott stepped to the side of the double-wide entrance to the dining hall. "Form two lines and take your seats." She rolled a gloved hand, gesturing everyone to hurry.

Staff waited along the walls. I took a seat, and Lucy plopped down beside me. I threw her a dirty look and angled my body away from her. The girl was insufferable. Why didn't she go find someone else to pester? I blocked out the chatter around me and stared out a window overlooking the street. I studied the cars, and people proceeding about their lives with little consideration of the injustice forced upon the children inside this building. If they were aware, why didn't they care?

Servers placed bowls of porridge before us, and a hush fell over the room. I glanced at the other girls before lifting my spoon and taking a bite.

"It doesn't matter how long I've been here, it still tastes like watered-down slop," Lucy said with a pout.

Across from me, the older girl with broad shoulders and a nest of frizzy brown hair paused her spoon halfway to her mouth. "Guess you ain't been hungry enough."

"Why's that?" Lucy scowled back.

"'Cause when you're picking your food from the streets you don't much care where it's coming from."

"How about you mind your business," Lucy sneered. The nitwit had no sense about her. The other girl could take her down with one swipe of her arm.

"When my ears can hear what you're nattering, that's my business. So if you ain't liking that porridge, send it on over here." She bent forward and made a swipe at Lucy's bowl.

"Leave off." She swatted at the girl.

"Then shut your yap." She bared her teeth, and Lucy gulped, dropped her head, and hurried to finish before the other girl got any ideas.

The girl leveled a hard glare at me when she caught me staring. "You got a problem?"

I bit back a remark, not looking to get myself locked up before I could secure my brother's information. I eyed the ogre. I'd seen her kind before: the loud type who sought to dominate and instill fear. No matter how big and mighty they thought themselves, they always fell the hardest.

"I was talking to you."

"No," I said.

"You bes' put your mind to eating before someone cleans up for you."

I shoved in a mouthful and swallowed. The slimy texture proved every bit as unappealing as Lucy had claimed. While I ate, I felt the older girl's eyes burning through me, and when I glanced up, she curled her lip and growled like a beast cornering its prey. *If only I had my slingshot. I'd deliver a blow between her shaggy brows and drop her to the ground.* But Miss King at the home in Liverpool had confiscated the slingshot, and in doing so, she may as well have cut off my left arm.

After breakfast the newcomers followed Miss Appleton

to the meeting room. She paused at the doorway and turned to watch us walk in. As I walked past her, she smiled and said, "Good morning, Miss Winters."

"Morning." I glanced past her to the headmistress standing at the front of the room with her hands clasped together.

I joined a row of girls and focused my attention on the key dangling from Miss Keene's neck. I wondered what door it opened.

After the last girl filed in, she addressed the room. "I trust your first night with us was enjoyable and that you slept well." With each word she spoke, she added an extra beat, and I suspected the habit could become quite annoying.

"Yes, Miss Keene," we responded. I moved my lips, but never spoke aloud.

"Today, each of you will visit my office and answer a list of questions before joining Miss Appleton for a tour of the building. Afterward you will attend your assigned classes, where your studies will commence."

A murmur arose.

Miss Keene held up a hand. "I understand most of you haven't had the privilege of attending school and likely can't read or write, but until your new families come to get you, your time will be spent wisely."

"What if we don't care to learn?" the loud-mouthed girl from the dining hall blurted.

Miss Keene looked at her. "Miss Digby, isn't it?"

"Beatrice is me name." The brazen girl rocked on her heels and held the headmistress's gaze.

"Well, Miss Digby. You will learn one thing around here, and that is we don't tolerate disobedience. Not the slightest trace." Her stern gaze moved over the girls in a warning. "Anyone who disregards the rules will be punished. Each act will determine the most suitable discipline." She removed the clipboard tucked under her arm. "In alphabetical order of surnames, each of you will visit me in my office, which is located by the front foyer. The first on my list is Miss Brown." She glanced up from the clipboard. "Miss Brown, lift a hand."

A girl who had bunked with William and I on the journey stepped forward.

"Ah, there you are. Follow me. The rest of you can wait here until Miss Appleton summons you." She left the room with the girl on her heels.

When my turn came to meet with Miss Keene, I paused outside the open door of her office. She sat behind a walnut desk, scrawling in a ledger, but her hand stilled and she glanced up. "No dallying; come take a seat." She nodded toward the chair in front of her desk.

I did as instructed and sat waiting until she finished her writing. The office had a different feel than the rest of the building; more inviting, one might say. Patterned gold and emerald wallpaper adorned the walls, and heavy green velvet drapes accented the windows. Pictures of lush countrysides in gold frames hung on the walls. On the desk lay a ring of keys—usually a permanent fixture at her waist. A framed photograph of an unsmiling girl with two dark braids, clad in a uniform like the ones we wore, standing on a train platform with a satchel clutched in her hands.

Miss Keene cleared her throat and I looked her way to find her staring. "Does the photo intrigue you..." she glanced at the ledger "...Miss Winters?"

No more than anything else in the dreary place. I shrugged and remained silent.

She gestured at the photograph. "I was nine there. It was taken by the first family who took me in upon our arrival in Winnipeg." She peered at the image as if recalling the day.

"You were an orphan?" My mouth unhinged.

"Yes. You see, Miss Winters, we aren't that different."

But I'm not an orphan, I wanted to say, but I wasn't looking to cross her. My reunion with William depended on my good behavior.

She continued. "Too many nights I sat huddled in the slums of London, trying to stay warm. Spent my life begging and stealing just to survive. That is no life for a child."

Neither is a life where you pluck children from the arms of their mums. I glared at her as she studied the photo a moment longer.

She shook her head as if to displace past memories and smiled with a hint of pride. My scowl deepened at the warmth in her dark eyes. Did she actually believe in an organization that would transfer children without their parents' consent? Children she knew full well weren't orphans. As it dawned on me, I wondered how her perceptions could've become tainted. I slumped in my chair as melancholy gripped my heart.

"Shall we get started?" she said and, without taking a breath, continued. "Tell me, Hazel Winters, what were your parents' names?" She held the pen on the page, waiting.

"Me dad's name was Alfred, and me mum is Colleen."

Her writing ceased, and she peered at me, all traces of cordiality evaporated. "We only provide boarding for orphans. It would serve you best to remember that. There will be no talk about families or your life before now. We don't want to trouble your new families with such dreary matters. Do we?"

I trembled under her cold inspection. "No, Miss Keene."

She fixed a smile on her face. "Now where were we?" she said with a sweetness that never passed her mouth.

Back where you chose to deny the truth. I kept my face unreadable, despite my simmering anger. If someone can't look into your soul, they can't touch the most vulnerable parts of you, and vulnerability was something I'd sought to shake.

"Did you go to church with your family?" she asked.

"If you consider 'iding out in the graveyard and listening to the cathedral's choir, I guess I've been to church."

She arched a brow and compressed her lips.

I sat taller and cleared my throat. "No, Miss Keene."

Her brow softened, and her expression turned to one of pity. "It's a shame. So many of you children come in here as nothing more than heathens."

I didn't want her pity or anyone else's. I recalled the robust lady, dressed in furs and a fancy velvet hat, who had referred to me as a heathen after I'd nicked her pocketbook.

"So I can mark a no to attending Sunday school," she muttered to herself. "Whereabouts were you staying in Liverpool?"

If I said with my mum, I would earn a look of disapproval. If I said in the gutters, I'd receive a look of pity. What did the woman want from me? "With me brother," I said.

"Your brother?"

"That's right."

"I need his name for my records."

"'Is name is William. And 'e is six. We've never been apart. I'm more like a mum to 'im than a sister." I wondered if I should have added the last part, but I needed her help to determine where Mr. Barnet had taken the lads.

"When did you last see your brother?"

"Yesterday. We came 'ere on the same ship. They brought me 'ere and took the lads somewhere else. Do you suppose I could see me brother?"

"Hardly," she said curtly. "Perhaps he will be adopted."

But he's got a perfectly good mum in England. We don't need no stranger trying to mother us.

"Is the boy frail?" she asked.

"A bit, I suppose."

"Sickly?"

"'E was a while back."

"Too frail to work on a farm and young, too. The boy's chances of finding someone to take him in may be slim. Families are looking for capable hands to tend their fields."

I gritted my teeth. She spoke as though we were merely mules.

"Well, that completes my questions. You can go and join the others for your studies."

"But me brother?"

"It's best you forget about him."

Forget about him? A fire flared in my belly. She may as well have told me to forget the need to breathe.

She stood. "Hurry now. The others wait." She walked me to the door.

At the threshold, I halted and peered up at her. "Miss Keene?"

"What is it, girl?"

"'Ow do you sleep at night?"

Her jaw dropped. "Pardon me?"

"I don't reckon it's easy to sleep when you spend your days tearing families apart."

She gasped before regaining her composure. "You watch your tongue, Miss Winters. Or I'll see you are dealt a punishment you won't forget."

I gulped at the glint of danger in her eyes. Had I crept too far into the lion's den? My shoulders slumped, and a look of satisfaction settled on her face.

I turned on my heel and walked into the hall to where Miss Appleton waited. She exchanged a look with Miss Keene and lowered her head in resignation. *Coward! You bloody coward.* Tears blinded me as I looked through the warden wishing, she, Miss Keene, and the nightmare I stood in would vanish.

CHAPTER 6

A FEW NIGHTS LATER, I STOOD BY MY BED, BUTTONING MY nightgown, when Gabby Lucy strode in and plopped down on the bed.

"Can I 'elp you?" I raised a brow.

"Saturday is coming." She sat swinging her feet.

"And?"

"They're coming."

"Who?"

"The visitors."

My heart seized. "So soon?"

"They come every second Saturday." She glanced around the room at the others. "The stock is plentiful this time, so many will come."

Nausea whirled in my gut, and I lowered myself down on the edge of the bed. I couldn't leave yet. I hadn't found out where they had sent William. I chewed on my lip as tears pooled and dropped onto my nightgown.

"Don't fret none. Maybe it won't be so bad." Lucy's shoulder nudged me.

I peered at her through blurry eyes. "But me brother."

"What about him?"

"I need to find out where they sent 'im. I must." Panic heaved in my chest.

"I told you. It's useless. You may as well consider him dead."

Her bluntness stabbed a blade through my heart. "Shut up!"

I leaped to my feet and lunged at her. "Shut the bloody 'ell up!" Pinning her wrists to the bed, I straddled her midsection. "I'll find 'im. If it's the last fing I do, I will find 'im."

Fear shone in her eyes. "I'm sorry. I didn't mean…" she blubbered, struggling to release herself from my hold.

A hand clutched the back of my nightgown and yanked me back. I clawed and kicked before the person overpowered me and snapped me back to my senses.

"You will be punished for this." Miss Keene glared at me. "You were warned I wouldn't condone the behavior of guttersnipes."

"Please. I must find me brother. 'E needs me," I pleaded with the soulless creature clutching me. Snot trickled down my face as uncontrollable sobs shook my body.

She released her hold on the back of my nightgown. Gripping my forearms, she shook me so hard my teeth rattled.

"Please." I clasped my hands at my chin as my hopeless weeping continued.

She lifted a hand and smacked me hard across the cheek. My head snapped backward. The shock and sting of her blow stopped my words and summoned silent tears.

"Miss Keene!" Miss Appleton strode forward and slipped an arm around my shoulders, pulling me in to her side. "The girl is distraught, is all."

Miss Scott entered the room and stood gawking at us.

"That is quite enough," Miss Keene said. "From both of you." She looked a warning at Miss Appleton, who flinched under her stare. "If you had been competent enough to handle the girls, none of this would have happened. Maybe I should've put Miss Scott in charge of the wards—she rules with a firm hand. Perhaps you aren't cut out for this job."

Miss Appleton's shoulders arched back, and she lifted her

chin. "You are wrong. I'm more than capable of handling the girls."

I snuck a look at Miss Scott, who stood tensely watching the situation. I was dumbfounded by the uneasiness I glimpsed on her normally stern face. It was like a crack in stone.

Miss Appleton glanced past Miss Keene and opened her mouth to continue, but Miss Scott shook her head as if to stop her. For the briefest of seconds she stood firm, but then her arm dropped, releasing me. "Do what you must."

Miss Keene smiled tightly in grim satisfaction. "I see you've come to your senses. It would not be wise for you to challenge my authority in my institute. We will discuss your behavior in more suitable surroundings." She eyed the girls who had gathered. "All right, girls, back to preparing for bed. Miss Winters will find herself in solitude. Upon my return, I expect you all to be in bed. Now step away, Miss Appleton."

One of the smaller children began to weep. Avoiding my pleading stare, Miss Appleton lowered her head and hurried to calm the child. My heart plummeted to my belly.

Miss Keene gripped my arm and pulled me toward the door. Her hold had me running on my tiptoes to keep my arm from being pulled from its socket.

"Miss Keene, do you fink it's necessary?" Miss Scott touched her arm on the way by, and Miss Keene came to a sudden stop.

"Not you too. Do I find myself immersed in a complete rebellion? The girls, now my staff." Her tone was lethal.

"It's just..." Miss Scott's words drifted as Miss Keene leaned closer.

"Breathe another word, and you and Miss Appleton will find yourselves removed tonight," she said through clenched teeth.

She straightened and continued to the door, where she paused and looked back at the girls. "I will not tolerate another outburst tonight. Do I make myself clear?"

An eruption of panicked voices responded: "Yes, Miss Keene."

The clicking of Miss Keene's shoes on the tiles as she marched me down the hallway coincided with the thrashing of my heart in my ears. At the door at the far end of the corridor, she paused and yanked it open. "You are about to learn what we do with girls that disrupt the order." Still clutching my arm, she descended the stairs into the unknown darkness.

No. Please, no, my brain screamed. I had feared the darkness for as long as I could recall. "I'm sorry, Miss Keene. I won't do it again. I give you my word."

"It's a bit late for that." She fumbled in the dark. "We don't need any more of Britain's trash."

There was a click, and light enveloped us. I lifted an arm to block the glare. As my eyes adjusted and she hauled me down a narrow corridor, heat kindled in my core.

"What's wrong wif you people?" I said.

She halted abruptly and spun to face me, jerking my arm tighter. "You people?" Her spittle freckled my face. "Said people took you out of Britain's slums and provided you with shelter, food, and a family."

"I'm not an orphan," I said. "I got me a proper family. We were 'appy."

"Happy?" She snorted. "How can someone like you know the first thing about being happy? Even your own families didn't want you."

Miss Keene's words sliced to the depths of my very soul. My conflicted feelings about my mum surfaced. "That ain't true." I balled my free hand and took a swing at her. "Take it back!"

"You can bet your bottom dollar it is. You might not be an orphan, but a number of parents leave their children at our organizations because they can't be bothered with the burden of them." Her lip twitched as she beheld the effect of her words.

I loathed her from the toes of her polished black shoes to the knot of hair where a horn should have sat. My gaze settled on the pencil tucked behind her ear, and for one troubled moment I envisioned my revenge. I shook my head, sickened by the mental image, and slumped in her grip.

She smiled. "Come to your senses, have ya? Very well, come along."

I walked beside her, the void in my heart expanding as wide as the Atlantic Ocean. Had Mum taken us to the home in Liverpool with the intention of never returning? She wouldn't do that to us, would she?

Miss Keene removed the key ring secured to her belt and unlocked a heavy metal door and pulled it open. Moonlight shone through a small barred window high on the wall opposite. It was scarcely big enough for a toddler to pass through, and the cement-walled room it illuminated wasn't much bigger than a closet. Panic thrummed through me.

"In you go," she said.

I planted my feet. "Please, don't do this."

As though I'd strained her last nerve, she gave me a hard shove. I stumbled, and before I could recover she shoved me again. I hit the floor hard, and the door slammed shut behind me.

"No!" I pushed to my feet and charged at the door. "Don't leave me in 'ere. I'll do anyfing." That last sounded hollow and empty as defeat overcame me.

"Good night, Miss Winters," she said, her words almost inaudible.

I turned and leaned against the door as my legs buckled, and I slid to the ground. "No, no, no…" I moaned, banging my head against the door until all sense had probably rattled from my skull. Pulling my knees up to my chest, I pressed my face against them and wept.

CHAPTER 7

T HE MORNING SUN SHONE THROUGH THE WINDOW, WARMING MY face. Body and neck aching, I raised my head, then pushed up from the cold cement and leaned back against the door. I took a gander around this makeshift prison fashioned for those foolish enough to disrupt the order of Miss Keene's establishment.

In the far corner, a gray wool blanket was the only bed, an old rusted chamber pot the privy. The room was the epitome of bare bones. Our shack back home had more comforts.

I stood, my legs numb from sleeping on the cement floor, moving stiffly. I walked to the window and craned my neck to peer at the bright blue sky, partly blocked by the fat white cat sunbathing in the grass. Resting my cheek against the wall, I thought of William. The ache to hold him and hear his sweet voice tore at me. Tears streamed as I hummed William's lullaby until my thoughts pulled to the day Mum had lost her job at the workhouse, and our landlord came looking to collect the rent. The vision of him lying sprawled out in the mud surfaced, along with how Mum had rushed me inside and told me to gather our things. Then we had fled, never to return to the wretched shack. Now, though, I would have done anything to go back.

Keys rattled in the lock, and I turned and pressed my back against the wall, bracing for whoever approached. The door swung open and my breath caught as I beheld the stern face of the tyrant. Under Miss Keene's inspection my knees knocked, and the need to elevate myself into her good graces took precedence.

She returned the ring of keys to her belt. The woman's need for perfection and order puzzled me. Not a hair on her head was out of place. Not a wrinkle marred the fabric of her crisp white blouse and ankle-length navy skirt that appeared to be from the past decade but revealed no wear. Even the buckle of the leather belt cinching her narrow waist gleamed. My gaze moved up, fixing on the key dangling around her neck.

"Well, what do you have to say for yourself?" The harsh snap of her voice pulled my gaze to her face. The channels etched alongside her unsmiling mouth deepened.

Jaw clenched, I knelt and clasped my hands under my chin, as I'd played it out in my head the night before. "I'm sorry, Miss Keene." I lowered my head and peered at the ground. "I was wrong. I shan't ever disrupt the order again."

"That's right, you won't." She paced around the room with her arms clasped behind her. "You were told what would befall any girl who did. Isn't that right?"

"Yes, Miss Keene." My eyes followed her gleaming brown shoes.

"What is to be done with you, is the question. One insubordinate girl causes a stir amongst the rest. You must be punished, and severely, as a reminder to anyone else who lacks common sense and steps out of line. With visitors coming, we can hardly withhold meals from you. Or give you the thrashing you deserve. No, we need you fattened and fit so that a troublemaker is removed quickly." She halted, then I watched her shoes spin to point at me. When her shadow stretched over me, my heart lodged in my throat, but I didn't look up.

"You will not continue your studies with the other children. You will spend the remainder of your days on your knees, scrubbing every last inch of this place. A lesson I too once had to learn for my rebellion against the headmistress."

You're a fraud. A bloody fraud. The devil himself. She warn't one of us, because if she was, she wouldn't have the stomach to govern an institution that enslaved children.

"You will wait here until Miss Appleton arrives with your breakfast and clothes. Then you will return upstairs to begin your task. If I hear about one more act of disobedience, I will keep you locked away until next month's visitors arrive. Do I make myself clear?"

"Yes."

"Yes, what?" she demanded, her voice clipped.

"Yes, Miss Keene."

She turned and marched out. I jerked when the door slammed, then the lock rattled, securing me in my prison. Bitterness ran rancid over my tongue. "Plonker!" I spat at her retreating footsteps. I pulled to my feet and walked to a corner by the window and sat down. Heaving a sigh, I curled into the wall and wept. If I expected to find my brother, I needed out of this bloody prison. I'd taken the last shred of pride I had left and placed it at the tyrant's feet, to no avail.

My tears at last spent, I remained curled against the wall and waited for Miss Appleton's arrival. I traced an index finger over the grooves and crevices in the wall while plotting what I'd do, once I was back upstairs. My finger paused as lines etched in the bottom corner of the wall captured my attention. I straightened, then lowered myself to get a closer look. Someone had scratched letters into the wall. I again felt frustration over my inability to read.

A key clattered in the lock, and I pulled to my feet. When the door opened and revealed Lucy cowering behind Miss Appleton, I launched forward, ready to strangle her. "What the bloody 'ell is she doing 'ere?" I bounced on my toes with animosity.

"I'm sorry, Hazel." She poked her head around Miss Appleton's shoulder.

"Like 'ell you are."

"Miss Winters, I suggest you watch your language," Miss Appleton said without a stitch of rebuke in her tone. She strode forward and held out a dull-looking blue cotton dress. "Are you all right?"

I squinted up at her. "What do you reckon? The old coot threw me in 'ere like I was a criminal."

"But, you disrupted the order…" Lucy's voice faded as I leveled a glare at her. The contents of the tray she held—a bowl filled with unpalatable slop and a spoon—rattled. My breakfast, I assumed.

"If I 'ear that word one more time, I'm going to do away wif myself. Besides, it's your fault." I turned away.

I heard footsteps behind me. "I should never have said that 'bout your brother," she said. "Sometimes I speak before I think."

"'Cause you're a gobby." I spun and jabbed a finger at her.

"Hazel." The gentleness in Miss Appleton's tone and the usage of my first name drew my eyes to her face.

I crossed my arms. "Well, it's true. She is loud and always nattering. She's a pest, like a flea you want to squish." I gritted my teeth on the last word. I wanted it to soak in good.

Tears welled in Lucy's eyes, and her bottom lip quivered. I looked from her to Miss Appleton, and the disappointment on her face cut a bit, but I pushed it away. What did I care about what the warden thought? She warn't no mate of mine.

"You ain't no better than them, so stop pretending to be me mate," I said to her, and when a glimmer of hurt crossed her face I waved a hand in frustration. "Leave off, why don't ya." I turned away.

Miss Appleton, having none of my sass, circled to stand in front of me. "Because if you don't want to spend another night in here, you'd best get dressed and upstairs. Now, off with that dress, and let's make haste."

I reckoned the hard day's work ahead was a mite better than being locked up in the dungeon. I unbuttoned my nightgown and slipped on the dress.

Lucy crept forward and held out the tray, but I shook my head, resistance on my mind.

"Eat up." Miss Appleton took the tray. "You will need your energy for the day ahead."

I ate what I could stomach and lifted an arm to wipe my mouth with my sleeve.

Miss Appleton cleared her throat, and I froze in mid motion before removing the white linen napkin beneath the tray.

"Well, now. We should get upstairs before Miss Scott comes looking." She turned and walked out, and I heard the click of her heels in the corridor.

I glanced back at the writing on the wall.

"I see you found it." Lucy's voice squeaked.

I snapped my head around, having forgotten she remained. The desire to know what the writing said had me at her mercy. "What do you know 'bout it?"

She walked to stand beside me. Then, thinking better of it, she took three paces to the right and stood peering at the corner. "I've spent my share of nights cooped up in here. Until I came up with the plan to follow the order and keep my ears and eyes open to any information."

I hadn't taken her for the sort to defy the wardens.

"I learned to read and write, and it's done me good. I got

myself in here so I could decode the message that kept me awake."

"What does it say?"

"It says 'Ellie A.'"

"A girl who shared the same fate?"

She shrugged. "Maybe."

"What else do you know 'bout the name?"

She regarded me sheepishly. "Nothing."

I glowered at her. She was as useless as I'd thought. I waltzed past her and strode from the room.

CHAPTER 8

Toronto, Canada 1890

I AM CHARLOTTE APPLETON. AN ORPHAN SCOOPED UP FROM LONDON'S *streets.*

On the dock, I stood trembling with my handbag clasped at my side. The guardians sent to see we made the journey across the sea divided the lads from the girls.

"Ellie, do you fink they will separate us?" I looked at my sixteen-year-old sister. She stood stiff and straight-faced, her eyes studying the guardians and the movements around us. "Ellie?" I pulled on her hand with the missing index finger—a reminder of our time on the streets and the bite of the butcher's blade.

She jumped. "What did you say?"

"Do you fink they will separate us?"

She scowled down at me. "Do you fink I'm God?"

Tears pooled in my eyes. I never liked it when she got cross with me, but the fear gnawing at me couldn't be tamed.

"Listen, I'm sorry." She rubbed the nape of her neck. "I wish I could tell you everyfing will be all right, but I can't. I told you Dad wouldn't die, for your sake, and—well, you know 'ow that went. You got to be tough." She scoured our surroundings. "This new life requires it."

Tough? I wasn't like her. Ellie had let out a wail when the butcher took her finger, but except while her bandages were being changed, she never revealed the pain it had to have caused.

I pressed my lips together to stifle a whimper.

"Oh, Charlotte, please don't give me that face. I didn't want this any more than you." Her voice quivered as she pulled me closer.

"I know." I buried my face in the protection of her brown cotton frock, the uniform for all the girls.

Ellie and I didn't bear any resemblance. She was tall with dark hair and a serious face, and my hair was blonde like our mummy's. Grown-ups often misjudged me as two or three years younger than my seven years because of my petite stature. I stationed myself at Ellie's side as soon as I could walk. Daddy often laughed and called me her shadow. The truth was, when I was next to her, life didn't seem so scary. But Ellie never smiled anymore. Not since the night the man, Walter, helped her bury Daddy's body.

Our mummy had died a few years ago, and Daddy had done the best he could to get by, but when he got sick we could no longer attend school. Ellie found a job at the workhouse, and I tended to Daddy. We sold all our possessions, and our flat sat empty. Our aunt and uncle knew of our troubles and lent us money from time to time, but soon they stopped answering the door.

When Daddy stopped breathing, I waited for Ellie to return from the workhouse. Panicked, she had paced the floor, trying to figure out what to do next. I had helped her wrap Daddy's cold, gray body in linens, and she told me to stay inside and not talk to anyone before she disappeared into the night, returning some hours later with a young man named Walter. Ellie had fancied him—I witnessed it in the softness reflected in her eyes when he stopped by in the evenings after Daddy got sick. The two would laugh and carry on in the main room of our two-room flat. Missing my friends at school, I had envied them.

I'd fallen asleep by the time they returned from burying Daddy's body, but I awoke to Walter comforting my sister in a way that sounded painful. I had covered my ears because I didn't want Ellie to be upset with me for interrupting. Walter had left shortly after, and sounds of my sister's soft weeping drew me into the main room, where I found her huddled in the corner with her legs drawn up to her chest. She moaned and rocked in a way that frightened me. I glanced at the buttons of her dress lying abandoned on the floor. I'd called her name, but she didn't look up, so I sat beside her and rested my head on her shoulder until her whimpers ceased.

She had never told me what happened that night, but I knew it was bad.

When the rent came due, we took what we could carry and left at dusk. In the following months we found shelter in barns, under bridges, and behind crates in alleyways. Ellie went to the workhouse each day, and I did as she instructed, keeping one eye open for the orphan snatchers. We lived that way until two men nabbed us one night. They took us to the Sheltering Home for Destitute Children, where we worked and learned skills to better our lives. Until the day came when the headmaster informed us that we would set sail the following day for Canada.

The journey had been long, and many children became sick. Ellie withdrew into herself like she had the night after Walter had visited. I missed the times when she'd smiled. Lately her mind seemed occupied. She quickly became angry with me when I asked her questions about where we were headed. Her behavior frightened me, and I'd stopped bothering her with my endless questions, but my tummy twisted and rolled with growing concern for what lay ahead.

The women in charge of the girls took us to a new home like the one in London. The headmistress wasn't the friendly sort. She was downright terrifying, and she insisted the younger girls must sleep in separate rooms from the older ones. Ellie had protested, and that got her locked up. That night many of us cried for our siblings, but the staff seemed deaf to our fear and loneliness.

At the home we met Agnes, a girl of twelve. Miss Grant, the headmistress, favored the girl, and like a treasured pet, she walked in the headmistress's shadow. She spied on us and reported back any misdeeds. Ellie hated her, and for it, she spent most of my two weeks at the institute locked away in the cellar room.

"Ellie, you got to stop acting up," I said one day when she sat down to eat breakfast.

She looked haggard, and dark circles haloed her eyes. She glared at Agnes, who stood beside Miss Grant with her shoulders rolled back and nose lifted. "I 'ate 'er," she said.

"No one likes 'er." I swallowed a bite of porridge.

"I won't allow the likes of 'er or Miss Grant to get the best o' me. Never again will I let anyone 'ave that kind of power."

"Don't you care 'bout me anymore?"

She didn't answer. With each mouthful she took, her eyes never left Agnes.

"Ellie, I need you." My lip quivered. "I 'eard talk 'bout families coming soon."

"That is good," she said.

Tears plopped onto my cheeks, and anger ignited in my belly. "I 'ate you. I wish you warn't me sister."

"What?" Ellie snapped from her trance and gawked at me. "What did you say?"

I repeated my words and didn't feel the least bit guilty for it, even when pain shone in her eyes. She deserved it because she had abandoned me. She was all I had. Her need to defy Miss

Grant and stand her ground with Agnes had proven more important than me.

Two days later, the families came, and as I stood weeping on the front step of the institution with my new family, the Mitchells, I glanced back at the foyer where a cold-faced Ellie stood.

For a decade or so, I stayed with the Mitchell family. Although I never went hungry, I understood that I was an outsider, indentured to the family to help run their home and care for the children and nothing more. The yearning to be reunited with my sister never dissipated. Remorse over the anger I'd shown her in our last days dogged me.

CHAPTER 9

Hazel

OR THE NEXT SEVERAL HOURS I HELPED THE LAUNDRESS. WHEN MISS Scott came to get me, I followed behind her in silence, displaying my new reformed obedience while revolution beat in my chest. As we passed Miss Keene's office, she stood in the doorway, eyeing me with pursed lips. I envisioned a riot of home children taking over the institute and dethroning the tyrant. We'd tie her up and force the slop they fed us down her throat. After we had a bit of fun with her, we'd throw her in the cellar room. I would take up position in her office and kick my feet up onto her neatly arranged desk. I smiled at the image. What a glorious day that would be.

The sunlight streaming through the glass-paned front door gleamed on the key around her neck. She followed me with her eyes and frowned at my interest, and I dropped my gaze. Why did she isolate that key from the ones positioned at her side?

The voice of the teacher instructing the other girls in arithmetic filled me with annoyance. I shouldn't have attacked Lucy and gotten myself locked up. In the short time I had been at the receiving home, I'd strained to understand letters and numbers. But I had yet to absorb what the teacher taught because William weighed heavily on my every waking thought.

Miss Scott left me on my knees with a bucket of hot soapy water and a basket of rags.

The pipes in the building groaned and thumped. "What you

complaining 'bout?" I grumbled, narrowing my gaze at the wall. I said, under my breath, "You ain't the one assigned to scrubbing these 'ere floors until she can see 'er reflection in them." I thought of the message Miss Keene had given Miss Scott for me. *Don't rightfully know why she'd want to see her own reflection anyway*, I thought as I slapped the soapy rag onto the white tiles.

I had gone but a few feet when the plumber hired by the tyrant trudged over my clean floors on the way to fix the indoor privy. I muttered and crawled on my hands and knees after him, cleaning up his mess.

Some time later, I straightened and brushed away the sweat pooling into my eyes before rubbing the dull ache in my lower back. "Excuse me," I said to a passing warden with all the politeness I could muster.

She halted and swung to look at me, wide-eyed. "Yes?"

"I 'ave to use the privy."

"You know where it is. Make it quick." She waved a hand and continued down the corridor.

I stood and wiped my hands on my apron before heading out the back door. At the corner of the building, I froze as I heard heated voices rising. I looked over my shoulder and scoured my surroundings but saw no one. The girls were at their studies…these voices belonged to adults. I crept forward and peeked around the corner and found Miss Scott pacing the lawn, and Miss Appleton with her hands planted on her tiny waist.

"She is insufferable, and some days I think you are no better than her."

"Don't ever compare me to 'er." Miss Scott paused to point a gloved finger in Miss Appleton's face.

"Fine." Miss Appleton's tone softened. "The girl was distraught over her brother. She didn't deserve to be locked away. You know better than anyone what that feels like."

"And you fink I could've stopped 'er?"

"No, I suppose not." Miss Appleton's shoulders slumped. "I'm frustrated, is all. We've been here for two years and have accomplished nothing. It sickens me with each girl that leaves this place." She thrust a hand at the building. "The organization claims to help impoverished children, and it may have started that way, but they can't control the situation once they put them on a ship. We were viewed as worthless bygones. Forgotten children. How can you condone Agnes's disregard for what is also her truth? Have you forgotten?"

My heart raced and my mind spun. Had I heard the women correctly? Had Miss Scott and Miss Appleton been home children?

"Of course I 'aven't forgotten." Miss Scott pressed fingers to her temples. "But like you, I 'ad no choice but to let 'er lock the girl up." There was remorse in her voice. "She would've viewed my protest as being incompetent to manage the place, and then our work 'ere is for nuffing."

"What's the use of keeping our own records if we can't make the smallest change by showing kindness to the lost souls that haunt the hallways?"

"You're right." Miss Scott hung her head. "She is always watching me. I must keep up the front, or we will both be out on our backsides without jobs. Need I remind you of the price we pay if that 'appens?"

"I'm quite aware of our responsibilities. Now we'd best get back to work before we are missed." Miss Appleton swerved around her and strode toward me.

I pressed myself against the building, the vines of the blue-flowered wisteria tickling my face. I didn't dare move. The women hurried past me, within an arm's length away.

The rest of the day, while cleaning every corner of the dining hall and polishing heaps of china, I pondered their conversation. If I were to collect more information on the wardens' claimed kinship to the place, I had to tolerate Lucy.

CHAPTER 10

T HE TYRANT PERMITTED ME TO EAT THE EVENING MEAL WITH THE
other girls. Ravenous from the day's work, I shoveled
the food in with little care for chewing. I coughed and
thumped at my chest when a piece of meat lodged partway
down my throat.

"No need to worry 'bout Beatrice getting your food," Lucy
said as I coughed the bite free.

I gawked at the empty seat across from me. "Where is she?"

"Locked in her room. Miss Keene caught her stealing from
the kitchen."

I studied the headmistress, who stood guarding the threshold of the dining hall. "Old 'en ain't got nuffing better to do than
lock people up?" I graced Lucy with a sideways glance.

She offered me a lopsided grin, as if we had become mates.
I stewed inside, but I warn't about to let her know it, because I
found myself in a bind. I needed her and I didn't like it one bit.

"Ever wonder what that key around her neck is for?" She
took a gander at Miss Keene.

"Got me wondering." I lowered my head, not wanting the
headmistress to catch us both looking.

Lucy leaned in close, and I jumped as her arm brushed
mine, but fought the urge to scoot over a hair or two. She leaned
even closer, and the warmth of her breath in my ear sent shivers
up my spine. "It opens her office."

My gaze gripped the key as if it were a gem taunting me

from the caves of the forbidden. The answers I needed relied on me obtaining the key. Oh, bollocks! The task was impossible.

Miss Keene's whistle blared, making us all jump. "All right, ladies. Supper is over. Run along outside. Soon it will be lights out."

Chairs scraped against the floor, and chatter erupted.

"Quietly." Miss Appleton ushered the girls along.

"Meet me by the big maple tree," Lucy said before falling into line.

When I stepped onto the back porch, the stickiness of the summer heat slapped me in the face. I looked at the ancient tree for any signs of Lucy but found the strange girl, Clara—the one who had been returned. She kept to herself, never speaking to anyone except the imaginary people she mumbled to at meal-times and in the hallway. The other girls laughed and called her Crazy Clara, but my heart pulled for the girl. I strode across the lawn to the tree and stood there to wait.

Angled away from me, Clara stood picking at a piece of tree bark. Her breathing grew rapid, accompanied by the urgency of her picking. I frowned, observing her odd behavior. The crimson staining her fingers gave my heart a jolt. Her frenzy intensified, and I turned to stop her.

"Clara." I touched her shoulder and she jerked, recoiling from my touch.

She whirled, baring her teeth, and hissed, her dark, unseeing eyes looking through me. Her mumbles, inaudible at first, made sense as her panic heightened. "Worthless. Whore. Street trash." Tears spilled over her cheeks as she repeated the words.

Had Lucy spoken the truth about the home they had sent the girl to? What had they done to her? My mind leaped to William, then back to the girl before me.

"You aren't those fings," I said, trying to console the deranged girl as though she could understand.

She cranked her neck side to side and centered her gaze on me. My heart pounded as her eyes widened. "You!" she said. "It's all your fault."

"You're wrong. I-I—" I took a step back as she advanced toward me.

She released a wild cry and lunged at me. I stumbled and sprawled backward on the ground. She jumped on me and clawed at my arms and face. I wriggled and tried to dislodge her, but her weight and strength overpowered me. I lifted my arms to block my face from her attack.

Miss Keene's whistle blared. "Grab that girl," Miss Keene shouted.

Shadows hovered over us, but I didn't dare lower my arms. Clara screamed and her assault stopped as her weight lifted from my midsection.

"Miss Winters, are you all right?" Miss Appleton bent and offered me a hand up.

I stood and brushed myself off while looking to where Miss Scott and another staff member held Clara with her arms pinned behind her back. The girl became crazed by the restriction. "Let go. Get off me. I will tell," she shrieked, her eyes wide with fear.

"You're scaring 'er," I said.

Miss Keene swung her head around to look at me.

I gulped but didn't back down. "She didn't mean any 'arm. She ain't right in the 'ead."

"So, this disruption of the order is your doing?"

I seethed at the term. What was this place, a cult? Couldn't they see Clara needed help to save herself from the demons in her head?

"It ain't her fault." Lucy pushed from the gathering of girls.

"Hazel was standing here when Clara attacked her, but it's like she said, the girl ain't right since she returned. She needs help."

Miss Keene's glare turned on Lucy, who swallowed hard but stood unwavering.

"Do you run this place now?"

"No, Miss Keene." Lucy bowed her head.

Miss Keene straightened and pressed her lips together. "Then I suggest you let me tend to the situation."

Lucy mumbled her understanding.

Miss Keene turned to address the girls. "All right, all of you return to what you were doing."

When we hesitated her whistle blew, and we scattered.

"Put the girl in the room," Miss Keene said. "She isn't fit to be with the others. I will contact Dr. Moore in the morning. Perhaps it's time we make other arrangements."

The conversation faded as I walked to the fence and looked at the fields, pulse racing in my ears. Sobs formed in my chest. What waited beyond this place?

Lucy came to stand beside me. "You all right?"

I nodded, not looking to cry in front of her.

"Maybe it won't be so bad out there," she said. "Maybe you will get a better family than Clara."

The tears came then, hard and unrelenting. "It's not me I worry 'bout, it's me brother."

"He is young. Six, you said?"

Through tear-filled eyes, I regarded her.

She offered a wary smile. "Maybe he will have a good life. I meant it when I said I was sorry 'bout what I said." She lowered her gaze. "I've been here so long I fall asleep to the weeping of girls longing for their siblings and families. It gets to ya after a while. I guess I kind of took a liking to you. You remind me of me oldest sister Katherine. I don't want you to end up like Crazy

Clara. But it still warn't right. If someone had said that to me 'bout my sisters, I reckon I would've laid a beating on them too, if my legs warn't my curse."

I hiccupped and dried my tears. "I'm sorry."

She shrugged. "Don't mention it. Now," she stepped closer, "do you want to hear my plan?"

"What plan?"

She leaned in, cupped my ear, and whispered.

My eyes widened. "'Ow do you reckon we do that?" I said when she stepped back.

She glowered and cast a look over her shoulder. "Keep your voice down."

"Sorry," I said sheepishly.

"Let me worry 'bout that. You be ready. All right?"

"Yes."

CHAPTER 11

Charlotte—1919

THE CHILLY WINTER WIND SNAPPED THROUGH THE AFTERNOON AIR, and I drew the fur collar of my long wool velour coat tighter—a gift Frederick, my fiancé, had given me last Christmas, and the most beautiful item I owned. I hurried down the sidewalk to the diner, gesturing my apologies and squeezing between pedestrians. Frederick had expected me twenty minutes ago, but electrical issues had stopped the streetcar on the tracks, and I had to run the rest of the way.

Breathless, I pulled the door open and walked inside, embracing the warmth. Greeted by the chatter of happy patrons and the scent of food, I felt my stomach roll with hunger. I glanced around the quaint diner decorated in dark wood, painted yellow walls, with misfit murals and artifacts.

A middle-aged waitress with a pleasant face looked up from filling a gentleman's glass at a nearby table. "Good afternoon. For one?"

"No, I'm meeting my fiancé here."

"I didn't see Mr. Taylor come in. And I've been here since seven." She glanced around the diner.

I frowned. Had he gotten tied up at the office?

"I'll clean your usual table. Give me a minute." She smiled and strode to the counter packed with the early afternoon crowd to return the coffee carafe to its base. Then she led me to a table by the window overlooking the main street before leaving to tend to customers.

I slid into the brown-upholstered booth and removed the burgundy cloche hat I'd borrowed from my roommate and friend, Delilah. Slipping out of my coat and scarf, I settled into the seat to wait. After several minutes had passed, I drummed my fingers on the checkered tablecloth, my concern growing over Frederick's tardiness.

We had met two years prior at a party to which Delilah had hauled me. He was a successful Australian investor who had moved to Toronto five years earlier. I had escaped the partygoers to find a moment alone in the lobby of the hotel. Engrossed in a painting by an artist I wasn't acquainted with, I hadn't heard him until he spoke.

"The artist certainly isn't Vincent van Gogh, are they?"

I had turned to find him leaning against a column with a cigarette pressed between his fingers, observing me. I suppose his knowledge of Vincent van Gogh's work had piqued my interest, but his inquisitive dark eyes and smirk had made me turn and walk away without a response.

Later that evening, I hauled a drunken Delilah outside. Struggling under her weight, I wondered how I would get her home.

"Need some help, little lady?"

Frederick had stood on the sidewalk. His smile flashed white in the streetlights. I missed a step and stumbled, and he rushed forward and caught Delilah and me before we hit the pavement.

I quickly removed myself from his grip. "I can manage," I'd sputtered like a fool, heat racing over my flesh.

At that moment, a cab pulled to the curb. Despite my insisting that I didn't need help, he had escorted us home.

At the steps of our apartment building, I'd thanked him and told him I would manage from there.

"As you wish. I do hope you will repay my kindness by meeting me tomorrow evening at a little diner I've come acquainted with." He'd delivered that with a mischievous smile.

Recognizing his manipulation, no matter how jovial, I stopped on the stairs. "You are very sure of yourself, aren't you, Mr...."

"Taylor. Frederick Taylor." He grinned and tipped his hat.

I had agreed to meet him, and the cheeky fellow I'd encountered the previous night had vanished, and I found a confident man with admirable intelligence. An immigrant like me, he spoke of his years in Canada, but I had never told him how I'd arrived. Throughout our courtship, I'd maintained the story I had created for friends and beaus: after my parents had died, my aging maternal grandparents had sent for me. I never mentioned Ellie, the vague memories of London, or the farm I'd been shipped off to where I learned I was a worthless object, a nobody, the forgotten problem of my birth country. For decades governments had played God with British children's lives. Off the backs of enslaved children, Canada continued to rise.

Remorse over my deceit weighed on me. Frederick deserved the truth, but I couldn't find the courage to tell him of the horrible shame I bore. Eyes dampening, I turned my gaze to the window. My thoughts turned to Ellie. Did she think of me like I did her? I hoped she hadn't carried the harsh words I'd spewed in the wake of my anger. I gulped at the memory. Some days, the yearning to see her again became too much to bear. I had never stopped thinking of her. What had happened to her? Maybe she had married and settled down. Had her life been better than mine? I hoped so.

Once my contract with the Mitchells had ended, I'd set out

on my own, taking up odd jobs like cleaning and mending. In my early twenties I met Gillian, a teacher and a lover of arts. Under her tutelage, I immersed myself in education with an eagerness to acquire the skills and development lacking from a neglected childhood. My dreams had never been grand. I longed for a simple life as an artist. Marriage hadn't played into the vision I had laid out for my life.

That was, until I met Frederick. He had ambitions enough for both of us and often spoke of returning home. Each time he did, panic rose. I couldn't leave without knowing where Ellie had gone.

A whiff of his spiced bergamot cologne tickled my senses before he spoke. "Care to tell me what is on your mind, Appleton?"

I turned from the window to find a smiling Fredrick peering down at me. Snow dusted his gray wool coat. He removed his hat and coat before slipping onto the seat across from me. An unruly lock of dark hair hung over his brow, and he smoothed it back. Dark eyes twinkling with delight, he kissed my fingers, stealing my warmth.

"It was nothing. I was thinking of Delilah and something she said the other day."

"Why do I get the feeling you aren't going to entertain me?" he said.

"Because it's women's business." The guilt of the lies between us weighed on my heart, but I shuffled it away. If Fredrick knew of my past, would he love me the same way? I didn't think I could handle his rejection. The need to love and be loved had guided my life, often steering me to poor choices, leaving me flawed and vulnerable. My beaus before Frederick had used my shortcomings and seized the last glimpse of self-worth I possessed. But Fredrick was different. He loved me. Truly loved me.

He recaptured my hand and held it while smiling with appreciation at the low-cut burgundy dress I'd also taken from Delilah's closet. "Is that new?"

"Maybe." I sent him a flirty smile, enjoying his full attention. I traced the back of his hand. I would never get used to the gentle comfort of the human touch, or the way I felt in his arms, like I was all that mattered in the world—a foreign and exhilarating sensation.

He laughed before his expression grew serious, causing my heart to thump faster. "Are we to have secrets between us?"

Panic thrummed. Secrets? What secrets?

My lack of response and gaping mouth furrowed his brow.

"Did I say something wrong?" he asked.

Heat touched my cheeks. "Of course not. I don't want you to think so poorly of me."

"I could never," he said. "Unless, of course, you caught feelings for another fellow. Then I may have to hunt both of you to the ends of the earth."

I laughed, which made his grin that much grander.

"I like the sound of your laughter. It is music to my heart. You're much too serious, Appleton. Your head is always off in the clouds. Sometimes I wonder if you hear me. We aren't even married, and you've already turned a deaf ear to me. These last weeks, it's as though your mind is preoccupied. You only half listen to me." He looked sad, and my breathing halted.

"I'm sorry. I don't mean to drift off," I said with all sincerity.

He glanced at our laced fingers, and the gentle stroke of his thumbs sent goosebumps over me. Next to his, my skin was pale. The giddy shyness that often overcame me in his company soared, and I lowered my lashes. I loved Frederick, and I wanted to be all he desired in a wife, but something more pressing gripped my mind.

I reached for my purse and withdrew the advertisement. I felt as if there were a herd of elephants on my chest, and the voices and noise of the diner faded as I honed in on his face. Two positions had come available at the receiving home I'd stayed at upon my arrival in Toronto. The one tie that held the answers to my sister's whereabouts. "There is something I've meant to speak to you about."

"Now we are getting somewhere," he said with a chuckle. His free spirit and good-natured attitude had been a soothing enhancement to my life. He released my hands and leaned back, resting his arm casually along the back of the booth. "Tell me, Appleton. What is on your mind?"

I swallowed back nerves and handed him the newspaper clipping. "I came across this job posting a few days back."

"But I thought you loved painting." His brow puckered.

"Yes, but I'm yet to be noticed for my work, and the little I earn isn't sufficient to pay the bills."

"What of the additional job you picked up as shop clerk at the clothing boutique? Does that not help?"

"There wasn't enough business, and Miss Chapelle had to cut my hours."

"You can't expect yourself to keep up with three jobs while waiting for someone to notice your paintings. It's not practical. We will be married soon. There is no need for you to work. Perhaps I can help you until then."

"No," I said firmly.

He frowned in confusion.

"I'm sorry." I stood, walked to his side of the table, and sat down beside him. "What I mean to say is, I don't want you taking care of me."

"But we are—"

"To marry, yes. Then we will act as husband and wife. Please understand." I searched his eyes.

"Very well, Appleton. I've come to know you as an

unconventional woman. We will do things your way." He read the advertisement before regarding me with a dumbfounded expression. "You want to work at an institute that houses orphans? You've always stated you've never cared for children."

I understood more about children's needs than most. More than Mrs. Mitchell had known about her own.

I squirmed under his gaze. "Well...I..."

"What is it you're not telling me?"

Tell him. Nerves swarmed, and I busied myself with the menu the waitress had left while I'd been awaiting his arrival. "Well, I guess I've always considered helping those without family. With my grandparents gone, and no living family, I can understand the orphans longing for something they no longer have. I'm not an expert on the needs of children, but I'm sure they require more than a bed and food in their bellies." Again, I cringed at the lie.

"That may be true, but answer me this."

"What?"

"Why is this the first time I'm hearing it?"

"Because I didn't want you to think I was unfit to be a wife."

"I will admit I'd hoped you would dedicate more time to us after we are married. Maybe if you're hired, you will fulfill the need and then after we—"

"But what if I choose not to?" I rushed to say. "Could you love a wife with such ambitions?"

"I am not one to stop anyone from forging their own path in life, but a job at the institution ties you down and the more you invest in the children's welfare, the more I fear you'll never leave Canada."

I turned to look at him. "I can never leave!" He jolted at my outburst. I tensed, then in a calmer tone, said, "Not yet." I reassured him with a smile. "In the future, perhaps."

"You sound as though you've given this some thought."

"I have."

"Well, I will not stand in your way."

"Are you sure you want to marry a woman so complicated?"

"Complicated?" he said with a chuckle. "Determined, yes. But I like a woman who knows what she wants. It gives you character."

I loved him at that moment more than the minute before, and my eyes fell to his lips. If we hadn't been in a public place, I would have stolen a kiss.

"Mind your manners, Appleton," he said.

I blushed at his awareness of my desires.

I returned to my seat, and we ordered. After the waitress brought our food, we engaged in conversation about the future and his dreams of returning to Australia. My unease continued. What if I never found Ellie? I wouldn't leave Canada without locating her. Would Frederick come to resent me?

"Well, I need to get back." He glanced at his watch before donning his coat and hat.

We strode from the diner into the incessant chill outside. On the sidewalk, he grabbed my gloved hand and pulled me to the side before turning to face me. Gripping my shoulders, he peered tenderly down at me. "You are quite the girl, Appleton, but you're my girl."

"I like the sound of that." I rested my palms on his chest and straightened a wooden button on his coat. "Be patient with me."

"I'm trying," he said with a grin that soon faded. "But why do I get the feeling you only offer part of your heart?"

I wanted to deny the accusation and state my love for him, but the truth in his words drew my silence. I loved him, all right—more than I'd loved any man before. But dedication to finding my sister would always come first.

Would I know Ellie if I saw her? I'd spent most of my life fantasizing about our reunion, but unearthing her seemed impossible. Maybe, after her contract was up, she had headed back to London or ventured off to other parts of the world. My heart twisted at the thought. Would she leave me behind? The hope of finding her had kept me rooted mere miles from where I'd spent my childhood as an indentured servant.

The day I'd spotted the Mitchells from across the street, they had a young girl with them, who I could only assume was a home child. Mrs. Mitchell was past childbearing years, and the girl walked silently behind them with her head down—a nobody, a possession. Something I could relate to. Thinking of my own emotional wounds kindled a passion to do something.

Frederick waved a hand in front of my face.

I shook my head. "I'm sorry." I rose on tiptoes and wrapped my arms around his neck, pulling his head toward me. I planted a passionate kiss on his lips for all to see. When we parted he looked dazed, but he managed a lopsided smile. "You're forgiven this time."

Warmth hugged my heart, and I laughed. "Good." I wasn't against using my womanly attributes to secure forgiveness.

"A fellow can't hold anger toward a girl willing to demonstrate her affection for all to see, now can he?" He gave my chin a nudge before turning on his heel. His whistle rose as he strode down the sidewalk.

I smiled and wrapped my arms around myself. Blanketed in love, I stared after him. *You are a good man, Frederick Taylor, and you deserve the truth.*

The next day, I stood on the sidewalk regarding the brownstone distributing house, another station on the journey to lives devoid of meaning, love, or hope for those deemed a burden by society. I climbed the steps as I had so many years ago, worry and fear replaced with a vision and determination to do what I could about the injustice inflicted upon those innocents so easily forgotten by the world. I also felt hope. The institute held the record of Ellie's and my arrival. If I obtained a position within, would I, at last, find her? Would I find a sense of belonging and self-worth?

I entered the lobby. Not much had changed. The potent scent of ammonia had been replaced with that of bleach. Like the outside, the place had aged, but it still possessed stark white walls, pristine cleanliness, and a lack of joy. The whispering of children walking the corridors and an instructor's voice rising somewhere nearby indicated life yet breathed within.

"Good afternoon. Can I help you?" An older woman with a limp crossed the lobby toward me from the library across the hall.

"Yes, I've come about the position."

"Applicants are asked to wait in here." She gestured at a small room to the right of the lobby.

I glanced at the closed door to a room on the opposite side, which had been the headmistress's office, before turning back to find the woman studying me. I smiled and walked into the room she had referred to and took a seat in one of the three empty chairs. "Am I the only applicant?"

"There is another in with Miss Keene right now and two more coming at 3:00 p.m."

"Thank you."

She turned and walked away. I sat clasping my purse with my gaze pinned on the closed door of the headmistress's office. The heels of my wool-lined black winter boots clicked on the floor. If I wasn't given the position, what then?

Because of my stolen youth, and the pain of Ellie's and my separation, I'd blocked most memories of the place. But as I waited, I recollected one of Ellie's final trips to the office, and how she had departed with her eyes red-rimmed and puffy from crying.

"Leave off, Charlotte. I don't 'ave time for your sniffling." She had brushed by me when I stepped from line to hug her around the middle. Later that night, she had found me on the back step and asked for my forgiveness. I'd eagerly given it, wanting nothing more than to be in her good graces. I wondered what had upset her, and the look of defeat on her face had made my heart pound. She wrapped an arm around my shoulders and pulled me closer before telling me that I would be leaving the institute the next day. We sat on the back step and wept.

Tears pooled in my eyes at the memory seared into my soul, and the demonstration of Ellie's overwhelming sense of responsibility toward me. "Oh, Ellie, I'm sorry," I whispered, as though the place brought me closer to her.

The headmistress's door opened, and women's voices drifted out. A middle-aged brunette woman clothed in a plain blue cotton dress, a gray wool coat draped over her arm, stepped into the hall.

"Thank you for your interest, Miss Scott. I will inform the applicants by day's end tomorrow." A woman with graying hair wound in a tight knot atop her head and dressed in a high-collared cream blouse and a black skirt followed her out.

"I look forward to hearing from you." Miss Scott stood with her back to me.

"I will let you see yourself out," the taut-faced woman said curtly before marching back into her office and shutting the door.

Miss Scott and I both jumped at the door's resounding thud. She turned, lifting gloved hands to place her hat on her head. I got a clear view of her and frowned. She looked familiar, but where had I seen her before? Perhaps at one of the social events Frederick hauled me to. Yet she didn't appear to be in the same social class as the usual attendees of those.

The woman glanced in my direction, halting her movement momentarily before striding to the doorway of the room where I waited. "You 'ere about the job?" She had a slight British accent.

"Yes."

Her hard expression unnerved me, but also gave me pause. Her brow furrowed as I gawked without care of her noticing.

"Is somefing wrong?"

"Do I know you?" I said.

She rubbed a gloved hand as though to ease away an ache before slipping into her coat. "Don't know how you would. I don't socialize with people much." She fastened one of the wooden buttons of her coat.

"Did you grow up around here?"

"What's with all the questions?" She narrowed her eyes. The woman's dry and standoffish personality left much to be desired.

"Sorry." I blushed. "I'm looking for someone."

"Who?"

I lowered my voice. "My sister."

Her eyes grew haunted before she shook her head and said, "I see. Well, best of luck with that." She adjusted the glove on her left hand, and I noticed the hollowness beneath the fabric of one finger.

My heart sped up.

"I need to be going. Good day to you." She turned and marched purposefully to the front door.

I leaped from my chair. "Wait." I hurried after her as she gripped the brass knob.

She spun around and studied me, leery. "Can I 'elp you?"

A door opened behind me, and Miss Scott glanced over my shoulder.

"I am Charlotte Appleton," I said for her ears only.

Her eyes widened in shock, and her lip quivered, but before

she could respond, I turned to find the headmistress regarding us with suspicion. "Hello, you must be Miss Keene. I'm here about the position." I strode toward the headmistress, but my thoughts remained on the woman behind me.

My name had struck her. Had I been right? My pulse beat in my ears. *Stay calm.* I fought to keep the mass of emotions gathering in my chest from appearing on my face, but my hands trembled. I wanted nothing more than to turn back and bombard Miss Scott with questions.

"Yes, well, come in then." Miss Keene pursed her lips, but before moving, she looked over my shoulder at the woman. "Is there something else I may help you with, Miss Scott?"

I swallowed hard and looked at the doorway where the woman still stood. Had life shifted in my favor and granted me a miracle? Could the woman be Ellie?

"I-I…no. I realized I must 'ave dropped my 'air comb." She patted the sides of her hair. "If you don't mind, I will take a look in there." She pointed at the assigned waiting room, and without waiting for Miss Keene to grant permission, she walked into the room.

We stared after her.

"Ah, just as I thought." She returned, holding up a silver hair comb. "If you ladies will excuse me, I 'ave somewhere to be."

An invisible hand gripped my heart as she strode to the door. Every part of me wanted to chase after the woman and risk appearing even more like a lunatic than I already had. I needed to know. But my feet stood fast. If I hoped to secure the job and make a minimal difference in the children's lives, I couldn't leave.

"What an odd woman," Miss Keene said in a monotone voice. "Perhaps the type of woman that could keep these children in line." She pulled her eyes from the door and rested her intense gaze on me. "Let's get on with it, shall we?"

"Yes, ma'am."

"Miss Keene will do," she said over her shoulder.

Seated inside, I looked around before a framed portrait on the edge of her desk caught my eye. My throat tightened. Why did the woman have a photograph of Agnes, the dreadful girl who had singled out Ellie to make her life at the home hell? I had forgotten and blocked many memories, but Agnes's face was one I'd never forget.

I forced back the nerves swirling in my gut and turned my full attention to Miss Keene. As Miss Scott had evoked familiarity in the hall, so did she. It had to be the home. I'd been on edge since walking inside. I frowned and roved my gaze over the headmistress. *Wait...* My heart skipped a beat. It couldn't be. I gave my head a shake, then chanced another glance at the picture. God in heaven! There was no denying the hardness in her eyes and the crooked way she held her mouth.

"Is there something about the photograph that causes you distress?"

"The child looks familiar, is all." My voice hitched with thrumming anxiety.

She folded her hands and leaned forward, scrutinizing me with a hard glint. "You look a bit pale. I won't have you fainting."

"I am fine. I missed breakfast today, is all." A night of worry had plagued me with nightmares, and nerves had stolen my appetite that morning.

"I have no tolerance for weakness. Tell me, Miss..."

Body trembling and my thoughts a jumbled mess, I blurted, "Charlotte Appleton."

"Appleton?" Her eyes narrowed. "That is a British name, isn't it?"

I gulped. Once Agnes knew my identity, she would send me on my way. "That is correct; my family immigrated here in 1750." I tried to hide my relief at my quick thinking. During my search for Ellie, while digging up records of Appletons in Canada, I had read about a Samuel Appleton immigrating to the country in 1774.

"I see." She eyed me a moment longer before seeming satisfied. She adjusted herself in the chair. "Well, let's get on with it, then. After decades of devoting herself to running this establishment, the former headmistress, Miss Grant, retired some years ago," she said with a hint of reverence. "I applied for the position, and to my delight, Miss Grant offered her highest recommendation to the board." A smugness pulled at her thin lips.

I clutched my hands in my lap. It took everything in me not to leap across the desk and wring her neck for the pain she had caused my sister. Agnes droned on with praise for the former headmistress and her work with the institute since she had taken over.

"Remarkable." I offered her a smile while feeling suddenly disheartened. It hadn't been Ellie in the lobby. For years, I'd studied the face of every woman around my sister's age in hopes of seeing her staring back at me. I had taken the years and maturity into consideration in my observations. However, when it came to Agnes, I would never have recognized her without the photograph. Ellie would've identified the girl in the picture even though Agnes didn't bear any resemblance until you looked more closely. She would never have sat through an interview or considered a position under Agnes's management.

"What interests you about working for our organization?" she asked.

"I am an artist and sometimes take on art students to teach—"

"The advertisement made no mention of an art teacher." She arched a sparse, peppered brow and took a thorough look at me. As though calculating that I was incompetent, she pursed her lips.

I set my jaw at the dismissal. Too often, people underestimated me for my petite stature and my gentle approach to life. I'd grown up knowing my thoughts and emotions were unimportant to those around me, and had spent my life riddled with self-doubt.

I focused on the reason I had come in the first place. No matter the turmoil stirring in me about working under Agnes, I couldn't forget the children. "I realize this, but what I want to explain is that, in my experience, children don't respond to a firm hand, but a gentle one."

She squared her shoulders. "I do not coddle the children. Order is of the utmost importance within these walls. Under my guidance, we have distributed over 288 children to families across Canada."

Yes, to where they are forgotten. You sentence them to lives where they are nothing more than livestock and become nothing but a record.

"Is that so?" I smiled in feigned awe. "You're to be congratulated. I'd imagine governing this place isn't a duty for the faint of heart."

A hint of red touched her cheeks, and her chest expanded as she basked in my compliment. "At the moment, we seek to hire two staff members. One will take on a supervisory position and report back to me. The other will attend to the children's daily needs, including bathing, meals, personal issues, and bedtime routines."

After Agnes finished listing the requirements and expectations, she questioned me for a few minutes before guiding me to the door. "I will let you know if I decide you would be an asset to our organization."

"Much appreciated." I stuck out a hand, which she looked at but avoided.

"Good day to you." She turned and walked away, disappearing around the corner.

"And to you," I mumbled into the empty foyer. *As cuddly as a porcupine, that one*, I seethed, and strode to the door, more than happy to put distance between us.

Outside, I hurried down the steps, part of me expecting to find Miss Scott waiting.

"Miss." A man clearing the snow from the pathway tipped his hat.

I nodded but kept up my pace. On the sidewalk, I looked back at the home before turning and walking down the street. I hadn't gone far when someone called to me.

"Psst."

I halted and glanced around.

"Over 'ere," a woman said.

I spotted Miss Scott hiding behind the trunk of the massive maple tree. My heart pounded faster. I looked back at the institute and surveyed the windows for prying eyes before continuing down the street. When the building disappeared from view, I paused at the hurried footfalls behind me.

"Keep walking." Miss Scott strode past me, and I hastened my pace to catch up. "Is it true?"

"What?"

"The name you claim."

"Why would I make that up?"

She halted and turned to study me, observing me from head to toe. "Are you 'er?"

My heart raced as I searched her face.

"Answer me." She gripped my shoulders and gave me a hard shake. "Are you..." Her words drifted as though she questioned the soundness of her mind.

Never allowing my gaze to leave hers, I said, "I was brought to that organization when I was seven with my older sister Ellie."

"Your sister?" Her voice hitched.

I bobbed my head.

Her face blanched, and tears dampened her eyes. "'Ow can it be, after all these years?"

"Ellie?" My voice cracked.

"Yes." Her tears fell in large droplets down her cheeks. "I've searched. God knows I 'ave." Guilt and shame twisted her features. "'Ow did you recognize me? You were so young. I would never 'ave known you."

"The index finger you lost when the butcher—"

She lifted her gloved hand and stared at it in awe. "I've spent my life loathing that reminder." She looked at me. "I never dreamed it would be the fing to bring you back to me."

"Oh, Ellie." I stepped forward and embraced her.

We stood there as the years of loneliness and heartache emerged in endless tears.

"I think we should find a quiet place to talk. There is a cafe around the corner," I said when we parted and dried our tears.

"I know the place. Getting out of sight is probably best. You never know if Agnes has spies watching us."

"So you recognized her, but not your own sister?"

"Well, she was older and 'asn't changed much. 'Er smug face has 'aunted me for years. And sadly, I've spent too long 'ating 'er, and blaming 'er for our separation and the anger I deflected onto you."

"We can't blame ourselves or each other for trying circumstances. But I must know: what caused you to seek employment at the institute?"

"You, of course." She looked at me as though insulted. "I've searched every face for the last thirty years for some sort of resemblance. When Miss Grant still ran the place, I came to inquire where they'd sent you. She told me the records were sealed, and wouldn't budge with any information. I've lived within blocks of here wif the 'ope you would one day come looking for me. So many times, I've walked by the place and fantasized of you exiting the front doors."

My throat thickened with emotion. "I too could never leave."

She paused and leveled a hard stare on me, but the intensity seemed aimed at a thought. "If Miss Grant wouldn't give me the information I sought, I intended to secure it myself." She fell silent for a moment before shaking her head as if to clear her mind. "Why did you come?"

"We have similar goals. I anticipated learning of your whereabouts and offering support and hope to the children."

She laughed—a bitter and hollow sound. "'Ope?"

I tilted my chin. "If we'd had someone with gentle encouragement, maybe there would have been a glimmer of hope and someone to help you when Agnes plotted to see you locked away."

When the cafe came into view, she looked at me and smiled. "I fooled 'er good. And if all goes according to plan, I will secure the job."

"But if your reason for applying was to find me, you no longer require employment there."

"Yes, well, the pay is a bit better than my job as a telephone operator. And if she 'ires me and not you, perhaps I can put in a good word. Agnes Keene will not 'ave the last say this time."

"So you advance solely fueled by your dislike for her."

"Yes," she said bluntly. "Does that bother you?"

I smiled uneasily. "How about we wait to see if we are granted the positions first."

"Agreed." She stepped forward to seize the door handle.

"Ellie?"

She paused and turned to look at me with an edgy glint in her eye. Something about the look felt familiar, a connection to the sister of my youth. I asked the question that perched at the back of my mind. "Why do you not bear our last name?"

She winced and lowered her gaze. "Well…I've spent a good many wasted years trying to forget."

"Forget what?"

"London. Mum, Dad, you…" She didn't look up. "Life before leaving England, 'im…the cell, and all the moments leading up to the day I left the institute." Her voice shook. "I believed if I were to survive, I 'ad to block out all emotions and memories of the past. The first fing I did after my contract was up and I'd earned enough money to visit a lawyer was 'ave my name changed."

"But why?" Pain at the revelation stabbed me in the chest. Our names were a vital connection to each other.

"Because I didn't want to be 'er. Ellie Appleton." As she spoke her given name, despondency slumped her shoulders. "I wanted to forget and desperately sought a fresh start. I needed to believe I mattered, and that I was somebody. I acquired the name Isabella Scott, and I thought it would make me feel different, but it didn't. No matter 'ow 'ard I tried, I couldn't escape the nightmares or the desire to belong to somefing or someone. It was too late by the time I got wise to my errors. So, in some weirdly distorted way, moving within walking distance of the institute gave me a sense of belonging. Don't judge me too 'arshly," she said.

I felt a deep connection to her sense of inadequacy and the pain that seeped through her tough exterior. I lightly gripped her arm. "No judgment. Let's get inside out of the cold. We have lots to catch up on." I smiled. "I'm engaged."

Her head snapped up. "You are?" The first sign of softness crossed her face. "Tell me more."

I laughed and linked arms with her, guiding her toward the door. "Once we have coffee to warm our bones, I will tell you anything you want to know."

CHAPTER 12

Hazel

OONLIGHT GLEAMED LIKE AN ELECTRIC TORCH ACROSS THE darkened room, threatening to reveal my alertness to the warden trudging the corridor. Lying on my side, I faced the door and waited for Lucy, and with every passing minute, panic thrummed. What was taking her so long? The girls' snores had risen an hour ago.

I held my breath when the clicking treads paused in the hallway, and in the small window of the metal door, Miss Appleton's face appeared. My galloping heart slowed. I considered her the lesser of the evils that governed the place, but nonetheless, she was the enemy. After surveying the room, she continued down the hall, and the ache of my lungs eased.

Another hour or so passed, and my lids had grown heavy when the door creaked open. I squinted in the dark and made out the mass of auburn hair, then heard Lucy's shuffle. *It's about bloody time!* I kicked back the bedding, rose, and quickly arranged lumps of clothing and towels under the blanket. When the next warden peered in, they wouldn't see an empty bed. My feet slapped against the cold floor tiles as I hurried to join her at the door.

Once we stood in the corridor, I spun and hissed through clenched teeth, "What took you so long?" I checked for any sign of the wardens while she closed the door and jabbed a key into the lock. "Where did you get those?" The jingling of the ring of keys had my pulse racing.

"To answer your first question, I had a task to take care of before I could get you out." Mischievousness glimmered in her eyes as she held out the key Miss Keene kept around her neck.

"You nicked the tyrant's keys." I stood dumbfounded by her skill.

She scowled, then her usual crooked grin returned. "The tyrant—a fitting name, I reckon." She covered her mouth to stifle a chuckle. "Right from her nightstand."

The key to the beast's lair! Perhaps I had misjudged Lucy. She had more courage and grit than I had anticipated. I felt a glimmer of respect. I returned her grin. A mate like her would have been useful back home.

She turned and tiptoed down the corridor.

"Where are we going?" I hurried to position myself at her side.

"Shh! Do you want them to hear us?"

I followed her to the lobby. She stopped at Miss Keene's office door. "You ready?"

"Ready as I'll ever be." My heart knocked harder. I checked the corners' shadows, half expecting Miss Keene to jump out and grab us. "If she catches us, it will be both our 'ides in the cellar."

"Then we bes' hurry before she wakes and notices the keys gone." She inserted the key, gave it a jiggle, and released a grunt or two in the process. "I think it's stuck."

"Move. Let me 'ave a go at it." I pushed her aside, but quickly caught myself and mumbled, "A bit on edge, I guess."

"Well, hurry then. Get on with it." She gestured at the lock.

I wiggled the key up, down, and to the left, then to the right before I heard a clink. I gave her a grin. "There ya 'ave it. Ain't a lock 'azel Winters can't master."

"Except the one to get you out of your room." Lucy positioned her hands on her hips before elbowing her way in front. Without hesitation, she turned the doorknob, and the door to the tyrant's den opened before us. Lucy stepped inside and turned to me. "Are ya coming, or you just gonna stand there in the open?"

I looked back down the corridor before creeping inside. Lucy shut the door behind us, and I turned and stubbed my toe on a hard object. I cussed and hopped around, but as a beam of light illuminated the office, I dropped into a crouch. My heart pounded against my ribcage.

"What ya doing?" Lucy turned an electric torch on me.

I grumbled and rose. "Stop swinging that thing around. You nearly had me eating me own heart, ya did."

Ignoring me, she strode to Miss Keene's desk and pulled open the top drawer. She thumbed through papers while I looked over her shoulder.

"You see anyfing of importance?" I asked.

"Not yet. I don't need you breathing over my shoulder. Make yourself useful and look in the filing cabinet for a bundle of ledgers."

I gawked at her without moving, and she swung the light into my eyes.

"Move, Hazel. I ain't looking to get caught."

"I'm sorry." I chastised myself for my rustiness and hurried to the filing cabinet. "'Ow do you know what we're looking for?

"When new shipments come in, she writes the names, ages, and origins of the children into a ledger she keeps with a stack of others. When she is done, she ties them with a leather band and places them in her top drawer."

"'Ow do you know so much 'bout what she does?"

"I told you, I keep an eye out. Till you went crazy on me, I never considered breaking in here and checking the records.

You got me to thinking that maybe all ain't lost. If I knew the whereabouts of me sisters, maybe when I'm old enough, I can find them."

"And you can. We will," I whispered back. "Can't see much. Bring that light over 'ere."

She joined me, and together we prodded around in one drawer after another.

"Nuffing." I kicked the bottom drawer, then winced in pain.

Lucy gave me a look lacking in sympathy and claiming me a fool. "You deserved that one now, didn't ya?" She shook her head and shone the light around the room.

I swallowed the insult on the tip of my tongue. I needed her, and I hated it. I preferred to tackle tough situations on my own because all blunders fell on my shoulders, and I only had myself to blame. Besides, I knew I could count on me.

"She must have put them somewhere else," Lucy said. "They have to be here somewhere."

"Perhaps she secures them in 'er room at night." I envisioned a massive raven with the eyes of Miss Keene, perched in a nest with the ledgers secured within its wings, the key Lucy held gleaming on its neck.

"No, they're here." She smacked a palm to her forehead. "Think."

"'And me that light." I swiped the torch and shone it over every inch of the room. "Wait a minute." I swung the light back to one of the countryside paintings. The artwork hung crooked. I strode to the wall. "Come 'elp me."

"What is it?" Lucy took the torch I held out.

I lifted the painting off the wall and set it on the floor.

"Well, I'll be," Lucy said, astonished. "A secret compartment. Doesn't appear to be any lock."

I arched up on tiptoes and ran my fingers along the wall,

pressing and feeling for movement. The wall had some give, and I pushed harder. My heart leaped when a small door swung open.

Inside sat a bundle of ledgers, tied as Lucy had described. I stood frozen before I released an outpouring of nervous laughter. By golly, we'd done it.

"Don't just stand there. Grab them so we can take a gander and get out of here before someone catches us." Without allowing me to do as instructed, she brushed by me and snatched the ledgers herself.

She set the books on the desk, untied the binding, and flipped open the first pages. She traced her finger up and down, thumbing through pages too swiftly for my liking.

"'Ow can you read that fast?" I peeked over her shoulder.

"I'm reading the first few letters, no need to read the rest. This book is dated 1918–1921. There you are. Hazel Winters, birthdate April 13, 1907. One sibling. Brother. William Winters, age six." She paused.

"What else does it say?" Impatience stirred in my chest.

"Nothing. That's all."

"It can't. It must say where they took him." I pulled the book from her grasp to take a look myself.

"You can't read, you meff. Give it back." Lucy's fingernails bit into my flesh, and panic flashed in her eyes. "I have to look for me sisters and my information. Your brother was never housed here, but they were."

"What in heaven's name are you two doing in here?"

I dropped the book, and it clattered to the floor. Lucy swung the torch around, and Miss Appleton lifted an arm to block the light.

"M-Miss Appleton, we're sorry," Lucy said, like she was about to break out blatting.

"Lower that light at once." Miss Appleton strode forward when Lucy obeyed. "Are you two looking to spend the rest of your existence in the cellar?"

Lucy gulped and shook her head.

"It ain't Lucy's fault. I asked 'er to do it. Guilted 'er into it after she got me locked up." I didn't know why I did it, but the words tumbled out.

I felt Lucy's eyes on me. "That ain't true. We did it together. We are clever girls, and we thought—"

"Enough," Miss Appleton said through clenched teeth, shooting a glance at the door. "You two get back to your rooms at once, before I report what you have done here."

I regarded the warden with suspicion before approaching her. "You ain't gonna go snitching on us, are ya?"

"No, but you'd best get out of here before I change my mind."

"Good." I lowered the hackles on my back and stepped back. "Come on, Lucy."

Without waiting for the warden to say more, we turned and raced for the door.

"Wait!"

We halted abruptly and swung back to her.

"How did you get in here?" she asked.

Lucy giggled nervously and dangled the key out for her to see. Miss Appleton snatched it out of her hand. "And the one for the rooms." She extended a palm.

Lucy lifted the ring from her pocket and placed it in Miss Appleton's hand.

"And the one you used to get into Miss Keene's room."

Lucy removed a bobby pin from her hair.

"Clever one, aren't you?" Miss Appleton said.

Lucy gave her a toothy grin.

"Go now. And hope I can get this back to her before she finds out." She wiped a palm on the fabric of her uniform.

We turned and raced from the office and down the corridor. At the door to the room I shared with the other girls, I slowed my pace and turned back as Lucy waddled past me. I gripped her arm.

She froze and looked at me, sadness etched deep in her eyes.

"For what it's worth, fank you." I tried to smile, but melancholy ate at the both of us.

She shrugged. "We tried, right?"

"Yeah."

She turned to leave.

"Lucy?"

She paused and swung back.

"I won't ever forget what you did for me."

She frowned. "But we didn't find what we needed."

"No." Glancing down at the fingers I twisted in front of me, I said, "But you showed you're a true mate back there, and I'm glad I know you." I blushed and inclined my head.

A small smile touched her mouth. "Reckon I'm glad too." With that she waddled off to her room, two doors down.

Later, discouraged and heavy of heart, I lay in bed, tears dampening my pillow. Turning over onto my side, I whispered, "I'm sorry, William. I tried. Really I did."

CHAPTER 13

Charlotte

N THE OFFICE DOORWAY, I STARED AFTER THE GIRLS, UNSURE WHAT TO think of Hazel's claim: *I got me a mum and a brother.* I'd had my suspicions, and experiences proving, the funded government organizations might not be putting the children's interests first. If Hazel's claim was valid, and she indeed had a mother, I was in over my head—knowledge of which had led to a sense of helplessness that had become stifling in the years since Agnes had hired Ellie and me.

I turned back to face the darkened room, redolent of Agnes's floral perfume. Like Ellie, I loathed her with each passing day. Oddly enough, she had taken a liking to Ellie, and positioned her under herself, never releasing too much control, but giving her more than any other staff member. The two had the same cold, emotionless stares. But no matter how much Ellie hurt inside, I believed she had a heart.

Hazel reminded me of my sister before Walter had taken her innocence, and before life had handed us more than we could handle.

If I could give Hazel a lifeline, information to adhere to for the years to come, I had to try. But the probability of providing a grain of hope seemed improbable. The brother hadn't been brought to the distributing home, which would mean Agnes wouldn't have any information on him. Luck and a miracle granted reunited Ellie and me, but the receiving home had been our one link. Assisting Hazel was as futile as attempting to pluck a star from the sky.

I clicked on the flashlight, and strode to the ledger on the floor, and picked it up. I laid it on the corner of the desk and flipped through the pages. As I had expected, the files bore no information that would prove useful in tracking Hazel's brother. However, I had noticed the entry of the girl's arrival. Scripted in Agnes's handwriting were her details. I frowned. The girl was marked as an orphan. Had Agnes intended to do so, or was it a logging error? Neglecting to record details correctly obscured the children's origins and inhibited them in any attempts to locate siblings. The injustice made me clench my hands.

"As if Agnes would divulge details if anyone came asking," I whispered. Hadn't Miss Grant also denied Ellie the information she sought?

I turned another page, and my fingers paused. A girl named Annie had been marked deceased, and a bold question mark stood next to the entry. The mark had been traced repeatedly, as if deep thought had captured Agnes's mind. I recalled the girl. She had entered the establishment a year and a half ago, and soon after, the Gagnons contracted her. Six months ago, the child was reported dead. All children underwent a health inspection shortly after arrival. The doctor had deemed her a simpleton, but otherwise she hadn't been ill—quite the opposite. She'd been healthy and lively with a fetching smile regardless of the decaying teeth. What had happened to her?

My heart jumped at the sound of footsteps in the hallway. Clicking off the light, I raced to the door, and as treads halted outside, I twisted the lock. I stood, holding my breath, when the handle jiggled. *Great, Charlotte. Just great.* No amount of explaining would deflect the attention from what I was doing in Agnes's office.

I would be out on my backside that very night. But after a moment the footsteps moved away, and I breathed a sigh of relief. I rushed back and shut the book, tied the bundle, and replaced it within the compartment before returning the painting to its prior position.

I waited an extra minute or two, then unlocked the door and peeked out to ensure everything was clear before stepping out and locking it behind me. I hurried down the corridor to Agnes's room. Breathless, my heart pounding, I bit down to ease my nerves and opened the door. My hand froze on the doorknob when I saw an empty bed. I scoured the darkness before glancing over my shoulder. Where was she? Not wanting to wait a minute longer, I hurried to the night table, deposited the keys, then turned to dart out, but halted. Had Agnes been the one at the office door? If so, she'd already know the keys weren't on the stand. I veered back, scooped up the keys, and slid them under the bed. Then I dashed into the hallway, closed the door behind me, and darted back the way I'd come.

When I approached the corner, I eased my pace and tried to steady my breathing—and ran headfirst into a solid form. My skull rattled from the impact. The person gasped and clutched me to catch their balance.

"Where are you going in such a hurry?" Agnes glowered down at me. The usual tight topknot worn by staff members had been loosed to drape in soft waves of gray-speckled dark hair over slender shoulders. Cloaked in a white nightgown and a robe, she almost looked angelic and vulnerable. I'd come to learn that Agnes's demand for order was her way of asserting control over her vulnerabilities. Like the children, the staff who took on the overnight stays had to turn in by a time she deemed reasonable.

I lowered my gaze and stared at her bare feet. "Sorry, Miss Keene. I went to the kitchen to get a drink. I've always been scared of my shadow."

"That's all well and good, but the kitchen is in the opposite direction from the one you were coming from."

I'd never been a quick thinker, and nerves conjured in my gut. *Think, Charlotte. Think.* "You're right." I elevated my gaze. "I-I went to the kitchen, then I heard a noise and thought I'd check in on the children." Yes, that would do—the perfect reason for me to be out of my room.

She pursed her lips. "And did you find anyone out of bed?"

"Yes, one of the little ones. She'd had a nightmare." I recollected how the panicked child had banged on the locked door of the children's room, crying for her mother, and how I could only console the girl through the metal door between us. "Her distress got me thinking."

"About what?" She stiffened.

"Maybe you should reconsider locking the children in at night."

She bristled.

"Children need comfort. They aren't animals to put in cages."

"Are you questioning my methods?" Her eyes narrowed.

My heart raced. "If it's order you seek, don't you think if the children felt loved and nurtured that they'd be less likely to act out?" I rushed on before I lost the courage. "It isn't easy leaving all you know behind, and if the children—"

"And what would you know about leaving things behind?" She arched a brow.

"After my parents died, when I came here to live with my grandparents, I had a tough time adjusting, as I'm sure you can understand. You must have gone through the same adjustments."

"The past is the past, Miss Appleton. I do not speak of it. Fear is for the weak. It's a tough world out there. As soon as you and the children realize that, the better you all will be." She peered around as though looking for something. "Any chance you have seen my keys? I've never been one to misplace something. I put them on my nightstand, as I do every night."

"No; but if I do, I'll be sure to bring them to you."

She nodded after a painful inspection of my face. "Well, you'd best see yourself to bed, Miss Appleton. Morning comes early."

"It certainly does. Good night." I darted past her.

I recalled Hazel and Lucy's looks of fear when I'd caught them in the office. My shock at finding them was counterbalanced by the hidden delight that the girls had settled their differences.

You ain't gonna go snitching on us, are ya? Hazel had looked me straight in the eye, unwavering under my authority. I smiled. The girl had spunk, and it would do her well in life.

At the room I shared with Ellie, I opened the door and glanced at the lump on her bed, relieved she slept. I crept inside but froze at a movement to my right.

"Where 'ave you been?" Ellie said from the rocker under the window.

I placed a hand to my throat. "You about scared me half to death."

The rocker squeaked as she began to rock. At first glimpse, in the moonlight trailing over her form, she resembled a ghost shrouded in a white linen nightgown and nightcap.

"I went to the kitchen. I couldn't sleep. On passing Agnes's office, I heard voices inside and saw a flash of light. When I went to investigate, I caught Hazel and Lucy going through Agnes's ledgers."

"What?" She stopped rocking and sat up straighter. "The girl never learned from being locked up?" Disapproval tightened her mouth.

I waved a hand of dismissal. "Did you?"

"I suppose not." She stood. "But if I could go back and tell my younger self anyfing, it would be: submit. Adults will seek to quieten the fire within 'er."

"You refer to Miss Grant?" Ellie never spoke of her time after she left the receiving house, and often I'd wondered what had happened in those years.

"One of many." She strode to her bed. "If Agnes catches you sneaking about, it will be the end of you."

"Too late for that," I said with a nervous laugh. "I ran into her in the corridor."

"And you lived to tell about it?" She shook her head and climbed in and tucked the covers up to her ears.

I climbed into my own bed. After a few moments of silence had passed, I rolled over to look at her. "Ellie."

"Yeah?"

"All the years we were apart, did you ever wonder why no one stepped in to help? Why no one from the receiving houses came to check on us? I mean, do the organizations not have a duty to the children that pass through these doors?"

She laughed, and a chill ran through me at the coldness of the sound. "'Ave you forgotten? We were orphans. We should be honored the organization saved us from the streets, and thankful for the families kind enough to take us in."

I tucked my hand under my cheek and tried to still the shaking of building anxiety. "You can't continue to bear the pain. It's like a cloak you can never shed if you don't heal. I'm here for you; to listen without judgment. I want you to know that."

Silence blanketed the room, and I didn't think she would speak until she did. "It 'appened before we came 'ere."

I thought of the night, barely a blur in my mind. My heart raced as I waited for her to continue.

I heard her soft sigh. "It's my fault. I was a fool."

"Don't say that." I lay still, not wanting her to withdraw, afraid to ask a question that had played on my mind for years, but knowing I needed to understand what had happened that night. "Did he rape you?"

She gasped, as though it was a fact she had been keeping in all these years. "You know?"

"I wondered."

"I worried you would. I spent my younger years trying to protect you." She paused, then in a quavering voice, she continued. "I noticed 'e 'ad taken a liking to me, and it made me feel good. An older man, finding me attractive. I've never been pretty. You were the pretty sister. You 'ad the delicate bone structure, blonde 'air, blue eyes. Anyway, as I said, I was flattered. I 'ad felt grown by providing for you, Dad, and me. When 'e came to visit, 'e was kind and never once gave me the feeling 'e was a monster." Bitterness tightened her voice. "But the night I asked 'im to 'elp me with Dad, 'e took to finking I owed 'im. And, when 'e came at me, I didn't know what to do." She was sobbing now. "Afterward I felt dirty. I carry the guilt with me even now. Shame 'as governed all me days. The shame of the rape at Walter's 'ands." Her voice caught at the mention of his name. "Shame for my part in it, and 'umiliation for the ones I encountered during my years at the family's home. Disgraced and made to feel worthless by a country because of where I came from. Rejected by our own countrymen and deemed no better than trash. I didn't ask to come 'ere. I didn't ask for our parents to die. They took us from the streets. I could 'ave cared for us. I wouldn't 'ave let anyfing 'appen to you."

I kicked back the blankets, leaped from my bed, and climbed into her bed, holding her while she cried.

"Why? Why me? Am I undeserving of love?" In her agony, she gripped at my back while sobs racked her body.

"You are loved, Ellie. I love you. You're my big sister, and you were always looking out for me."

"But I said 'orrible fings to you. Awful fings. Then this damn place separated us, and I've spent the last firty years reliving my final words to you. That almost seemed worse than the rapes." She hiccupped, laying her cheek against my chest.

"We found each other, and never again will we be separated," I whispered into her hair.

"But if you are going to marry Frederick, you can't keep this job. An 'usband wants 'is wife at 'ome."

"Frederick is understanding. He knows how important it is to me to help the children."

"You are but one person against the whole of the British and Canadian governments. What can you possibly do?"

"It isn't the government I seek to stop. Because, as you said, I am one woman against power too great. But what I can do... what we *both* can do is help the children we encounter. If we can save but one child, our work won't be in vain."

"And 'ow do you suppose we do that?"

"By continuing to keep our own records and checking in on the children we can."

"And if Agnes finds out? We will both lose our jobs. And I need the money."

"What is money when the children's innocence is at stake? When you left here, didn't you ever yearn for someone to come and rescue you?"

"Every night."

"Then help me," I said. "Help me give the children hope."

"All right." A shiver went through her. "Charlotte?"

"Yeah?"

"Did anyone violate you?"

I tensed at her question, then answered honestly. "No."

"Good." She relaxed in my arms. Her voice thick with sleep, she mumbled, "I worried."

I kissed the top of her head and pulled her closer. "No need to worry anymore. I'm grown. We will face life together."

I lay there holding her, lulled by her soft snores, until sleep came.

CHAPTER 14

Hazel

THE FOLLOWING SATURDAY, MISS KEENE ORDERED US TO RISE EARLY, bathe, and dress in clothes laid out for us. From the waiting room across from the lobby, I watched all morning as other girls entered and left with their assigned families, or exited weeping over not being chosen. I recalled Lucy's mention of the library system. If a family didn't select me, I would be shipped off to another receiving home or returned to England. Neither seemed like a favorable option. Distance would limit the chances of me finding my brother. If our reuniting had a glimmer of hope, I had to leave with a family.

When my turn came, I pinched color into my cheeks to imply health and smoothed my dress and hair before knocking on the door.

"Come in," Miss Keene's voice called.

I squared my shoulders, opened the door, and strode into the room with more confidence than I felt. A man and a woman sat with their backs to me in front of the headmistress's desk.

"Welcome, Hazel." Miss Keene rose from her chair behind the desk and came to stand beside me. She placed a hand as cold as her disposition on my arm. "I'd like you to meet Mr. and Mrs. Gagnon. They've come seeking a girl about your age to help manage their youngsters and household chores."

Pins poked my flesh as the couple turned in their chairs.

"Kinda skinny." The balding man with blue ribbons of veins meandering across his bald head eyed me from the tips of my shoes to my head.

"Oh, hush, Samuel. We didn't come to fetch another boy for your fields." The thickset woman with a stomach swollen with child swiveled to inspect me. "Come here, girl. Let me look at you."

I obeyed and stopped in front of her, hiding my trembling hands in the folds of my skirt.

Her meaty hands gripped my face. "Open up. The last girl I got came with a mouth full of rotten teeth, and ill from the start. No wonder she didn't last long."

I gulped. What had happened to her?

I glanced at Miss Keene, and she jutted her chin out. Grudgingly, I opened my mouth. Mrs. Gagnon poked her finger inside and wiggled it around as though seeking a critter to pluck from its den. Her tongue flicked up over her burgundy lip as she explored. The urge to clamp down on her finger scurried through my mind, but I minded my manners and focused on quelling my gag reflex.

"All is intact," she said. Heat rushed over my cheeks as she ran her hands up and down my body, squeezing my limbs before giving me a hard shake. I gritted my teeth and registered a glare at her. "She appears to be sturdier than she looks. But she got the devil in her eyes. I have much work ahead of me to cleanse her, but the Almighty has placed these poor souls in my care for me to do His calling. I am no stranger to trials and tribulations. We'll take her."

Panic thrummed in my chest. What calling was she referring to? By the looks of her, she was the one with the devil in her eyes. I had walked into the room in pursuit of a home, but fear enveloped me as I looked upon the couple.

"Very well, I will get her papers together and she will be ready to go within half an hour," Miss Keene said. "Hazel, go and gather your things and meet us in the lobby."

On the verge of tears, I spun and hurried from the office before they spilled over my cheeks. In the dormitory, I used my cuff to wipe my tears before pulling the suitcase from beneath my bed and placing the few belongings I had inside. My fingers paused on the folded linen napkin from the dining hall, which concealed my greatest treasure. I lowered myself onto the edge of the bed and stroked the linen with my fingers.

Inside was a photo of me and William that the organization had taken our first night at the home in Liverpool. When everyone slept, I'd snuck down the hall to the main office and found the door locked. After picking the lock, I'd crept inside and spotted the files for the day's arrivals in the center of the desk. I'd flipped through the documents until I'd come to the photo of William and me.

I tucked the napkin into the bottom of the suitcase and went to retrieve my hat and coat. As I did up the wooden buttons, I heard footsteps behind me. I spun to find Lucy with tears gathering in her eyes.

"Guess you will be leaving?"

"Yes, and the couple seems downright appalling. Well, the mister may be all right, but the woman…" My words faded as my tears flowed.

Lucy shuffled forward and wrapped an arm around my shoulder.

"I-I'm skeered." I peered at her through my tears.

Seemingly lost for words, she nodded. "Guess I will also be leaving."

I tensed at the news. "You nabbed yourself a family?"

She lowered her gaze. "Nah, they are sending me to another receiving home."

"But your sisters. 'Ow will they find you?" Panic rose at the disheartening thought.

She slumped down on the edge of a bed. "Probably ain't ever gonna see them again. I was a meff to hope."

"No, don't say that. We must stay strong. We must." I used the back of my hand to brush away the tears before joining her on the bed. "I know I've been dreadful—"

"Wasn't any more than I deserved."

Drained of emotions, I laughed because I didn't know what else to do. "You may 'ave deserved a little, but not all. I'm glad we sort of became mates."

She cocked her head at me, and a gleaming smile revealed the gap between her two front teeth. "Mates?"

"That's right. I reckon if we 'ad met on the streets, I might 'ave let you join my pack." I nudged her shoulder with mine.

"Your pack?" she said in awe. "You were the leader?"

"You could say that." I thought of my solo adventures on the streets and decided not to tell her otherwise. She needed to feel wanted, the same as I needed her friendship. Then perhaps life wouldn't feel so empty. I thought of Brock and how he'd tried to get me to join his gang of boys. Maybe if I had I could have earned more coin, and Mum wouldn't have taken us to the home in Liverpool.

The sound of someone entering the room drew our attention. Miss Scott stood with her hands clasped in front of her and an odd look on her face. A look that stated her unease.

"'Azel, Miss Keene 'as sent me to retrieve you. Your family awaits."

I rose from the bed and strode to her, suitcase in hand. Looking up at her, I squared my shoulders. "They ain't my family. No one will ever replace my family." I stomped my foot.

Nervousness danced on her face, and she bobbed her head

like I was the one in authority. "You are right, young 'azel. You 'old onto that truth." The tenderness in her tone took me by surprise, and I frowned at her. "I am not the enemy," she added.

I snorted. "All wardens are the enemy." I strode past her and showed myself down the hall to the lobby.

"Ah, there she is." Miss Keene's foreign smile gleamed like polished silver, but she didn't fool me. I had experienced the rot in her soul.

"Make haste, girl. We have a train to catch," Mrs. Gagnon said.

"I believe she said her name was Hazel." Her husband placed a straw hat on his head and opened the heavy oak door to the outside.

Mrs. Gagnon scowled at him. "I didn't ask for your input. You're not to be putting your opinion in when it comes to me managing the girl. You tend to your responsibilities in the fields and let me tend to matters of the home."

"As you say, Peggy." He dipped his head and stepped outside to hold the door.

"Hazel!" Lucy rushed into the lobby with Miss Scott on her heels. Miss Scott gripped Lucy's shoulder to stop her, but stood regarding me with a look that resembled sadness. What did she care what happened to me? After all, warn't this what they all wanted: to ship off the orphans and street rats? Something told me death would be better than what awaited some of us. And at that moment, I wondered if that someone was me.

Lucy lifted a hand and waved, then called, her voice cracking with tears, "Take care of yourself."

"You too." I braced myself for what was to come and swung back to Mrs. Gagnon.

Her sour expression deepened. "Well, what are ya waiting for? Let's go."

Maybe the babe stretching her midsection until her stomach looked like it would burst was the reason for her moodiness, I thought as I hurried to join her. Her hand gripped my arm and pulled me toward the door. As the door closed behind me, she rushed me down the steps.

Miss Appleton was walking up the walkway, her arms weighed down with brown paper bags of groceries. "Hazel?" She gawked at me. "Wait." She addressed her plea to Mrs. Gagnon.

"No time to wait. We have a train to catch." Mrs. Gagnon brushed past her, and Miss Appleton stumbled back, landing on her backside.

"In you go." Mrs. Gagnon gestured at the open door of a car, where the mister stood waiting.

Squished between her and Mr. Gagnon, I glanced at Miss Appleton as Miss Scott helped her to her feet. I turned my attention to the sign on the lawn and studied the arches and strokes of the letters and numbers one last time before the cab pulled away from the curb. My heart thumped wildly at the prospect of what lay ahead.

CHAPTER 15

Charlotte

SPRAWLED ON THE LAWN WITH THE GROCERIES SCATTERED AROUND me, I stared after the familiar woman clutching Hazel. She shoved her into the backseat of a cab, and I gritted my jaw at the lack of tenderness displayed in her handling of the girl.

"Come, Miss Appleton, there are tasks to attend to," Agnes said from the front steps.

I glanced at her as Ellie hurried toward me.

"You all right?" she said under her breath while helping me to my feet.

"What, you mean after Bloody Mary blew through?" I scowled at the woman, who waddled around the car to the other side, plopped down beside Hazel in the backseat, and slammed the door shut. "Not a stitch of manners in her."

As the car pulled away, I cast one last look at Hazel. She sat squashed between the man and the woman, with her head bowed. Unease rolled over me. Everything in me told me to run to the girl and pull her from the car, but Agnes's restless tapping of her foot on the steps warned of the danger in doing so. I fought back tears of frustration and hurried to gather the scattered groceries.

Agnes turned and went back inside, seeming satisfied with Hazel's departure. Foreboding lodged in the pit of my stomach.

"Did you fink she would stay forever?" Ellie bent to retrieve a bag of rice.

"If Agnes hadn't sent me to the store to fetch supplies that could have waited until our wholesale order came in, I'd have been here."

"To do what?" Ellie said, devoid of emotion. "You can't stop the inevitable."

"Perhaps not. But I could have said something. Tried to reason with Agnes that the woman doesn't seem fit to take a child. But the well-being of the children isn't of her concern." My thoughts turned to the ledger and the records I'd seen. "Do you recall the girl Annie who came here soon after we started working here?" I envisioned the girl: big blue eyes, frizzy brown hair, and sturdier than most children that entered the establishment.

"The older girl who wasn't quite right in the head."

"Yes, but she was healthy nonetheless. Took orders well, too. She simply lived in her own world."

"All right, where are you going with this?" Ellie glanced at the doors. "Agnes is watching; we better 'urry."

"Well, she's dead."

"Dead?" Her eyes widened. "'Ow do you know?"

"Because the night Hazel and Lucy got into Agnes's office, I saw her details, and she was marked dead."

"Why is this the first time I'm 'earing of this?"

"Because I've yet to process the information myself. There was no cause of death mentioned, and it seemed as though Agnes questioned the death herself."

"What makes you fink that?"

"There was a question mark beside the record that had been traced several times. If only I could speak to the Gagnons, I could question them myself." I picked up the sack of coffee beans.

"Gagnons..." Ellie said in a hollow voice.

I glanced at her and noticed her ashen complexion. "What is the matter?"

She looked down the street. "That's who left with 'azel."

An invisible hand seized my throat. That was why the woman had seemed familiar. Nausea rose in my belly. *Oh, Hazel.* Tears burned at the corner of my eyes.

The door squeaked. "Ladies, do I need to separate you?" Agnes said.

"Coming, Miss Keene," Ellie said in feigned reverence.

I stood, too numb to move. Ellie, ever level-headed, blocked me from view as she turned and hurried up the steps. Agnes stepped back to open the door wider.

I grappled with the urge to revolt, to break ranks with Agnes's precious order. There was no wisdom in that, I knew.

But as Agnes turned to walk inside, I said, a bit too loud, "What happened to Annie?"

She froze and turned back, gripping the doorframe as though my question had taken her off guard. "What concern is it of yours?"

"I was wondering, is all. The Gagnons come here to seek two house girls in a matter of two years. Contracting more girls is odd, don't you think? Usually families seek more boys, to work their fields."

She cocked a brow. "I grow tired of your endless questions. I must warn you, Miss Appleton: do your job and don't pry into things that aren't of your concern, unless you aspire to be removed from the establishment." Then, as though brushing me off, she waved a hand and strode inside.

I gawked after her, a wave of lightheadedness washing over me. If Agnes also had questions about Annie's death, why would she hand Hazel over to the Gagnons without further investigation into the matter? I whispered a prayer for the girl's safety. Determination anchored in my chest. I wasn't sure how, but I would find out where the Gagnons lived. Maybe Annie had died of natural causes (although I had no idea what they would be), but until I knew I wouldn't rest.

I climbed the steps and walked inside, but as I passed Agnes's office, I paused at the sight of her pacing the floor, muttering to herself. She stopped at the window to look out.

"Miss Keene," I said.

She spun around, a look of panic on her face.

"Is everything all right?" My concern over Hazel, and Agnes's odd behavior, pulled me to the doorway.

She marched forward and slammed the door.

A hand gripped my elbow. "Are you insane?" Ellie pulled me down the corridor. "Do you want to be fired?"

"Of course not."

"I need your 'elp with Clara."

"What is it?" My concern shifted from one child in need to another.

"She refuses to come out."

"From where?"

"You 'ave to see it for yourself." She marched at a pace that had me running to keep up. At the closet where the cleaning supplies were stored, Ellie paused, gave me a worried look, and opened the door.

I gasped. "Where are her clothes?" I bent and placed the bags on the ground. "Clara," I said softly. "It's Miss Appleton."

She sat curled in the corner of the closet, rocking and talking to herself.

"What is she saying?" I looked up at Ellie.

"I don't know."

I looked back at the girl as she started clawing at her flesh. "Get them off of me," she wailed.

"What, Clara? What is it?" I reached for her, wanting to offer comfort, but thinking my touch may bring her more distress, I withdrew my hand.

On closer inspection, I noticed she had rubbed her skin raw, and the hot poker marks marring her flesh never ceased to summon rage within me. No one would ever know the depths of what the girl had suffered. How she'd survived it, I didn't know. Annie's face flashed before me, and I quickly dismissed it as Clara gripped handfuls of her hair and pulled out strands.

"Get off of me," she wailed and scurried deeper into the corner.

"The poor soul is troubled. Been in there all morning after bathing time," the laundress said matter-of-factly on her way by.

"And you left 'er 'ere?" Ellie clutched her arm. "Can't you see the girl is clearly distressed?"

The laundress adjusted the pile of clean linens she carried and glanced at Ellie's hand before shaking her arm free. "Of course I do. We all do. The doctor said there isn't anything to be done. The girl has lost her mind. She won't be our problem for much longer."

"Why is that?" I asked.

"Because Miss Keene has put in a call, and the asylum in Kingston is coming for the girl."

"She is locking her up?" I rose.

"Appears so." The laundress shrugged as though Clara's welfare mattered little.

Did we not have an obligation? Regardless of Ellie's and my personal reasons for helping the children, the staff members' lack of empathy and the normalcy of their emotionless approach was astounding. I seethed but remained quiet. I grabbed a folded white sheet from her.

"Hey, we have a new shipment coming in. I need that for the beds."

"Too bad. Skedaddle." Ellie narrowed her eyes. "Off with you now."

Eyes widening, the laundress stepped back before grumbling

under her breath and marching off. Under Ellie's management, the staff toed the line, and for this, Agnes found her of use. Me, not so much. She didn't like me; I could feel it every time she looked at me. Agnes hated weakness, and she viewed me as weak. Perhaps because of my soft mannerisms and gentleness toward the children, she believed me a compromised link in her precious order.

Clara's distress elevated to screams and flailing arms.

"We 'ave to get 'er calmed down before Agnes 'ears 'er, or it will be both our 'eads on a platter," Ellie said.

I shook open the sheet and knelt before Clara. "I'm not going to hurt you. We need to get you out of here and somewhere more comfortable," I said, as though she would understand. The girl lived in the sanctuary her mind had created because reality had become too hard to bear. A twinge of guilt jabbed at me. We had no choice but to use restraint to keep her from harming herself more. I draped the sheet over her, and Ellie helped me get the flailing girl to her feet.

"What is the meaning of this?"

We spun to find Agnes standing behind us with a puckered-up face and hands clenched at her sides.

"Nuffing we can't 'andle," Ellie said.

"I should hope not. What if families had been here to hear such a ruckus? They would think this is an establishment of horrors."

"Isn't it?" I said under my breath while trying to keep my grip on Clara.

Her eyes trained on Clara, Agnes curled her nose in disgust. "Get her out of my sight. I can't stand to look at her. The girl is clearly possessed."

I glared at her. *This is all your doing. If you hadn't given her to that family, she wouldn't have suffered as she has.*

"Is there a problem, Miss Appleton?" Agnes had turned her gaze to me.

"No, Miss Keene." I lowered my eyes, feeling like I was failing Clara as I had Hazel. Discouragement weighted my footsteps as Ellie and I led the girl away.

In the sick room, the nurse on duty helped us get Clara into a bed. Ellie lay across her flailing body while we strapped down her wrists and ankles. The nurse gave the girl a sedative, and soon she settled. "She will sleep now," the nurse said before moving on to the young girl with a fever that I'd brought in early that morning.

"I hate her," I said when the nurse was out of earshot.

"You and me both. Agnes should rot in 'ell for what she's done."

"She took on a responsibility to these children, but her need for control has clouded her judgment."

"No, sister, it's who she 'as always been—a walking poison to all those she comes in contact with." Resentment ran rancid in Ellie's statement.

"And that poison has scarred your heart."

She cranked her head around to give me a grim look that had made others tremble. "Be careful, sister."

"It's the truth. As long as you allow the past to eat at your heart, Agnes will have a hold on you."

Her hands clenched at her sides.

Deciding not to push the matter further, I left her to go and monitor the children in the yard.

There, moving away from the children and the other women watching them, I removed the small leather journal from my apron pocket and jotted details of the day's occurrences: Hazel's leaving with the Gagnon family, and the news of Clara's impending move to the asylum. Since my arrival at the institute, I'd recorded the children who had entered, registering their names, ages, and siblings. When I could without the risk of discovery, I listened outside Agnes's office on distributing day to gather information on the families who came to contract the children.

"What you writing?"

I jumped and closed the book, then tucked it away before turning to smile at Lucy. "It's nothing. What can I help you with?"

She lowered her head and picked at her fingers. "Guess Hazel leaving has me a bit in the dumps. Suppose it doesn't matter much now anyway…"

"Why do you say that?"

"I'll be leaving soon."

My heart dropped. I'd come to enjoy Lucy's prattling. "Leaving? Has a family inquired about you?"

"No, Miss Keene told me that I'm being sent to Nova Scotia to another receiving home. I've come to believe no one will want me. Let's not forget: not even our own parents wanted me and me sisters."

"That isn't true." I anchored my hands on my hips and gave her a disapproving look.

Her eyes flashed. "What do you know 'bout it? You warn't there when they deposited us on the institute's steps like we were a burden they'd rather be done with. I recall it like yesterday." Misery and hurt reflected in her eyes.

I dropped my hands and opted for a softer approach. "You shouldn't speak so lowly of yourself. I'm sure your parents had no other choice and that they loved you very much."

She sucked back a quivering lip and looked away before observing me uncertainly. "I won't deny you've been kind to us, more helpful than the rest of the lot. But it doesn't take a fool to see your mind sails a million miles away. I reckon it's as Hazel said—you're too busy writing in that little book to offer anything else."

My hand went to the notebook tucked inside my apron pocket. I had tried to use the utmost discretion when jotting down details. I feared what Agnes would do if she got her hands on it. "I do care, and it's not what you think."

"Really?" She crossed her arms and gave me a hard stare. "I don't believe a word you say." Lucy had always been a pleasant girl, popping out from nowhere to ask, "What ya doing?" I assumed her sour disposition spoke to her disheartenment over Hazel's and her own impending departure.

I surveyed the yard and building for anyone watching us, and the thumping in my chest eased a tad at finding no one. I gripped Lucy's shoulder. "Walk with me."

"What for?" Her moodiness continued, but she obliged me.

"I need you not to mention the book to anyone."

"I ain't gonna tell no one 'bout your blasted book," she grumbled, her last word catching. She peered up at me. "What's in it, anyway?"

"The book doesn't matter."

She huffed. "It's like Hazel said: this place is a prison, and you all are the wardens bent on tearing families apart."

The girls' opinion of us dismayed me. Had I failed in my mission? "I can't say I disagree."

She stopped and looked up at me, then shook her head as though expecting a different answer.

"I know it seems impossible, but not all wardens are cut from the same cloth."

"You saying you're different?" Her laughter was mocking. "For a while I thought you may be different, but now I'm not so sure. Reckon you're the same as Miss Keene, Miss Scott, and the rest. For so long, I've wanted someone to come for me, but the more I notice, the more I realize that may not be a good thing. Did you get a gander at that woman who took Hazel?" Her contempt turned to unconcealed concern, and a shiver rushed over her.

Oh, I did, all right. I envisioned the groceries and myself sprawled over the front lawn. "I did."

"It can't be good. If you claim to be different, what do you suppose you're going to do 'bout it?"

"What do you think I can do?"

"You're an adult. You can do a heap more than we can." Her demeanor grew urgent. "You ain't going to give up on Hazel, are ya, Miss Appleton? I got this feeling in me gut that those people ain't good."

You and me both. "Well, I don't know…"

"That ain't good enough. The way I look at it, you're 'bout the only one who can help Hazel. You could check in on her." Desperation widened her eyes.

"I don't have access to the information on where the children go after they leave here."

"But we can get the information." She clutched my wrist.

"How?"

"We go back into the lion's den."

"But I thought you didn't trust me."

She shrugged. "Reckon I ain't got no choice. I suppose, compared to the others, you may have some heart to ya. Hazel needs us."

"I want to help her."

"Then prove it. Let me help you help Hazel."

"And if we are caught? It will be the cellar for you, and I'll be out of a job." *Have you gone mad?* I couldn't believe I was considering involving the child in an adult situation.

"So you are like the rest. All you care 'bout is your job and upsetting Miss Keene. For a moment I hoped…never mind." She dropped her head and kicked at a stone.

No, you don't understand. It's so much more than that, I pleaded silently. "Lucy." I touched her arm, and she recoiled. Tears cascaded over her freckled cheeks. "Please." She turned her back to me. Desperately wanting her to know she hadn't lost an ally, I blurted, "You know the writing on the wall in the cellar?"

She swung back, her eyes narrowed, but there was a gleam of interest. "What 'bout it?"

"It was written by my sister."

Her mouth unhinged. "Your sister? She was a home girl?"

I nodded.

"Here?"

"Like you. She stayed here for far too long. But I believe it was because the headmistress didn't like her."

Enlightenment relaxed her face. "She locked her up?"

"Yes. In the weeks after we arrived, she spent more time in the cellar than with the other girls."

She let out a whistle. "Well, ain't that something. I've always felt a strange kinship with the phantom girl in the cellar. Spent many days and nights envisioning the misery she must have suffered." She glanced around before leaning in to say in a soft voice, "But if you and your sister were home children, what made you want to work in a place that separated you and locked your sister away?"

I turned my back to the others in the yard. "To connect siblings." I removed the notebook from my pocket and pointed at what I had written. "See here."

Lucy scanned the pages. "You're recording our information?" she said in awe.

"Yes, in hopes that one day I can help siblings reunite."

"Don't you think you'd do better by helping stop the

children from ever leaving or coming here in the first place? After all, you're an adult. You have the power to stop all this."

I tucked the book away. "It isn't as simple as that. Up against the government, I'm as helpless as all of you in the matter. Home children are common around here, and no one sees the wrong in what they are doing. I would not only have to overpower a government but change every citizen's mind as well. You must believe me when I say that if I could, I would. I've tried my best to show you all kindness…" My words dropped off as I heard how feeble my plea sounded.

Lucy's expression softened. "Doing something is better than doing nothing, I reckon." She offered me a lopsided grin. "I was angry earlier. You ain't that bad."

I smiled at her. "You're too kind. Let's get back to Hazel, shall we?"

She bobbed her head eagerly.

"We need to learn the Gagnons' location if I am going to help."

Face brightening, she leaped forward and threw her arms around my neck. "I knew I could count on you."

Teetering, I caught my balance and patted her back. "You're a smart girl, Lucy. Hazel is lucky to have a friend like you." I pulled her back and rested my hands on her shoulders.

She grinned. "It was nice to have a mate, even if it was only for a short spell."

"Now off with you before the others become suspicious," I said.

"Too late for that. Here comes Miss Keene." She turned and tottered off.

I took a deep breath and swung to face the storm headed my way. Jaw set, Miss Keene marched toward me like a drill sergeant bent on punishing a new recruit.

"Miss Keene." I presented a broad smile. "What can I help you with?"

"You forget your place, Miss Appleton."

I tensed, and my brow puckered. "Pardon me?"

"That girl and her public display of affection to a staff member—it jeopardizes your position. The children must know they are but soldiers in the order."

That day, I regarded her with sympathy. At some point in her life, she'd switched off her emotions. To feel, one had to be vulnerable. Fear of rejection was an emotion most could relate to. Agnes had built the wall of protection so high around herself, I'd come to believe that regardless of her outward display of power and strength, she was still the young, helpless girl from years ago and would never be free—a soul lost to the trauma of a stolen childhood.

"No, Miss Keene, they are children. They seek attention and love. Kindness can heal the fracture in the hardest heart. Don't we all deserve love and compassion?" I patted her arm on my way by.

"I won't tolerate…" Her voice faded behind me as I strode across the lawn and up the porch stairs.

Ellie grabbed my arm, panic alive in her eyes. "You poke the bear, sister."

I turned and positioned myself at her side. "I simply searched for the vein of humanity within her." I rested my gaze on Agnes, who stood astonished and confused. Then she lifted her whistle and blew, and the children fell into line.

Later that night, as Ellie changed into her nightgown, I sat at the desk and wrote in the notebook: *Hazel left with Peggy and Samuel Gagnon. Lucy to be shipped off to a receiving home in Nova Scotia.*

CHAPTER 16

Hazel

URING THE DRIVE TO THE TRAIN STATION, THE MISSUS reprimanded her husband and me by turns. Each time she ventured off on another tangent, Mister would sit up straight like a choir boy on Sunday. I snuck a peek at him and saw the spark of indignation in his gray eyes, but one look from her and he ducked his head and muttered, "Yes, dear." I wanted to kick him and tell him to stand up to the heifer.

The missus's recent bath in rose perfume, mixed with sweat, roiled my stomach. She dwarfed Mister in height and girth. Her tongue's bluntness could move you to tears if you didn't brace for its lashing. Her yellowish-green eyes peered through you as emotionlessly as if you were an object in her way.

Mister sat with his elbows resting on his knees, his hands fumbling with his straw hat. His wispy gray comb-over made him appear some years older than the missus. From what I'd gathered, they were farmers, and he preferred the fields to time in the city and people's company, least of all his wife's. I can't say as I blamed him. My nerves vibrating, I sat staring out the front window. What lay ahead in a home where the new taskmaster ruled even her husband's movements? I stroked the letters of the home onto my knee until the missus's hand struck it. I bit down on my lip. *Don't cry. You mustn't let her see you cry*, I told myself.

We boarded a train, and I took my assigned seat by the window. The missus sat beside me, and I cringed as her thigh pressed against mine. Mister opened his newspaper and blocked us from his view. The missus closed her eyes, and soon her loud snores pulled frowns and annoyed glances from the other passengers.

As the train pulled out of the station, misery coursed through me, and I fought back the tears as I thought of William and the distance separating us. I rested my cheek against the cool of the wall and spoke a silent promise. *I will find you. If it takes me a lifetime, we will be together again.*

Over the next hour, I thought of Mum and daydreamed that she had kept her promise and returned to the organization to retrieve us, and in the fantasy, I suppose life didn't seem so dismal. My thoughts turned to William. Had a family come for him? Maybe a couple who had wanted a child to love. I envisioned William at play, laughing, and his hand clasped in that of a smiling man. The image gave me comfort. I glanced at the Gagnons, and with both occupied, I traced the letters and numbers of the receiving house on the window until sleep pulled at my eyelids.

I awoke at the jab of an elbow as the train pulled into the station.

"Up with you." The missus tried to hoist herself up. "Samuel, do you mind?"

"Sorry, dear." He offered an arm.

She grumbled and elbowed her way down the aisle, deaf to the protests from passengers. Mister tucked the newspaper under his arm, placed the straw hat to his chest, and mumbled apologies for his wife's rudeness while hurrying after her.

Soon I sat in the backseat of the Gagnons' green automobile as the town disappeared behind us. The breeze from the missus's open window cooled my sticky flesh from the afternoon's heat, but it also blew her pungent scent back at me. I eyed the sweat dampening the curls at the nape of her thick neck and the large dark mole peeking above the collar of her brown gingham dress.

Turning to look over the fields speckled with dairy cows that lined the dirt road, I envied the beasts their freedom to graze and breathe the fresh air outside of the car. The one pleasant aspect of Canada was the quality of the air. The car moved along, rattling my skull with each pothole, but nothing could dislodge the cavern in my soul. Melancholy had snatched the hope right out of me. The unknown vastness of the land that stood between William and me daunted me. A piece of me longed to be back at the receiving home, regardless of how obnoxious Lucy had been. She and I had started to become mates, and Miss Appleton—well, she too had begun to grow on me.

After some time, Mister turned the car down a long driveway, and he glanced over his shoulder and offered me a kind smile. "Welcome home, little missy."

The missus snapped her head around to regard him and arched a bushy brow. As if she had snatched the sun from the sky, his smile faded, and he returned his eyes to the driveway. The trees gave way to a two-storey house with chipping yellow paint and white shutters. To the left of the house, by a dilapidated barn, an old tractor sat engulfed in tall weeds and grass. In the background stood another barn, which appeared newer.

On the house's front step, a fat dog lay sleeping in the sun. A dark-haired girl sat on a porch swing with a toddler bouncing on her lap. Two young girls raced across the lawn in a battle of sticks. I gawked at the screen door to the house, expecting another brood of children to storm out. The missus didn't strike me as the sort to like children, yet her middle was swollen with another.

"Out with ya, now." Missus threw open her door, and with a grunt or two, she gripped the car's doorframe and hoisted herself out. The vehicle shook in the aftermath.

"Daddy." The girls dropped their stick swords and raced toward Mister.

He spread his arms wide, and they jumped into his arms, almost sending him toppling backward. The delight in his echoing laughter made me smile.

The girl from the porch swing joined us, her scowl and emotionless eyes matching her mother's. "This the new one?" She nudged her head in my direction.

"It is." Missus removed the toddler from the girl's arms and curled her nose in disgust. She held the baby dangling in front of her. "When did you last change him?"

"This morning." The girl kept her eyes on me. "She gonna last longer than the last one?"

"She had better." Missus's tone lacked warmth even with her children. "Don't stand there, girl." She thrust the baby at me.

I seized the boy and looked into his large blue eyes. He cooed and displayed a drooly grin, but the foul scent he emitted gripped my nose.

"Nora, take her inside and show her where Joey's diapers are at."

"I'm not going to be responsible for her, am I?" Nora said.

"Off with you." The missus gave her a smack to the back of the head.

Nora marched toward the house, grumbling under her breath. Balancing the baby and my satchel, I hurried after her.

Inside, we stepped over shoes scattered in the foyer and walked through a sitting room. Clean clothes were piled high on the brown plaid sofa, overflowing onto the floor. Dust and cobwebs hung from lampshades and picture frames. Newspapers and dirty dishes were scattered from one end of the room to the other. We walked through the kitchen, and the disorganization and filth at the front of the home continued. The scent of braising beef mixed with the unpleasant smell of the passenger whose chubby legs gripped my waist churned my stomach.

At the back of the home, we climbed a steep set of stairs to the bedrooms. Nora paused outside a door at the far end of the hall. "This is Joey's room. You will sleep in here with him and the twins."

I peeked into the room, at the slanted ceiling descending to a double bed and a chest of drawers. White linen curtains stained with dirty handprints hung over the large open window. An underlying scent of urine assaulted my nostrils.

"What ya waiting for? Get in there and clean Joey up." Nora shoved me.

I gripped the baby tighter and struggled to catch my balance before sending a scowl in her direction. "Keep your bloody 'ands off me."

"Keep your bloody hands off me." She screwed up her face in mockery. "It'll do you good to watch yourself, unless you want to end up like the other."

I recalled the girl her mother had mentioned in Miss Keene's office. What had happened to her? I glanced at Nora, but her eager look, as if she yearned to tell me, kept my lips sealed.

"Where are 'is nappies?"

Disappointment tugged at her pale face. She pointed at the top drawer.

I retrieved a nappy and a washcloth. "Wa'er?"

She nudged her head at the window, a gleam of enjoyment in her dark eyes. "Go fetch it from the pump."

I gritted my teeth, pushed past her, and retraced my steps to the main floor.

As I stepped off the bottom step, I ran smack into the missus, and the impact knocked the wind out of me. Stunned, I stood gawking at her.

"Where do you think you're headed?" The thick vein that kept her brows from joining pulsed.

My heart thrashed against my ribcage. "I will change 'im straightaway. I need to fetch wa'er from the well to wash 'im."

A shadow fell over us, and from the corner of my eye I saw Nora standing at the top of the stairs. The missus balled her hands on her ample hips and scowled up at her daughter. "Got no time for your games. Show the girl where we keep the water for cleaning, or you will find yourself changing him instead."

Nora gulped. "Come on, then." She turned and stomped off.

I climbed the stairs and followed the echo of her muttering. In the room next to the children's, she stood at a chest of drawers, pouring water from a ceramic flowered pitcher into a glass container. "Here." She nodded at the dish. I retrieved it and left.

Back in the children's room, I lay Joey on the bed. He proceeded to coo and have himself a grand old time while I struggled to clean him. After I'd finished, I lifted him and sat on the edge of the bed. He offered me a toothless smile, and I smiled back. The babe was too pleasant to have been birthed from the heifer's womb, or to have a sister like Dreadful Nora.

"Girl!" Missus's bellow vibrated the walls.

"Coming," I said, but my words stuck in my throat. I hoisted Joey onto my hip and hurried from the room.

Downstairs, the missus took the baby and handed him off to Nora. "Get these dishes cleaned up." She pointed a knobby finger at the mountain of dishes piled on the olive-green countertop and stacked past the rim of the white cast-iron sink. My heart dropped at the task ahead. "Don't dally. The kettle is heated for you, so get started."

She lowered herself into a rocker in the corner to observe me as I worked. When the twins raced through the house, she bellowed for them to go outside until it was time to eat. The squeaking of the rocker soon faded, and her heavy snores mounted. The woman slept more than an infant; no wonder her home was in such disarray. I scrubbed at the hardened food coating the dishes, and with each whistle of her lips my agitation grew.

Through the window over the sink, I observed Mister speaking to a young lad in the field. They exchanged words, and Mister clapped him on the back in a gesture of gratitude. I found myself wishing my tasks were minding the cows and tilling the land, although I didn't know the slightest thing about taking care of the critters or working a farm. But I suspected the days would be more pleasant than being stuck in the house with the missus and Nora.

An hour later, my fingers had withered from the water, and I'd hardly made a dent in the stacks of dishes. I jumped when the missus let out a loud snort and stirred before sitting up.

"Ain't you got those done yet?"

"I'm going as fast as I can, Missus."

"Mind your tone. You won't fare well with a cheeky attitude. I have a special place for those of you that forget what you are."

I turned to face her, wiping my hands on the apron, which didn't appear to have seen the laundry in some time. "What we are?" As soon as I'd spoken, I wished I could take it back.

Her eyes narrowed, and she stood. "Are you hard of hearing or just plain stupid?" She closed the distance between us, and I cringed back. My legs shook as she towered over me.

"Sorry, Missus." I lowered my head, hiding my clenched fists in the folds of my dress.

She clutched my shoulder, and I winced under her talons. "The Lord himself said in Ephesians 6:5, 'Slaves, obey your earthly masters with fear and trembling, with a sincere heart, as you would

Christ.'" She seemed to relish the words. "I see defiance in you that needs to be broken. Something I will take pleasure in. You too will know you aren't part of this family, you don't have a voice, and no one cares if you live or die. You are a slave, remember that." The coldness in her tone charged me with fear unlike anything I'd ever experienced before.

She was crazy—straight-up mad. I didn't know a word of the Bible, as my parents hadn't been churchgoers, but if God had such an outlook, I was glad I'd stayed clear of Him.

She patted my shoulder before turning and letting out a bellow that dampened my underwear. "Nora!"

"Yes, Mama?" She entered with Joey asleep in her arms.

"Put him down and set the table."

Nora hurried to obey, placing Joey on a blanket in the corner.

I topped up my dishwater with hot water from the kettle and continued washing the dishes. Movement outside the window drew my gaze, and I noticed Mister and four lads entering the yard from the fields. I assumed they were home lads, three younger and one older. The oldest wore no shirt, revealing a muscled upper body from days in the fields. He removed his hat, unveiling dark hair, and wiped the sweat from his brow with the back of his arm. As if sensing my gaze, he looked to the window and nodded with a serious expression.

Long after, I lay in bed, sandwiched between the twins and Joey, and thought of the field lads and their stories. How long had each of them lived at the farm? Where did they come from? Another face entered my thoughts, as it often had since I'd seen him in the hallway in Liverpool. His blond hair and dark eyes stirred in my mind too often for my liking and swirled a mass of strange feelings in my chest that I'd tried to bury. But like most times, I failed to shake him. I fell asleep, and Brock dominated my dreams.

CHAPTER 17

N THE WEEKS THAT FOLLOWED, THE WORDS THE MISSUS HAD SPOKEN my first day resonated. She savored my suffering, and it was as though she set out each day to inflict new tortures on me. I fought against her attempts to demoralize me, but pieces of my soul chipped away. She made me feel dirty and ashamed of my existence.

My days consisted of working from morning to night, and I fell into bed long after the family slept. Food was rationed, and often my portion came from the scraps on the family's plates. I contemplated escape. I'd leave while they slept. I had made my way around the slums and streets of Liverpool brilliantly. I was smart enough to take on whatever lay beyond the boundaries of the farm. But as I thought of my brother, reasoning plucked the desire from me. If I became a wanderer, I'd never find him. And if something happened to me, what good would I do him dead? If I intended to see him again, I had to endure. I'd gathered enough from the receiving home to know that children who left with families were contracted until they turned eighteen, which meant, under servitude to the Gagnons, I had less than three years.

At mealtime, while the family ate, I stood in my assigned position in the corner with my head lowered and hands clasped in front of me. My stomach rumbled with hunger as they devoured a spread of dishes more delectable than I'd seen in all my days. The family ate like King George and Queen Mary themselves but behaved like hogs. Mister had the refinement of an English gentleman at heart and showed tenderness to his children. I'd witnessed him trying to school the twins in manners until the missus quickly and shamefully reprimanded him with no regard for the presence of the children. It didn't take long to see she had snatched his manhood, and trapped under the reign of the ogre and the burden of a house bursting with children, he succumbed to his responsibilities.

"Take the twins upstairs and get them ready for bed, and take him with you," the missus said one evening, stabbing a finger at the baby. She had sat in a chair, nattering on the phone for an hour. Her conversation had consisted of gossiping and complaining about her children, Mister, her friends, and even me. She never referred to me by name, and the worthlessness that transmitted carved away at my sense of merit. In her eyes, the field lads and I were less than animals.

"Yes, Missus." I bent and picked up Joey, who hadn't quite found his legs and used the furniture to make his way around the sitting room.

"And then I expect you to come back and get these dishes done." Her voice rose behind me as I opened the screen door and walked out onto the back porch. I grumbled to Joey, and as if understanding, he bobbed his head. I smiled and kissed his forehead. How could a babe so beautiful in spirit have sprung from the ogre's womb?

The sun still sat high and scorching in a blue sky, unobstructed by tall buildings and factories. Sweat dripped down my back, and Joey's grip around my hips dampened my cotton plaid dress. I walked about the property, looking for the twins and calling their names. After several minutes of searching, I returned to the backyard.

"What ya looking for?" a deep voice said.

I spun to find the older lad I'd observed in the weeks since my arrival, standing by a shed that looked like a slight breeze could knock it over.

"The twins."

"They're around here somewhere. Saw them playing by the barn." He looked me over. "Been wondering when we'd meet. You're too thin to last long with the way the missus treated the last..." His words trailed off as though he'd reconsidered what he had been about to say, and unease flickered in his eyes.

"You don't look too skinny."

"It ain't out of the kindness of their hearts. It's because they need me to work. If I ain't fed, the fields don't get worked, and the cows go unmilked."

"'Ow long you been 'ere?"

"Arrived in Canada when I was eight. Now I'm sixteen, I think." His brow furrowed, as though he was trying to recollect.

"You don't know 'ow old you are?"

"Don't reckon so."

I thought of the endless questions I'd drilled into William's head. Would he too forget, as this lad had? The thought filled me with fear. "You're a fool to forget." I adjusted Joey on my hip.

"Ain't no time to think," he said with a snort. "It's 'bout survival. What does it matter anyway?" He eyed me curiously.

"'Cause our identity is the one fing we 'ave. The one fing the Gagnons can't take."

He shrugged. "I look to the day I walk out of here. Who I was before don't matter much 'cause I ain't that kid anymore. Take my identity; see if I care. I'll form another."

"'Ave it your way," I said. "You stay 'ere from the first?"

"No, this is my third home."

"Why so many? Are you trouble?" I asked the questions that I'd compiled from days of pondering about the field lads.

"At first I suppose I was, but after a while I realized it warn't worth fighting them. I'm trapped in this country whether I like it or not. At least at this place I get fed, but I can't say it will be the same for you."

"I'm used to 'unger," I said, with more sass than was needed. "What they call you?"

"Mrs. Gagnon calls me you, him, or boy. Whatever comes to her mind, I reckon. Mr. Gagnon calls me by me name."

"What name is that?"

"Graham. What's yours?"

"'Azel."

"You'd best get the twins, or I'll tell Mama that you've been chasing after the help," Nora's whiny voice said behind me. I turned to look into her scowling face.

She looked past me at Graham. "Evenin'." Her scowl faded, and her cheeks flushed pink.

"Evenin', Nora." Irritation tinged his reply.

"You care for a walk by the brook?" Nora swayed ever so slightly.

"Don't suppose I can. I have cows to milk."

Her scowl returned. "Daddy always keeps you busy." Her displeasure turned to me. "We should have gotten another boy to help in the fields instead of you."

"A lad, or a girl to help take the load off of you. Which one you wanting?" Graham asked.

Her shoulders slumped, and I took my leave before she unleashed her despondency on me.

As I walked, I considered Graham. He seemed pleasant enough, and anyone who could put Nora in her place deserved a bit of respect.

Running footsteps approached behind me, and I glanced over my shoulder to find Graham racing to catch up. "Don't you 'ave cows to milk?" I turned to face him.

He grinned and wiggled Joey's outstretched hand. "I do."

"It appears Dreadful Nora 'as taken a fancy to you."

"Dreadful Nora, eh?" He chuckled.

I blushed. "Yes, giving people names 'elps me deal wif the ones I don't like and life's situations, you might say."

"And have you fixed me with a name?"

"No, I 'aven't figured out if I like you yet." I jutted my chin out.

Amusement gleamed in his eyes. "Is that so? What do you say 'bout that, Joey? Women are hard lot to figure out."

I stood taller at his reference to me as a woman and marched on toward the barn. He passed me and strode through the open doors, and cautiously I followed. I jumped when he cupped his hands and yelled up at the loft, "Daisy. Susie. If you're up there, get on down here."

Giggles came from above, and a head poked out of the hay, followed by another. "What you want, Graham?"

"Hazel here's come looking for you. Come on now; don't need your mum cross."

The twins hurried to the ladder and made their descent. When they stood before me, I said, "Your mum wants you inside and ready for bed."

"I wish Mama would let me sleep with Nora," Daisy said. "At least she doesn't pee the bed." She glowered at Susie.

"Go on now. Bes' not to keep your mum waiting," Graham said.

The girls darted by me and raced to the house, and after mumbling a goodbye, I hurried after them. Joey giggled and slapped at my shoulder as though to make me go faster. I arrived, winded, at the back porch as the twins scampered inside.

"Where have you been?" Missus marched toward me.

"I-I—"

"No need to explain. Nora told me you were off flirting with that boy."

I gawked at Nora, who stepped around her mum with a vindictive smile.

"No, I-I—"

"Save it. You stay away from him if you know what is good for you. I don't need you knocked up."

Satisfaction crossed Nora's ugly face.

"Yes, Missus." I bowed my head.

"I expect you two to come when called." Missus cuffed the twins on the back of the head, and they let out wails. "Now, off with you."

The girls hurried to get out of her way and disappeared around the corner.

"Go on, get after them. I won't tolerate laziness."

The irony of her statement had me biting my lip.

She dismissed me by turning her back. "Nora, come rub my feet," she said.

I slipped past her and continued through the house. The task of minding the children became more pleasing as I imagined Nora rubbing large calloused feet with curling yellowed toenails.

Upstairs I washed the twins and helped them into nightgowns. After they climbed into bed, boots echoed on the stairs, and soon Mister darkened the doorway.

He offered me a nod before entering the room and taking Joey from my arms. "Hello, my boy." He kissed the top of Joey's blond head before lowering himself down on the bed. The twins peered up at him with eager expressions. The love between Mister and his children made me long for my dad.

"Are you going to read to us?" Susie asked.

Mister smiled. "Have I missed a night?"

Daisy hung over the side of the bed and pulled a book from

beneath it. Mister, with some effort, kicked off his soiled boots and clambered up onto the bed to rest his head and back against the wall. The twins cuddled into his sides while Joey munched on his chubby hand. My eyes misted.

Mister opened the book and glanced at me. I took a step back and looked around the room for a task to busy myself with.

"Sit for a while, missy." He nudged his head at the edge of the bed.

"We don't want her," Susie said.

"Hush, now." Mister gave her a look, and she compressed her lips and wiggled tighter into his side. The child acted starved for affection. I suppose, with a mum like the missus and Mister's time spent in the fields, there wasn't much love to go around.

I glanced at the door, half expecting to find the missus's scowling face.

"It will be fine," Mister said before he started to read.

I crept forward and sat, and soon the children and I became lost in the soft drawl of his voice. I recalled my dad reading to me. He would sit in his favorite armchair and say, "Come, my 'azel girl, let's see what adventures await us." Some time later, Mum would wake us, and Dad would carry me to bed, tuck me in, and place a kiss on my temple. Tears gathered in my throat as I allowed abandoned memories to rise—the pain of what I had lost left a hollow feeling in my chest.

"I knew you'd be up to no good."

Heart pounding, I jumped to my feet and eyed Nora standing in the doorway.

"Lazy as they come, I see." She crossed her arms.

"Be quiet, Nora," Mister said.

Her mouth dropped. "But she isn't here—"

"Enough," Mister said with more harshness than I'd witnessed in him.

"Mama won't be happy."

"When is she ever?" he grumbled. "Come and join us or get out."

Nora gulped, and tears swelled before an unnerving look centered in her dark eyes. She turned and stormed off.

I eyed Mister, whose face had reddened as he sat staring at the empty doorway. "Too much like her mother," he said to no one in particular before concentrating his attention on me. "For your sake, you'd best go down and see what Mrs. Gagnon wants."

I nodded and left the room. My legs leaden, I made the descent to the main floor. In the kitchen, I prepared to wash the evening dishes. I eyed the housefly resting on the plate of the Gagnons' pickings, my hunger pangs replaced with the nerves swirling in my stomach as I awaited her arrival.

The floor squeaked under the missus's weighted footfalls, alerting me. As I turned to face her wrath, there was a flash of movement. Before I could block the blow, my head snapped back, and I cried out.

"You think because I'm heavy with child, you can cozy up to my husband?"

The blur of her strike cleared from my eyes, and I beheld her red face, the vein pulsing in the middle of her forehead. "No, I…" My words faded as I caught sight of Nora grinning from the sitting room doorway. My dislike for Nora and her mother fueled my anger.

"Don't look at my girl as though it's her fault. You have no one to blame but yourself, street whore." Her nostrils flared as she inched closer. "Spread your legs for all the menfolk, do ya?"

My backside pressed against the counter, and I swallowed hard, panic rising. "No, Missus. I ain't that kind of girl. I ain't ever—"

Her hand came again, and I lifted my arm to block the blow, but the strength behind her swing sent excruciating pain up and down my spine. "I didn't ask you to speak. I am the master in this house, and it's best you learn that."

My tears came in floods. She grabbed a handful of my hair and reefed my head back to force me to peer into the eyes of the devil herself. "You speak when I say. You rise on my command. You eat, piss, and breathe when I say. Understand?"

"Yes, Missus." My sobs were loud in my own ears. I hated her. Hated the scent of her. The look of her. The very air she breathed.

"You gutter rats should be thankful we open our homes to you. Nothing but thieves and whores." She yanked my head back farther.

"Peggy!" Mister's voice reverberated through the kitchen.

She craned her neck to look at him, and I looked over her shoulder at where he stood, stunned, in the doorway. Hope rose in me.

"You stay out of this, Samuel."

"The girl didn't mean any harm. I told her to sit a spell." He shot Nora a look that clearly indicated his displeasure with her. Under his glare, the girl lowered her head.

"Don't give her the eye. She did right by telling me the favor you show. Need I remind you of what happened the last time you involved yourself?"

His gaze snapped back to the missus, and his face turned ashen. "Very well." He turned and walked from the room.

No, please, I wanted to call after him. Come back. Don't leave me.

Missus bent her neck side to side and centered her glare on me. "Got him turning on his own children, do ya? That will end here and now. I am weary, so tonight you will sleep with the children. Tomorrow you will sleep in the barn with the others."

"But, Mama," Nora crept closer, "if she doesn't sleep with the children at night—"

"Then you will." Missus released me and turned on Nora. "I won't hear any of your sass, or you will find yourself in the barn too."

"With the animals?" Nora said with a gasp.

"That's right, with the animals." She gestured at me.

Nora pressed her lips together and fought back tears.

The missus strode to the table, lifted the plate of leavings, and held it out to her. "Take this out to the hogs. The girl won't eat tonight."

Nora took the plate and left.

"Finish up here. I'm going to bed," the missus said over her shoulder and walked from the room.

I stood washing the dishes. Tears streamed down my cheeks and disappeared into the curve of my neck. Nora entered the house and went upstairs without a word to me.

An hour later, I climbed into bed and wiggled between the sweaty bodies of the children. Joey whimpered and I pulled him close, and he settled. My chest heaved, but no more tears fell— the dishwater had accepted my sorrow. I recalled the missus's words. The need to know what had happened to the last house girl became overwhelming. What fate had befallen her?

CHAPTER 18

MISSUS'S THREAT TO SEND ME TO THE BARN DIDN'T HAPPEN because Joey became ill, and she wanted me in the house at night to tend to him.

I had been with the Gagnons a month when I met the rest of the field lads. That evening the family gathered around the table, and the missus dumped an extra portion of mashed potatoes onto her plate.

I served the twins and Joey's helpings, and as the meal commenced, the missus shoveled in mouthful after mouthful, moaning and carrying on like it was the first time she'd eaten that day. No one spoke, except for Joey, who chattered and gestured at his family. Mister smiled at him with affection, but the awkwardness of mealtime continued. The missus inhaled the third helping before pushing back and resting her hands on her stomach. She released a loud belch, causing us all to look at her.

I dropped my gaze, but not before she caught the lowering of my brow. "You got a problem?" she said.

"No, Missus."

"You can't fool me. I saw that look on your ugly face. You think you're too good for my family?"

My pulse raced.

"Peggy, the girl—"

The missus's fist slammed onto the table, making the silverware and dishes bounce, and we jerked back.

"Fetch me a clean plate." She gestured at me.

I hurried to do her bidding and returned with the dish trembling in my hand.

She grabbed the plate, scooped a spoonful of potatoes onto it, and held it out to me. "Here, take it. You can take my seat." A broad smile expanded across her face.

I eyed her with suspicion. I'd never been permitted to eat with the family, and only after my tasks were done, often long after they had retired for the evening, did I eat. By then I was too tired and hungry to care that the twins and Joey had played with their food. I didn't have the option to be fussy.

I reached for the dish and she grinned, pulled it back, made a weird noise with her mouth, and spat into the food. "There, that should suit." She shoved the dish at my chest. "Now sit and eat."

Riddled with fear, I gripped the plate. She grabbed my shoulder and forced me into the chair with bone-jarring force. "Now eat." Her crazed eyes gleamed.

I looked at Mister, but he kept his gaze downcast. I gritted my teeth and dipped my fingers into the potatoes. *Do not cry. Don't let her win.* I took a mouthful and swallowed. She stood over me while I took a few more bites before she emptied the last of Joey's tray on top. I glanced at his smiling, snot-nosed face and his fingers coated with food he'd happily squished moments before. My stomach turned, but determination fueled the next mouthful and the next. I forced back the need to gag. I would not let her see the depths of the humiliation her actions inflicted.

Mister threw his napkin on the table and exited the room. The twins hurried after him.

The missus grabbed the plate and said, "Now get up and take the food out to the others."

Eager to flee, I gathered the basket filled with stale biscuits, last week's ham, and potatoes, and walked out the back door before I allowed my tears to spill.

The doors to the barn lay open, and the lads sat waiting at the entrance. Graham's mouth stood agape, and he clambered to his feet at my approach.

"What brings you out here?" he said. "Mr. Gagnon usually brings our food."

"Not tonight." I stood in the shadows so he wouldn't see I'd been crying.

But as though sensing my dismay, he said, "They treating you all right in there?" He nodded in the direction of the house, which was hidden from the barn.

"Sure." I looked from him to the other three.

He grinned, revealing a chipped front tooth I hadn't noticed the last time we'd met. "Let me introduce you to the boys. This here is Timmy." He pointed to a pale lad with striking blue eyes.

"Hello," he said with a cheerful smile.

I waved, not in the mood for niceties.

"And that is Farley."

I nodded at the lad with large ears and brown hair shielding his eyes.

He blew at his hair before brushing it back with a dirty hand. "You gonna wish you were in the fields with us, if you don't already," he said. I figured he was twelve years old or so.

"Not now," Graham warned with a lift of his brow.

The lad huffed and fell silent.

"Get from behind Farley, Emory. No use playing shy." Graham gestured, and a lad with more freckles than clear flesh and a mass of auburn hair stepped from the shadow of the other boy. He kept his head down and mumbled a hello.

"He don't like people much." Timmy strode closer and lifted the cloth to peek inside the basket.

"Do too," Emory said. "I just don't like strangers."

"She ain't gonna hurt ya. She's one of us." Farley marched forward and joined Timmy.

I pushed the basket at the boys. After taking the food, they sat cross-legged on the ground and started eating like they hadn't eaten in weeks.

"You eat?" Graham asked.

"Yes." When I'd packed the basket, my mouth had salivated, but after what occurred inside, I'd lost all appetite.

"Now hold on. Save some for Graham," Timmy said.

"We don't have to share our rations with you too, do we?" Farley eyed me from behind the flap of hair.

"No," I said.

"Do they feed you in the house?" Timmy asked. "'Cause they never fed Annie."

The lads fell still at the statement.

"Annie?" I looked from the younger lads to Graham.

"The house girl before you," he said reverently.

Was she the girl the Gagnons had mentioned in Miss Keene's office, and the one they'd alluded to as my similar fate if I messed up?

"The missus permits me to eat the scraps left on the plates after the evening chores are done." The lads gawked at me, and I shrugged. "I gathered slop thrown into the streets to eat, and many times went 'ungry. It can't be as bad as that, right?" For my own sake, I tried to dismiss what had happened inside. Only hardship would befall me if the missus got to thinking I was a snitch.

"Living in there with her, you will come to wish you were back on the streets with the ache in your belly." Graham bent and retrieved a hunk of ham and offered me a piece.

I shook my head and stepped back.

"You ain't been here long enough if you can refuse food,"

Farley said. "Can't imagine the missus taking a liking to ya. She don't even like her own."

The missus's bellow came to us and I swung to leave, but Graham gripped my arm, and the warning in his eyes snatched my breath. "It would do you well to sleep with one eye open while under her roof."

I jerked my arm free and raced for the house. Timmy's words resounded in my head: *They never fed Annie.* I pushed away the harrowing mental image of a girl wasting away and bounded up the back steps and into the house.

CHAPTER 19

Charlotte

IF SHE FINDS OUT WHAT YOU ARE UP TO, IT WILL BE THE END OF US both!" Ellie gripped my arm while eyeing Miss Keene through the open door to her office, where she sat speaking on the telephone.

"The Gagnons should never have been allowed to have Hazel. Annie was in good health when she left this place."

"But Miss Keene—or any other staff member—never visit contracting families. What if Mrs. Gagnon contacts Miss Keene and puts up a fuss about the new regulations you say she put in place?"

"It's a chance I have to take. I thought you of all people would help me. Especially after what happened to Clara. I can't believe she…" The reality was too devastating to speak. My core trembled at the news Ellie had shared moments prior.

"Miss Appleton? Miss Scott?"

We pulled our heads apart at the crack of Agnes's voice.

Agnes circled her desk and walked into the lobby. "It seems lately I find the two of you with your heads tucked together more than not." She looked from me to Ellie. "Care to explain, Miss Scott?"

Ellie straightened. My heart raced, and my stomach roiled. "I'm afraid I 'ave disturbing news." Ellie stepped away from me.

Agnes dropped her arms and narrowed her eyes. "What?"

"While you were busy, news came from the asylum in Kingston."

Alarm reflected in Agnes's eyes. "What sort of news?"

When Ellie hesitated, she strode forward as though intending to shake the information from her.

Ellie squared her shoulders. "They sent word that Clara 'as 'ung 'erself."

Agnes stopped in her tracks, floundering at the news. Face ashen, she gripped the back of a nearby chair. "Are you certain?"

"A Miss Turner brought the news 'erself."

"Why not call?" Agnes said, as if in a fog.

"The telephone lines were down yesterday, and today you've been tied up in calls all morning."

She lowered herself into the chair, her eyes turning to the window, where the leaves of a massive maple rustled in the morning breeze. After a moment she looked at me without a whit of emotion. "Miss Appleton, isn't it your weekend off?"

"Yes." I gulped, my throat feeling thick.

"Then off with you." She waved a hand in dismissal. "You don't need to stand around listening in on private organization affairs."

I bristled but kept my composure, dipping my head in respect. "My apologies, Miss Keene." I clutched my black canister purse tighter and hurried for the door.

Outside on the landing, I took a deep breath, squeezing my eyes shut. *Oh, Clara. I wish I could have saved you.* I choked back a sob. *What are you doing, Charlotte? Why did you come here if you can't help them?* I was a fool to think my presence at the institution could make a difference.

At the sound of a horn, I jumped and opened my eyes. Frederick waved from his newly purchased Nash Touring. His stock investments had soared, and recently he'd bought an old estate in Liverpool, of all places. He bent his head and shouted out the open passenger window, "Appleton, you coming?"

I hurried to the car. He smiled, revealing gleaming white teeth, and the twinkle in his dark eyes made my heart flutter in my chest. Leaning over, he opened the door, and I slid in and shut it behind me.

He sealed a peck on my cheek. "I thought you were going to make me die of heat exhaustion out here."

I smiled, but I couldn't displace the despondency over Clara's death.

"What has you so glum?" He rested his arm on the back of the seat as he pulled away from the curb.

Staff members had to sign a confidentiality agreement upon their hiring at the institute. "You know I can't speak to you about work." I wanted to tell him, and desperately so, and to seek comfort in his embrace.

His fingers tightened on the steering wheel and his jaw set. "Yes, I know."

"I'm sorry, I wish I could. You have your policies for your clientele," I said, hoping the reminder would stop any further questions.

He shot me a look of annoyance before another question rose. "Who was that woman you had your head conjoined with?"

My heart sped up. "Spying on me, were you?" I said with as much lightheartedness as I could muster. I had yet to introduce him and Ellie, and although she had insisted, I feared the lies that lay between him and me.

"A fiancé is forced to use every measure possible when his soon-to-be wife is full of mystery and has come to show more interest in work than him."

I felt a twinge of guilt. He had been patient, but I feared his patience was growing thin with my pushing back the wedding twice. What was I afraid of? Hadn't he proven his love for me? Yet I continued to shut him out of the most vulnerable parts of me.

"That was Miss Scott, my work colleague." My nerves thrummed as I broached the matter I'd wanted to discuss with him for weeks. "There is something I've meant to ask you."

"Oh, and that is?"

"Miss Scott finds herself without a roommate and unable to afford housing on her own. You and I agreed after we married that I would give up my apartment."

"That is what married people do, do they not?" Sarcasm tinged his tone.

I wiggled in my seat. He waited for me to continue. "Well, I was thinking, you have that guesthouse that needs some fixing up, and I wondered if you'd consider renting it to her at a lower price."

His lips parted and he swung his gaze to me before returning his attention to the busy street. A moment or two passed in silence, and my palms dampened with anticipation.

"I fear Miss Scott will move in before you finally become my wife."

I ignored his remark as hope buoyed. "It would work out splendid. We could take the train to work and come home on the weekends."

He heaved a sigh. "How long do you expect to remain at the institute after we wed?"

"We've spoken of this. I—"

"How long?" The firmness in his tone demanded an answer. "No more, Charlotte." His use of my first name informed me of his dismay. "I want a straight answer. I can't take any more of this. When do you plan to quit?"

I fumbled with the clutch on my purse, not daring to look at him. "What if my answer was...never?" I asked, and he inhaled sharply. "Would you still marry me?" God knows I had tried the man. I'd put him through more than anyone should expect of another.

Painful silence stretched before he said in a weary voice, "Perhaps I am a hopeless fool, but to imagine life without you is too much to bear." He looked at me. The love radiating from his eyes wrapped up my heart and sealed it as his forever. "If I must share you with your commitment to those children, I will."

I smiled, slid across the seat, and leaned into the crook of his arm, resting my head on his shoulder.

"But on one condition." He kissed my temple.

I waited.

"You agree to marry me right away."

I sat up and looked at him. "Forgo the large wedding?" My heart leaped with joy at another obstacle avoided. His insistence that we invite all of our family and friends had troubled me from the beginning. His endless questions and persistence in meeting people in my life had become the focus of several of our conversations. I had hoped meeting Delilah, my roommate, would have been enough, but it hadn't been.

"If we are to move forward swiftly, we have no time to plan a big wedding," I said.

"I want to marry you before the grave summons me," he replied, amused. "Something simple and quaint will do."

"Then that settles the matter. We will wed at the courts." I sank back into the crook of his arm while struggling to mask the delight of bypassing another obstacle, but my breath caught at his next words.

"I thought this would be the perfect opportunity for me to finally meet your family. We have courted for two years, and I don't know if you have any siblings, cousins, or living relatives. Besides your mention of your grandparents, you've avoided the subject. I've come to wonder if you're on the run from the law," he said with a laugh, but I heard the underlying hurt.

I brushed off my guilt and laughed. "Hardly."

We agreed to marry the following month, and Frederick was in high spirits for the rest of the day. That evening, he took me to the Winter Garden Theatre, where we enjoyed the vaudeville luminaries.

The next morning I boarded a train that would take me to the Gagnons' hometown. An hour later the train pulled into the station, and I hired a farmer to take me to the family's farm.

"I know them, all right. They live about three miles from me. Guess I could take ya for a small fee." He wiped his dirty hands on his stained checkered shirt.

I dug into my purse and withdrew a half dollar. "Will this do?" The coin could have purchased enough potatoes to feed the children for a month.

"It will do." He snatched up the coin and tucked it into his trouser pocket before gesturing for me to follow him. "Come on, now. I got cows to milk, and they don't wait on nobody."

I climbed in and stifled a gag at the overpowering scent of manure. Bits of hay and what I hoped was mud coated the floor. As we drove along, he told me about his wife, children, neighbors, and all the town gossip.

"So, what is your business with the Gagnons?" He swatted at a hornet with a sweat-stained cap.

"I work at the institution where they recently acquired a girl."

"Is that so?" He looked at me and shook his head before turning the truck down a dirt road. "Got themselves five or six of those poor souls. I hate to see the children suffer on England's streets, but they may be better off that way than with Peggy."

My chest tightened at his view of the Gagnon woman, but I sat unmoving, waiting for him to continue.

"Now Samuel, he's a decent enough fellow. We are sort of friendly in passing, but Peggy, why she could pummel you with one strike. Saw her take her purse to poor old Samuel once. What he saw in the woman I don't know. Suppose he already had three kids and couldn't leave. The woman sure can put out children, and she doesn't have a motherly bone in her body. From what I hear, she works those orphans until they can barely stand."

His insight into the woman heightened my concern over Hazel's well-being, and the next twenty minutes passed at an agonizingly slow rate.

"This here is the drive." He pulled the truck to a stop. "If you don't mind getting out here, I'd best be on my way. My Mildred will have the afternoon meal on the table, and although she ain't nothing like Peggy Gagnon, she won't take kindly to me being late."

I climbed out, closed the door, and said through the open window, "Thank you. Now, you have yourself a good day." I stepped back and he drove away, leaving me in a cloud of dust.

I looked at the long, winding driveway with the yellow house at its end, surrounded by green and yellow fields. Then I eyed the road leading back to town. "And how do you suppose you're getting back?" I said with a huff, and inwardly rebuked myself for not thinking the trip to the Gagnons' farm all the way through.

When I reached the front porch, I climbed the rickety steps and knocked on the screen door. "Hello?" I called.

"Don't dally, girl, go see who is here," a woman said.

I heard shuffling inside, and then Hazel stepped into the hallway. She froze at the sight of me, and I offered her an awkward smile.

She strode forward.

"Hello, Hazel."

"Did you come for me?" she said in a soft voice, as though she couldn't believe her eyes—or so she wouldn't alert the woman in the other room of who had arrived unannounced. The hope shining in her eyes created a lump in my throat.

"I've come to check in on your living situation."

Her shoulders slumped. "Oh."

My heart tightened. "How are you faring?" I noticed the weariness in her face, the eyes haloed in dark circles.

"I'm alive, if that is what you mean," she said dryly.

"Please don't be angry with me. I wish—"

"Oh, for heaven's sake. Who in tarnation is it?" The woman's grunts and weighted footfalls signaled her impending arrival.

"It's Miss Appleton," Hazel said over her shoulder before locking eyes with me. "She ain't gonna like it that you're 'ere."

I squared my shoulders, preparing for the bull of a woman thundering toward us with a scowl that raised the hairs on my neck. "Let me worry about her."

The woman swatted Hazel away as though she were a pesky housefly, and the girl cowered into the wall. I clenched my jaw and focused my gaze on the woman.

"You? Ain't you the woman from the receiving home in the city?"

I elevated my gaze to take in the woman in her entirety. Built broad and tall and hairy, there was nothing womanly about her. I took in the food stains splattering the bodice of her dress, the heavy brows invading her face, and her cracked lips. Her yellowish-green eyes bored into me, but although nerves churned my insides, I wouldn't be intimidated. "I've come to check in on Hazel. The well-being of placed children is of great importance to us."

"Ain't ever had any of you pay us a visit before." Her brows dipped. "And Miss Keene made no mention of you poking your nose around in my business."

"We have implemented a new policy," I said.

"Approved by the government?"

"No, this is strictly a home-to-home situation. Here is the contract Miss Keene had you sign when you contracted Hazel." I removed the forged document from my purse, unfolded it, and pressed the paper against the screen for her to view. My heart hammered, hoping she wouldn't call my bluff and notice her and her husband's forged signatures.

"What you fixing to look at?" She glanced from the document to me.

Relieved that she didn't ask to examine the contract more closely, I folded the paper and placed it back in my purse. "May I come in?"

She hesitated. At the sound of a child crying, she leveled a hard look at Hazel. "Don't just stand there, go and fetch him."

"Yes, Missus." Hazel hurried away.

I gawked after her then stepped back as Mrs. Gagnon swung open the screen door.

"Ain't got all day." She stood tapping her foot.

"Thank you." I entered and stood beside her in the small foyer. "I won't take up too much of your time. If you allow me to sit with you a while and watch the girl's interactions with the family, that should satisfy the questions needing answering."

"Questions?"

"Yes, but nothing too lengthy or imposing, I assure you."

"Says you." She spun and marched back the way she'd come.

I made the sign of the cross and followed after her. Clutter and chaos filled the interior of the home. Two young girls with unkempt hair and dirty faces raced through the house, screaming and knocking over anything not bolted down. I grabbed a teacup and saucer in their wake before it toppled to the floor from a nearby stand. Mold had formed on top of the liquid within the cup.

Hazel paced the far side of a living room, holding a small child. The boy, flushed and appearing feverish, clawed at the fabric of her bodice and rubbed his snotty face into her chest, seeking comfort. Hazel patted his head and spoke softly to him.

"Go on now, take the boy upstairs. His whining is insufferable."

I looked from Hazel and the boy to Mrs. Gagnon. Although I never had children of my own, it didn't take a parent to understand the baby needed his mother and sought one in Hazel.

"Yes, Missus," Hazel said and left.

I had hoped to spend time with Hazel and get the answers I feared Mrs. Gagnon wouldn't provide. The woman had frustrated that desire with the girl's removal.

"Oh my," I said when one of the wild children ran smack into me. I grabbed the girl to steady her.

"Sorry, miss," the dark-haired girl said with manners I hadn't expected and peered up at me with mischievous eyes.

I smiled. "It's quite all right. You didn't hurt yourself, did you?"

Mrs. Gagnon clutched the girl by the shoulder, and she winced. "She's fine," she said for my sake. "Daisy, you and Susie get on outside before you find yourself in the fields with your father."

The girl bobbed her head and ducked past her mother as though expecting a clobber on the way by.

After the girls headed outside, Mrs. Gagnon turned her scowl on me. "Well, let's get it over with, so you can be on your way and I can get on with my day." She strode to the sofa and cleared a spot amongst the soiled and clean clothing, newspapers, and trash. "What ya waiting for? Have a seat." She jutted a hand at the sofa.

"Thank you." I cringed as I sat down.

She waddled to a rocker—the only cleared piece of furniture I'd noticed inside the home. It moaned under her weight, and I imagined her spending most of her day there while Hazel played mother and housekeeper to the family. One glance at the kitchen table told me the hallway and sitting room were only the beginning of the home's disarray. It would take several housekeepers and a few months of work to make the house presentable.

"Is there a problem?" Mrs. Gagnon's voice pulled my focus back to her.

"No," I said, and withdrew a clipboard and pen from my bag. "Thank you for seeing me. I will start by asking you how Hazel is faring."

"She is as good as can be expected." She stroked her swollen abdomen.

How could the woman possibly think of bringing another life into the world when she obviously couldn't handle the ones she had?

"Where does the girl sleep?"

"With the children."

I squirmed beneath her unnerving stare. "And mealtimes?"

She regarded me as though she didn't understand my meaning.

"When does Hazel have her meals?"

"When her chores are done." The coldness in her tone was mirrored in her unfriendly eyes.

I jotted a note on the paper. "When does she rest? And does she have any days off?" I never lifted my eyes.

She snorted. "Do you think I'm running a charity here?"

My pen stilled, and I looked at her. "Pardon me?"

She sat forward and pinned me with a disapproving look. "This is not a hotel. My husband and I are not in the service of charity work. The girl works for us. She is clothed, fed, bathed, and given a place to sleep. That is more than she had outside the institute."

"That may be true, but I hope you remember Hazel is still a young girl that can only handle so much toil. If you wish for her to continue to be of help, I would suggest you consider awarding her leisure time to be a child."

"We're farmers. There ain't no awarded time for leisure, as you call it. My husband is in the fields from morning to night."

I wanted to ask her what she did during the day. It undoubtedly wasn't tending to her children or keeping a clean house. My guess, from the worn floorboards under the rocker, was that the chair was the place to find her. "I'm aware of how hard you must work to keep a farm running; I'm simply concerned about Hazel's mental state and health. She looks weary."

"We're all tired. Joey's been sick and keeping the whole house awake at night. Probably caught some kind of illness from the girl, is my thinking. She has got a touch of what he has, but the rest of us are fine."

"I see," I said. *Or she is sick from caring for the child.* I gripped the pen tighter. "Well, I think that will sum up my questions." I rose, and she followed. "Would you mind letting me speak to Hazel before I leave?"

"I would."

"It would only take a minute."

She took a couple of steps forward. "I said no. Now, if you

don't want me ringing up Miss Keene and putting a complaint in about this here visit, I suggest you get on out of here."

I lifted a placating hand and tucked the clipboard into my bag. "I assure you there's no need. Thank you for your time, and I will see myself out."

"You do that." She trudged into the kitchen, leaving me standing in the living room.

"Very well," I said to myself and strode outside.

I paused in the driveway and looked back at the house, and my attention was drawn to an upstairs window. Hazel stood peering down at me.

I offered a small wave and mouthed, "I'll be back." I hoped she understood, but she turned away too quickly for me to be sure.

Relief embraced me as I walked down the drive. Other than exhaustion, Hazel's overall physical health appeared in order. I had hoped to ask her about Annie, and if she had information about what had happened to the girl, but Mrs. Gagnon had made sure to keep her away, which may have been for the best; I didn't want to worry the girl for no reason. Hazel's responsibilities to the Gagnons were too many.

I would return. When? I wasn't sure, but I wouldn't leave Hazel, in case she needed me.

CHAPTER 20

Hazel

ALL HAD BLANKETED THE COUNTRYSIDE IN SHADES OF CRIMSON, orange, and gold. The maple trees out front had shed their garments, which lay in heaps on the ground. I sat on the front porch peeling apples the field lads had gathered in the orchard. Joey lay asleep on a blanket beside me. The lad had become my shadow, and the one joy I'd found on the farm. I often watched the field lads and yearned for their friendship, but the missus restricted our interaction.

A month had passed since Miss Appleton had come to the farm. After I'd found her standing on the other side of the screen door, my heart had leaped with the hope that she'd come for me. However, it hadn't taken but a second for her words to dampen my spirit. She hadn't come for me—no one was coming. She'd sounded like she cared, all right, but not enough, because as quick as she came, she had left. Watching from the upstairs window, I had wanted to cry for her to come back, but who was I fooling? She wasn't my friend. All she cared about was soothing a guilty conscience, and I warn't about to be pitied by no one.

In my time at the Gagnons', I had learned shame: the shame of my origins, of being a home child, for my very existence, and I hated them for it. The missus was bent on breaking me. Each time her hands struck and her words sought to hurt, or she objectified me as "girl," "street rat," and "gutter trash," I retreated inside of myself, seeking to protect the flame of my self-esteem. *I am good. I do matter. I'm not what they say I am.*

The twins' squeals of merriment rose as they emerged from beneath mountains of fallen leaves. I dislodged my despair and smiled, imagining William joining in their play, his blond curls tousled and webbed with leaves, his cheeks rosy from exertion.

"What you smiling about?"

Lost in my daydreaming, I hadn't heard her come out of the house.

"Mama won't be happy when I tell her you're dawdling."

I twisted to look at her. "Shoo, you little gnat. I'm sick of you and your threats. What's the worst she can do? Kill me?"

She dropped her mouth open like a gaping plonker. "Well…"

"Well, nuffing. I ain't skeered. There is nuffing your Mum can do that can be worse than what I already been through. You got it?"

Her eyes widened with disbelief.

"Now leave off, so I can get these apples peeled. Unless you want to put your 'ands to work instead of your mouth and 'elp."

She glowered and stormed back inside.

"I didn't think so," I said quietly at her retreating back.

Later that evening, the missus's water broke, and her wails and carrying on grated on all our nerves. That brute of a woman's labor lasted a few hours before the new Gagnon screamed life into the world.

The midwife stepped from the room to inform Mr. Gagnon, "It's a boy."

He beamed with pride. "I will have my team of farmers yet."

"And if you and Mama have any more, we will need a bigger house," Nora muttered from her position on the couch.

In high spirits, he laughed and hugged the gremlin.

I felt a twinge of jealousy, yearning to love and be loved. I had taken for granted the simple touch of William and Mum. I looked away and placed the shirt I had been folding on the chair before reaching for the next item.

"Why don't you sit awhile?" Mister said.

I lifted my head and looked at him, then to Nora. "Me?"

"Yes," he said with a grin. "A son is a reason to celebrate."

Nora rolled her eyes and glowered at him.

"Indeed, but the missus wouldn't like it."

"She is in no state to do anything about it," he said.

Nora dropped her arms, and her mouth flopped open at his disregard for the missus. She would snitch on me as quick as nothing.

"I-I—" I started to protest.

"I won't hear no fuss. Come. Sit. It's an order." He pointed at the couch next to Nora and strode from the sitting room to the kitchen.

I hesitated a moment before obeying, making sure to avoid Nora's scowl.

"Mama will hear of this. I'll see to it," Nora said through gritted teeth.

I never looked her way. Keeping my eyes pinned on the kitchen doorway, I said, "I don't doubt it. I've always summed you up as a snitch. Where I come from, swine like you are worse than gutter rats. The lowest scum in all of England."

She gasped and pulled back. "You wait until Mama hears what you said to me."

I didn't have the energy to argue with her. "Tell 'er. See if I care."

She opened her mouth to speak, but Mister returned with a glass jar of candy he kept in one of the upper cupboards. He removed the metal cover and retrieved a piece. He handed one to

Nora, who snatched it and popped it in her mouth. He took out another and held it out to me.

"Mama won't like you favoring her," Nora said.

I gave her one look and snatched the candy before Mister could retract it. I moaned in pleasure as the sweetness rolled over my tongue.

Mister grinned, his eyes sparkling at my delight while Pesky Pants sat beside me, glowering like someone had ruined her day.

I smiled back.

CHAPTER 21

T HE GAGNONS CALLED THE BABY HERBERT. I DIDN'T LIKE THE name. Of all the ones they could have given the lad, they chose the ugliest, but I suppose when you populated the earth with as many children as they had, you run out of names. The name suited the baby because he was a homely little thing, and colicky to boot. The missus had to breastfeed him so he spent the nights with her, but during the day I paced the floors and the grounds, bouncing the baby and trying everything I could to calm him.

One evening when I walked to the barn to bring the field lads their evening meal, I found Emory perched on a stump outside the barn, drawing pictures into the dirt with the toe of his boot.

"What you making?" I took a gander. The sketch appeared to be a woman with bushy hair and an unbecoming face. "That bad, eh?" I moved to stand beside him and get a better look. "It's missing somefing." I set the basket of food and the water pail on the ground before picking up a stick. I added a dot to reflect the furry wart on the tip of her chin and emphasized the scowl he'd given the missus's image. "There. That should do."

Emory's head snapped up, and as he looked at me, a grin broke across his freckled face. "You don't like her either?"

"Not since the day I laid eyes on 'er."

"You reckon Mr. Gagnon is trapped like us?"

"Maybe so."

His smile faded, and he dropped his head. "I want to go home. I miss me mummy and brother."

"They alive?"

"Mummy works in the workhouse, and me brother had a terrible accident, and his legs don't work. Mummy took us to the home for orphans and left us. Never said she was coming back. Me brother said it was too hard on her, caring for a cripple and me. I know I ain't but eight, but I tried to help take care of us. Got me a job as a rat catcher for a tavern." He sat up a little taller. "Did right good, I did. I gave Mummy the coin I earned, and she patted my head and smiled. But it didn't last. I had to rise early to walk an hour there, and one day the owner caught me napping on the flour sacks and took me by the britches and tossed me into the street."

"I'm sure your mum was real proud of you. We do what we got to do for our families now, don't we?"

He bobbed his head, but tears welled in his eyes. "I worry 'bout me brother. I don't suppose he is much good on a farm, and when we left England he stayed behind."

"I 'ave a brother too. 'E is six, and 'is name is William. What's your brother's name?"

"Tate."

"Well, I'm sure Tate is set to library duties or giving the new arrivals the 'ome tour. Perhaps 'e got the better lot in this arrangement."

His face brightened, and he used the back of his hand to wipe away tears. "You think so?"

"That I do." I gave his shoulder a nudge. "Now, you come and 'ave your meal wif the others."

He smoothed away the image of the missus with his boot and gave me a cheeky grin. I laughed and tousled his hair before walking toward the open doors of the barn.

He raced to keep up and fell into step beside me. "Reckon things 'bout to get a heap more miserable around here."

"Why do you say that?"

"Graham will be leaving soon."

"Oh?" I halted just inside the threshold, my stomach somersaulting with the news.

"Mister told him today that his contract is up soon. Said he could stay on for a wage, but Graham said he ain't looking to stay here a moment longer. Can't say I blame him. Mrs. Gagnon doesn't like any of us, but she got special hate for me."

"What makes you think that?"

He shrugged. "She says I'm a bastard 'cause Mummy had me out of wedlock. Farley says that means her and me daddy weren't married. Haven't you noticed how each week she picks someone to punish?"

No, I suppose I hadn't. I'd assumed the missus centered her vendetta against the world on me. A person so saturated with poison that she couldn't say a kind word to her children or her husband assured me that she had no empathy for the living. She continuously reprimanded Mister about minding his fields and the lads and to leave me to her. Busy inside the house, I hadn't paid much attention to the happenings outside.

"Before me, it was Buddy, and before him…well…you know who." He dipped his head and shoved his hands into his pockets.

I had yet to hear the reasoning behind Annie's disappearance. The lads had mentioned about the missus not feeding her, but that had been all. To my knowledge, the Gagnons hadn't returned her to the receiving home. So where was the girl?

"Was Buddy another lad before I came?"

"Nah, he was a dog. Followed Mr. Gagnon home one day, and Mrs. Gagnon never liked him." He looked up, and his brows narrowed. "Used to kick him for no reason at all. He was skeered of her, just like the rest of us. One day she took to yelling at Mr. Gagnon because the crop didn't turn a profit. She marched out onto the porch and did a few circles until her eyes fell on Buddy napping in the sun. She raced back inside and returned with a shotgun." He shuddered at the memory. "Shot him dead; she did it for no cause at all. Called him a lazy good for nothing." His eyes pooled. "Now I'm the one she picks on. I spend more time in the cellar than any of the others."

"The cellar?" I recalled the times I'd looked through the kitchen window and seen the missus open the cellar doors and peer inside. Never had I dreamed someone was within! I'd thought maybe darkness was her weakness and fear kept her from descending. My gut plunged at Emory's revelation.

Graham strode up behind us with the other boys and took the basket and water pail. "The lads are hungry."

"The slop she feeds us lately isn't worth eating. I ate better on the streets." Farley strode forward to take a look in the basket. Timmy followed on his heels.

"Did ya, now?" Graham said with a chuckle.

"No, but it tastes better than anything from her." He looked to the house and spat on the barn floor. "Keeping Emory locked away for the last three days causes more work for us. Besides, look at him; he can't bear to lose any more weight. He ain't but a rack of bones already."

"Go eat." Graham cupped the back of Emory's head and gave him a gentle push to join the others.

They used their fingers to shovel the stew into their mouths. I thought of Miss Keene and Miss Scott and the groove that would form between their brows at the display of poor manners.

Graham studied me. "What's the matter?"

"Is it true 'bout the cellar?"

"Indeed."

I rubbed my arms to ward off the chill generated by what Emory had revealed. It was all so hard to believe, but then I recalled Clara at the receiving home. Horrible, unthinkable things had happened to her.

"What 'appened to Annie?" I blurted. "Did she kill 'er?"

Before he could answer, a fuss between the lads drew his attention.

"There ain't hardly enough, and it tastes funny," Farley said.

"Ain't fit for the hogs." Timmy licked his fingers clean.

"That's 'cause we're less than hogs to her," Emory said.

"I'm sorry. That is what the missus gave me. She keeps the cupboards locked and a close eye on all the food." I had scooped the layer of mildew off the top before placing the stew in the basket.

"Well, she ain't nothing but a heifer," Farley said with a huff. "Probably lays on the settee with heaps of food piled around her, using her meaty hands to wipe up the drippings."

The lads shared a look and broke into laughter.

I lifted a hand to stifle the giggle at the mental image he created. He didn't realize how close he was to the truth. Nora waited on her mum for most of the day, serving her endless amounts of food. I'd come to wonder if a babe had grown inside the missus or if the mound of her midsection reflected her gluttony, but then the newest Gagnon had emerged.

"You lads better keep your voices down. You never know when Nora is larking 'bout." Emory glanced at the open doors.

"Mrs. Gagnon's mouthpiece," Timmy said with an exaggerated roll of his eyes.

I smiled before turning to exit the barn, but the warmth of a hand stopped me.

"You care to take a walk?" Graham said.

"The missus said I ain't to be mixing wif you all." Although the Gagnons had piled into their car and left an hour before, I could feel her eyes on me even from town.

"She ain't gonna know. Heard one of the twins say Mr. Gagnon was taking them for a lolly ice," he said.

"Lolly ice." Someone repeated, and the others groaned.

"What I wouldn't do for a lick." Timmy's tongue flicked out over his lips.

"I'd cut off my right arm," Farley said.

Graham's laughter resounded. "And then what good would you be."

Farley waved a hand in dismissal, and Graham looked at me and grinned. The way he looked out for the lads reminded me of Brock. Since the day in the graveyard, I had wondered if, had I been kinder with Brock, we would have been mates. I sighed. What did it matter now? He probably hated me for causing the gravedigger to grab him, and rightfully so.

"You all right?" Graham asked, his eyes alight with concern.

His intuition and attention to my emotions both intrigued and puzzled me. Were my feelings on display for all, or just with him? I didn't like it one bit. "I was finking of 'ome." I hoped his intuitive eye would turn to other matters.

"Come," he said.

"I need to get back. Goodbye, lads." I stepped out of the barn and hurried toward the house.

Graham jogged to catch up. "What harm can a short walk cause? We will be back before the family returns."

I halted and sent a look toward the drive. Maybe it would be all right. "Fine, 'ave it your way."

He grinned in triumph.

As we walked, I studied him. When he caught me, he smiled self-consciously. "What?"

"Nuffing. You remind me of someone, is all."

"The someone you're thinking 'bout when your expression goes from relaxed to tense?"

I bristled and looked away to hide the heat rushing over me. *Get out of my thoughts, you bloody imposter.* "I do not," I said.

"You sure do. It's a bloke, isn't it?"

"None of your business."

"Tell me."

"I shan't"

"It is. I knew it. Took a fancy to this bloke, didn't ya?"

I punched him in the shoulder. "No. You remind me of someone, is all. I always thought 'e claimed the prize for the most annoying person, but I'm coming to believe that may be you."

He laughed and walked backward so he could get a good gander at me. Attempting to pry into my deepest thoughts, he was. Well, I wouldn't allow it.

"Tell me 'bout this bloke I rival with for first place in Hazel Winters's books," he said.

I pressed my lips together and focused on one of the naked maples until his continual stare got the best of me, and I halted and threw my hands in the air. "Why do you care?"

His jovial demeanor faded. "You are a tough one, Hazel Winters. You planning on going through life alone?"

I continued walking. "Better that way. Then no one can pluck out your 'eart."

"Reckon nobody understands that better than the lads and me." His tone turned serious. "But the way I look at it, we need each other. And together, this here existence don't seem so miserable."

His words hit me hard, and I gulped back the emotions clotting in my throat. I heaved a sigh and said, "There was a lad named Brock. 'E and 'is gang moved into my district some

time back and soon after started encroaching on my territory."
I paused, recalling the day in the graveyard, and how I'd dishon-
ored the dead and plucked the golden trinket from the deceased
child's hands. What would Graham think of me if I told him
the truth? I cringed at the thought of his disapproval. I didn't
know why I cared, but I did. Only one person knew of the sin
that haunted me—well, him and God, if He was up there. I gave
the heavens a bit of a gander, feeling smaller at the reflection.
Graham stared at me intently, as though pleading with me to
finish, so I continued. "One day I got myself into a bind, and 'e
came to my rescue. And in doing so, got 'imself nabbed. 'E told
me to run, and when I looked back, the bobbies 'ad 'im." The lie
wasn't that far from the truth.

"Seems like a decent enough bloke," he said appreciatively.

I shrugged. "After the bobbies caught 'im, they locked 'im
up until they could decide what to do with 'im. The day Mum
brought me brother and me to the institution, I saw 'im in the
'all. I guess 'e suffered the same fate as us."

"You've caught feelings for the bloke."

"What?" I stopped and glowered at him. "'Aven't you 'eard
anyfing I've said? Brock and I were not mates. We were rivals."

"But he risked being captured for you. That isn't what rivals
do."

He'd touched on a detail I had pondered for many a day and
night. Why had Brock risked everything for me? My guilt deepened. "Enough about 'im." I shuffled all thoughts of Brock and
the accompanying guilt away, and we continued our stroll. "Tell
me what 'appened to Annie."

"She died."

"'Ere?"

"Yes." His jaw tensed. "At Mrs. Gagnon's hands. You must
be careful. She is mad, and that damn cellar is her cage."

I shivered. The depths of cruelty the missus was capable of frightened me.

As we walked, Graham spoke of his friends back home and life before his parents died. In our memories, we shared a union of sorts.

"Emory said you will be leaving soon."

"That's right. Fixing to move on out of here by spring. Guess I'm almost eighteen," he said with a cheerless laugh. "Who would have thought."

"What about the lads?"

"What about them?"

"You would just leave?"

"What would you have me do? Stay until they're grown? No." He shook his head. "What stops the Gagnons from bringing in more home children? If I care for them all, I'll never be rid of this place. And I've dreamed of leaving here from the day I arrived."

Every part of me wanted to protest, but how could I begrudge him his freedom? Oh, bollocks! The plonker had stirred feelings in me, and I rebuked myself for letting down my guard.

"I wish I could take the lads with me. Believe me, I do, but I can't attach myself to hope. Don't reckon I'll see any of you, once I leave."

Why did his words about his leaving fill me with despair? Our time together had been limited, but knowing I wouldn't see his friendly face about the place stole the spirit right out of me.

Upon our return to the yard, I saw the Gagnons' car coming up the drive. "I got to go." Panic surged through me, and without waiting for a response, I raced toward the back porch.

"I'll see you soon," Graham called after me.

I darted up the steps and into the house, and the screen door slammed behind me. In the kitchen, I paused to catch my breath. At the sound of the children's chipper voices and the missus's bark,

I straightened and hurried to the front porch. The missus flung open the door and charged at me with the flames of hell alight in her eyes. My heart pounded, and I braced myself.

"Out hanging around with those field boys, are ya? Let that older one have a go at you, did ya?"

I gawked at her. "No, I—"

She struck me across the mouth, and I screamed. "I will teach you what I think about whores." She dragged me toward the back door, her nails biting through my cardigan and the sleeve of my dress.

"Peggy, what in tarnation are you carrying on about?" Mister chased after her.

"The girl thinks she can act like a whore on my property. We leave the house for a minute, and she's out prostituting herself. I saw her with my own eyes, coming back from the woods. Thought she'd race in the house before we caught her." The missus came to a sudden stop, and Mister plowed into us.

"I'm sure you're surmising things. Isn't that so, missy?" Mister turned a concerned gaze on me, looking hopeful that I'd confirm his words.

The missus spun and glared at him. "I told you from the start to not put your opinions where they aren't needed. You're too soft, Samuel. If you don't rein them in, these heathens will be fornicating and breeding."

Ain't no more room for breeding. You do a good job of that yourself. I clenched my hands into fists.

"Now out with you." The missus shoved me out the screen door. I stumbled on the steps and tumbled to the ground with a hard jolt. "Get up." Her eyes flashed, and she glanced at Nora. "Go fetch me a bucket from the well."

I gawked from Nora to the missus. Graham and the lads stood some yards away.

"Up," she shouted.

"Peggy," Mister said again.

"Shut up, Samuel."

He cursed and spun on his heel and marched back into the house.

No, please don't go, I wanted to call after him, but as the missus descended the steps, my attention flew back to her.

"Take that dress off."

"But I—"

"Do as I tell you or you will live to regret it." Madness gleamed in her eyes.

Tears spilled over my cheeks, and I undid the first button.

"Hurry it up."

After I had unfastened the last button, I stood clasping the dress closed.

"Take it off."

A sob escaped me, and I shook my head. "Please, no."

"Take it off, or I'll ensure you never see tomorrow." She clenched her teeth and charged at me. Her hands reefed at the fabric and I soon stood in only my undergarments. "Those too." She pointed at my drawers.

"Please, don't do this. I'm sorry."

"You'll be sorry, all right."

Nora returned with the bucket. She looked nervously at her mum. "What you meaning to do?"

"Mind your own, girl," she said to her daughter.

I saw compassion flicker in Nora's eyes for the first time, but it left as quickly as it had arrived.

I removed my undergarment and stood attempting to shield my nakedness from Graham and the lads. My flesh burned, and I lowered my head, gasping when the cold water splashed over me. She tossed aside the bucket and strode over to stand inches from my face. My nostrils revolted at her stale breath. "If I catch you with those boys again, you will pay with your life. I have no problem returning to the home for another girl. Do you understand?"

Too numb to think or speak, I stood shivering.

"Do I make myself clear?" She grabbed at my hair, which had grown long enough to cover my ears and cup my jawline.

"Yes," I said.

She stepped back, and I squeezed my eyes shut as sobs racked my body.

"Let this be a warning to you, boys. If I catch any of you near this girl, you will be punished, and it won't be as gentle." She turned and marched back inside.

Dropping to my knees, I wept. My shame and humiliation was displayed for all, and with it, a bit of my soul broke.

"Here." A young voice tinged with hatred said.

I looked up through my tears into Emory's eyes.

"Take it." He held out my dress.

I took the garment, and he pivoted and raced off. I shielded myself with the dress and locked eyes with Graham. He stood rooted, his face a mask of empathy and pity. I dropped my head, and as if the wind carried her voice, I recalled the words Miss Appleton had spoken in the yard: *A sound mind is a necessity to survive. Set your mind so you may face what comes.*

Could it be she understood more than I wanted to believe?

CHAPTER 22

FTER THAT DAY, I STEERED CLEAR OF THE FIELD LADS, PARTLY OUT of humiliation and partly because I feared what the missus could do to us. As I walked about each day, my body was in a constant state of tension, and a slight tremor had seized my hands. Some days I felt like I was losing my mind, and all human senses seemed to heighten, but food took on a metallic taste. During the night, I'd wake up with my heart pounding out of my chest and covered in sweat, scouring the dark for a killer. Not finding her, I would lie back amongst the children and pull Joey closer and cry. Surely life wasn't meant to be so miserable.

Time passed, and I clung to the foolish illusion that someone would come for me. Like a casualty of the *Titanic*, I flailed in the frigid ocean while trying to survive until help arrived. But like those who had sunk to the ocean's bed, their hands still outstretched for a loved one's grip, my hope faded.

Snow blanketed the ground the day I noticed her hiding behind the old maple tree some distance from the house. I stood over the barrow machine in the kitchen, loading the linens from the notorious bed-wetter now scurrying around the yard like a wild banshee, her matted blond hair falling in her face and her sister following on her heels. Joey had started walking; bundled in a hat and a blue coat much too large, he resembled a waddling snowman as he tottered after his sisters. His delighted squeals shifted the deadness inside of me, and my heart smiled.

"Dallying again, I see." Nora walked into the room and

stood glowering at me. "Mama won't be happy if you don't get moving."

I'd come to believe the girl sought to dump her misery on me—it seemed the worse she treated me, the better she felt. I had become numb to her threats. I bent and picked up the basket of damp clothes, resting the load on my hip, and grudgingly turned to face her.

She circled the barrow washer, running a hand over the top like it was a prize possession. "Bet you never had one of these before."

I didn't feel much like talking, but I figured once I amused her for a moment or two, she'd go back to pestering Graham until Mister told her to leave off. "My family 'ad one."

"You had a home?" Her brow puckered. "Mama said you were orphans and that no one wanted you."

My hands tightened on the basket, and I dropped my gaze to hide the fire kindling inside me. It warn't true. I wouldn't allow her to snatch away my memories of the love of my family. The Gagnons could take everything else, but not that. I wouldn't allow it.

"Well, answer me, girl."

"My parents died." The taste of the lie roiled my gut, and I stewed at the injustice. The organization had whisked us across the ocean, telling us to forget our parents and the life we'd had before. To pretend we were orphans needing to come to a land of opportunity. I'd rather have died in the gutters than come to Canada. I loathed the day I stepped foot in the country.

"Well, you owe us, then. We helped you."

As the missus's parrot continued her nattering, I bit down hard not to react to the smugness in her words. *I owe you nuffing. The bloody organization offered us up as slaves to work your farms. We 'ad no choice.* Like the strings of a fiddle, my nerves thrummed with every insufferable minute in Nora's presence. "Ain't you got anyfing better to do wif your time than pester me?"

"You'd best watch how you speak to me." She crossed her arms over her budding chest.

Something snapped inside me, and common sense fled. I strode past her and on my way by, I paused inches from her. For once I towered over my tormentor. "Or what?"

She took a step back, her mouth agape.

"I didn't think so." I shoved past her and walked out. I felt triumph, and a bit of my spirit soared. I knew Nora would have the missus punish me for my burst of rebellion, but I didn't care.

"You can't talk to me like that." Her voice, weak and uncertain, followed me.

I waved a hand in annoyance and walked down the hall, passing the sitting room where the missus's snores rose from the settee. The baby slept in a bassinet in the corner of the room. The times when he did sleep, the intensity of his colic-induced screams that had been seared into my head would make me think I heard him crying.

I carried the basket to the room at the front of the house that held a cast-iron stove and a clothesline strung from one end of the room to the other. I set the basket down and picked up one of Mister's shirts and shook it out before pinning it to the line. I'd turned to pick up another item when I glimpsed a figure darting behind the old maple tree at the beginning of the drive. I frowned and strode to the window to get a better look. Scanning the front yard, I discovered no one. Had I imagined it?

Perhaps it was a deer. In the early mornings, a variety of animals entered the yard to graze on vegetation poking through the snow. I recalled the day a beast the size of a house strode by, not two feet from the sitting room window. I had swallowed my own heart in my fright. That was the first time I'd seen a Canadian moose. I couldn't get accustomed to the critters that ventured from the woods. In Liverpool, hordes of rats had been as common as the animals that roamed the Gagnons' yard. One night soon after my arrival at the farm, I had stumbled upon a skunk while heading out to the privy. The stench of me was too much for the family to bear, and I found myself sleeping under the back steps until the scent diminished.

A flash caught my eye, and my gaze turned back to the maple tree. And I saw her. She stood watching the house, bundled in a burgundy coat, her blonde hair tucked beneath a matching velvet hat.

Miss Appleton? My heart leaped. What was she doing here? I glanced over my shoulder for Nora or the missus, and finding no one, I looked back. If she had come to check on me, why didn't she walk up to the front door?

I returned to hanging the laundry, and when I finished, I glanced at the window, and to my surprise, Miss Appleton hadn't left. The fool would freeze to death, and I didn't want that on my conscience. I slipped into a coat in the hallway and gripped the doorknob.

The missus's voice rose behind me. "And where do you think you're going?"

My hand froze on the doorknob. Heart leaping into my throat, I said, without turning around, "The privy."

"The outhouse is out the back," she said.

I turned reluctantly to find her eyeing me with suspicion. "I thought I'd stretch my legs by taking the longer way." My reasoning sounded crazy to me and her both.

The groove between her brows intensified, and crossing her arms over ample breasts, she stood tapping her foot. "Why does it not surprise me you would deem yourself deserving of a leisurely stroll?"

"My apologies, Missus. I will take care of my business and be back before you can blink an eye."

The baby's cries lifted, and she looked more annoyed than ever. "Make it quick, girl. I will feed the baby, and then I expect you to take him upstairs. I have a throbbing headache, and can't endure his endless screaming."

I slipped past her, cringing on the way by, half expecting her to take her agitation out on me. Instead she marched into the sitting room, and I continued down the hall and out the back door.

Near the privy, I found Emory splitting wood. He'd been at it all morning. He lowered the ax when he spotted me. "Good day, Hazel." He offered me a weary smile.

"'Ello." Heat radiated from my cheeks at my last memory of seeing him, when I knelt naked in the yard.

Loading his arms with wood, he swayed, struggling under the weight, and looked as though he would topple over. He steadied himself and walked to the pile of wood stacked beside the privy.

I studied the reedy lad. I'd come to know him as the quiet sort who stood back and listened more than having an opinion. Like me, he was smaller in stature.

He returned for another load. "Be careful." He glanced at the house, but never let his gaze fall on me. "She is watching."

"Fank you." I opened the door and stepped into the privy.

The chill gripped my legs as I dropped my drawers and sat on the cold wooden seat, thankful the winter had swept away the pungent smell the privy oozed in the hotter months.

When I returned inside, Miss Appleton was gone.

CHAPTER 23

Charlotte

I HURRIED DOWN THE DRIVEWAY, BLOOD PUMPING SENSATION BACK TO MY iced fingers and toes. After the house disappeared from sight, I slowed my pace. I trained my eyes on the sky, and how the sun had tucked behind the clouds.

Hazel was alive and appeared well, and in that, I gained some comfort. I had hoped to intercept her outside without the Gagnons' knowledge, but the opportunity hadn't presented itself. After my last visit, I had worried Mrs. Gagnon would call Agnes and inform her, but she never had. If she had, Agnes would never have let it go unmentioned.

Frederick and I had married, and he'd taken me on a honeymoon to visit his parents in Australia. We had returned last week, and the urge to check in on Hazel had weighed on my mind. Spotting her leaving the house to visit the outhouse, I had leaped for joy.

At the end of the drive, I picked up my pace, wanting to find warmth from the cold that seized my breath and danced on the tip of my nose. I was happy when the rental car I had parked a short distance away came into view.

Inside the car, I started the engine before removing my leather gloves to blow on my hands. It was my day off, and I had been relieved when Frederick informed me that he would be at the office all day. Ellie had moved into the guesthouse, and I loved having her near, but she had to work and couldn't drive me to the train station. I had persuaded Delilah to take me. She'd asked too many questions about what I was up to, but I had avoided telling her.

Pulling the car onto the road, I headed toward town. The train left at noon and I couldn't miss it because the next one didn't leave until five. If Frederick returned home to find me gone, he would become suspicious of why I hadn't told him I had plans to go out. He had apologized profusely that work drew him away on a day we had planned to shop for a new sofa. He had insisted we purchase a few items to make the home feel like mine.

The road felt more like a buggy trail than a drivable road, and with the freshly fallen snow, the car had to plow a path. My fingers gripped the steering wheel, and my palms dampened as I bounced and swayed at the mercy of the road while keeping my eyes sharp to what lay ahead. Large snowflakes hit the windshield and the light wind from minutes ago picked up.

As a city girl, I never saw the need to purchase a car, and on my salary, I could hardly afford one. But the truth of the matter was I never cared for driving. Fredrick had teased me that I drove like an elderly woman out for a Sunday drive.

Ellie had exclaimed at how lucky I was to capture the attention of a man like Frederick, with the means to care for me. I wished for my sister to find a man who would make her happy, but she insisted she enjoyed her life as a spinster. I believed she never wanted to open herself to being hurt. God knows we had both endured our share of heartache, but life without Frederick seemed unimaginable. When I reflected back on my life before him, I suppose I had been happy enough. I found pleasure in my painting and companionships with friends and colleagues. Then Frederick had swept me off my feet, and life added a layer of bliss I hadn't experienced before and filled me with thoughts of a future together. The hope of finding my sister had long faded.

Then I saw the advertisement and knew life held more for me. When Ellie and I had reunited, I thought life was complete. Since starting work at the receiving home, I had discovered my real purpose and felt a kinship to the children unlike anything in any other aspect of my life.

Awareness of Annie's mysterious death while in the care of the Gagnons had intensified my concern for Hazel, and she never strayed far from my mind. The desire to help the girl became ever-pressing. I wanted her to understand she wasn't alone.

I glanced out the driver's window to the field and recalled how I had hoped someone would come to rescue me. How I had yearned for a loving touch and words of kindness. My desire to be loved had led me down a dark path for several years. Men came and went, leaving me feeling dirty, used, unwanted, and as small and vulnerable as I had felt in my youth, until one day I realized a man couldn't satisfy the emptiness within me. I never told Ellie of my promiscuous ways because she hated all men, Frederick being the exception. In her eyes, all men had become Walter. Life's circumstances had left us all a little broken in one way or another.

My thoughts occupied with Hazel and my sister, I hit the pothole I had barely avoided on the way to the Gagnons' farm, and the car swerved. Heart thrashing, I tried to regain control, but black ice under the dusting of snow pulled the car toward the ditch. *No!* The snowbank's impact flopped my body around like it was a rag doll, until my forehead hit the steering wheel and my world went black.

Some time later, a gentle hand shook me. "Ma'am."

Confused, my vision blurry, I lifted my head, becoming aware of a dull ache. I raised my fingers to touch the coolness trickling over my eyes.

"Ma'am, you've taken a good hit to the head," a man said. "Take it easy, and don't move too fast."

I held out my dampened fingers before me as my vision cleared, and I saw the blood. As I turned my neck, pain radiated down my spine, and I moaned.

"Banged ya up real good," the voice said. "What you doing out here on a day like today?"

I lifted my gaze and found an older man eyeing me with concern. His face seemed familiar, but...wait! He was the Gagnon fellow. He couldn't know I had come, or Mrs. Gagnon would surely call Agnes.

"I came to visit my cousin."

"Surely you could have picked a better day," he said. "Looks like we got a blizzard sweeping in."

I looked at the windshield and found a layer of snow had gathered. How long had I been out? "I need to get to town. I have a train to catch." Panic tightened my chest.

"What time does it depart?"

"Around noon."

He pulled back the cuff of his coat and glanced at his wristwatch. "If you don't leave now, you will never make it in time. Let me give you a lift."

"But the car."

"Don't worry about it. I'll speak to Pete and tell him what happened. He will have someone come out and take the car back."

I recognized the name as the one on the name tag of the man who'd rented me the car. "I don't know—"

"You want to catch your train or not?" he said in a matter-of-fact tone.

If Fredrick got home before me, he'd ask questions I wanted to avoid. "Very well, thank you." I reached for my purse and stepped from the vehicle. My head spun, and he gripped my arm to steady me.

"Take it easy."

He led me to his truck and helped me inside before circling to climb behind the wheel. He turned the vehicle and headed back in the direction of town. If he recognized me, he never let on, and on the drive he spoke candidly of his children, never once mentioning Hazel or the field boys—nor his wife, for that matter. He was gentle in manners and personable, the complete opposite of his wife. Although I felt a hint of sympathy for him, I wanted to believe a man of his demeanor wouldn't allow anything to happen to Hazel. But what about Annie? Had the girl died of natural causes, or had something unimaginable happened and he'd failed to step in? How could one stand by and not speak up against injustice?

As promised, he dropped me off at the train station, and I boarded just in time.

Upon returning to the city, I hired a cab to take me home. When we pulled up outside, my heart skipped a beat when I saw Frederick's car sitting in the driveway. What was he doing home early?

"Ma'am, we are here." The driver had turned in his seat at my delay and sat regarding me with a look of puzzlement.

"Oh, yes." I dug in my purse, paid the driver, and exited the car.

I walked up the drive, my mind grasping for an explanation of where I'd gone.

Inside, I walked through the house, calling out his name when I didn't find him. I looked in the backyard before returning inside. Where was he?

Passing a hallway mirror, I noticed the gash on my head. On the train, I had cleaned myself up and come up with a brilliant plan for how I would explain the injury.

I continued my search and halted on the threshold of our

bedroom. Frederick was perched on the edge of the bed. Beside him sat the small wooden chest with the secrets to my past. He held a paper in his hand, and his lips moved as he read.

No! I gulped back the fear strumming through every muscle in my body, and walked quietly into the room. "Frederick?"

He lifted his head, and the pain in his eyes cut to the very depths of my soul. "Why didn't you tell me?"

"I-I wanted to."

"But I've asked you time and time again."

"I know."

"It all makes sense now." He pressed fingers against his temple.

"I'm sorry."

He lowered the paper. "You were a home child."

I stood rubbing my sweaty palms together in front of me and chewing on the corner of my lip. I nodded.

"From what age?"

"Seven."

"Ellie Scott." His eyes widened. "I thought there was something familiar about her. Is she related to you?"

"She's my sister." Tears streamed down my cheeks. "Frederick, I'm sorry. Truly sorry for not telling you."

"I don't understand. Why the big secret? I love you; haven't I proven that?"

"Yes, time and time again." Shame, like a familiar coat, embraced me. "You must believe me. I wanted to tell you."

He stood and hooked his hands on his waistband before pacing the floor. "How can I believe that? It doesn't make any sense. Why keep it a secret?" he asked again.

"Because…"

He spun and threw his hands in the air in frustration. "But why?"

"Because I was ashamed!" I shook as I released the pain hidden inside me. "I've spent my whole life being embarrassed about who I was—not wanted by anyone, made to feel dirty and no good. I've tried to forget where I came from and who I was because they ingrained it in me."

"Who?"

"The government. The receiving home. The family. When my contract was up, I wanted nothing more than to forget it all. To be somebody in life. To find peace. To love and be loved." My voice shook.

He strode forward and gripped my shoulders. "Take a breath. It's okay."

I shook my head and buried my face in my hands. "I'm sorry, Frederick. So sorry."

He pulled me into an embrace, and I clung to him and sobbed. He stood there holding me, whispering his love into my hair until I calmed and laid my cheek against his shoulder. Exhaustion claimed every part of me.

He pulled me back to search my face and lifted a hand and wiped my tears with his thumb. "You are my girl, Appleton. I'm here to love and protect you without judgment." The endearing term he used for me even after I'd taken his last name warmed my heart.

"I thought if you knew you wouldn't want me."

"Why not?"

"Because I'm wasted goods. You're a good man with much success. If your friends and colleagues were to know about me, I feared they would think you were making a mistake, falling in love with me."

"And if they did, what would it matter?" he said. "It only matters what you and I think. Our journey in life is together. Friends and colleagues come and go, but our relationship is forever. How can I be a good husband if I don't truly know you? I want the real you, not a version you've created, a pretty little package tied up with a bow. No, I want to know the good and the bad."

My tears fell in silent floods. "I love you more than I've ever loved anything." The vulnerability in my confession had me squirming inside, but I elevated my gaze to meet his. "Can you forgive me?"

He eyed me tenderly. "It depends."

I frowned. "On what?"

"If you're going to tell me how you came by that gash on your head, and if we sit and you tell me everything over a nice cup of coffee."

"All right." I smiled. "I will tell you all about it. Anything and everything you want to know. I promise."

"Good." He grinned and lowered his head, sealing my mouth with a warm, passionate kiss.

CHAPTER 24

Hazel

'D BEEN WITH THE GAGNONS ALMOST A YEAR WHEN GRAHAM POUNDED on the back door. "Mrs. Gagnon! Come quick."

I pulled open the door and his pallid face knotted my stomach. "What is it?"

"It's Mr. Gagnon." He bent and rested his palms on his knees while trying to catch his breath.

The missus's weighted footfalls hurried up behind me. "Who is it, girl? Best not be one of those field children. They know the rules. None are allowed near the house." She pushed me aside, and when she caught sight of Graham, she froze. "What is it?"

"It's your husband, Missus. I-I—he is dead."

"Dead?" Her voice hitched, and her legs buckled. I reached to steady her but crumpled under her bulk. She leaned against the wall for support, and all color drained from her face.

No, it couldn't be. My throat seized up. Then a thought occurred. "The doctor. 'As anyone sent for the doctor?"

Graham wiped his hands on his trousers, eyeing the missus, then me. "You ain't listening, Hazel," he said with an intense urgency before softening the delivery of his next words. "There ain't gonna be any need for the doctor. He ain't breathing."

Sickness churned my stomach. The mister, gone? Despondency enveloped me. He had been the one hope of protection, and left in the hands of the missus…I couldn't bring myself to think about what would happen. I blinked away tears. What did his death mean for the field lads and me?

We buried the mister a few days later, and for a week after his burial the missus stormed around the house and unleashed abuse on us all.

Graham's contract was up, but he agreed to stay on until after the harvest. I knew he'd decided on account of the field lads and me, kind of like he was waiting around to see what Mrs. Gagnon would do with us, now that Mister was gone. I felt a sense of kinship to Graham and decided he was a decent bloke. But for his sake, I hoped he could break the chains of bondage placed on him for far too long.

———◇✳◇———

It was midsummer when the blue car drove up the drive. The missus strode to the window at the sound of an approaching vehicle.

"He is here!" She released the curtain and hurried to the door.

For days the missus had looked forward to her brother Mr. Tremblay's arrival. Nora's disposition became sourer than ever, and she seemed to withdraw into herself. Between the missus's admiration for the bloke and Nora's dislike, I had lain awake at night, worrying about what would transpire with a new mister in the house.

As the car pulled to a stop out front, Nora plopped down on the couch and stared blankly ahead like a dead person. I didn't understand what the girl was carrying on about. Perhaps another adult to answer to had upset her. I assumed she found pleasure in bossing the younger children and me because she was the oldest child and the missus's spawn.

"No, Joey." I turned away from the sulky girl and removed the lad as he reached for the giant cactus in the front window. The bloody plant had captured my attention soon after my arrival, and for my curiosity I'd ended up with needles implanted in my fingers for days.

From the window, I watched Mr. Tremblay embrace his sister. He stood half her size, with slicked-back hair and neatly pressed clothes; he didn't resemble the missus at all. Perhaps the bloke wouldn't be as appalling.

"You are a sight." The missus clapped his back, and he winced from the blow. "I'm glad you're here. Come inside." She pulled from his embrace and strode back toward the house.

I retreated from the window and busied myself with tidying the shoes blocking the entrance.

"Move out of the way." The missus kicked at me on her way by.

Mr. Tremblay's freshly polished shoes halted in front of me. "And who may you be?"

I kept my gaze down. "'Azel, Mister."

He bent and thrust out a hand. "Nice to meet you."

I gawked at the groomed nails and hesitated before extending my hand. His touch was gentle, but weirdly so. I lifted my eyes to look into gleaming dark eyes, and saw an eeriness that chilled my blood. I didn't know what it was, but goose pimples raced over my flesh. When his thumb took to stroking the top of my hand, I reclaimed it, pulled to my feet, and stepped back.

"And you," I said.

He laughed and straightened and looked at Nora, who still sat on the couch with her shoulders rolled forward and hands clasped tightly in her lap.

"Is that my little Nora?" He brushed past me.

She cringed, but never returned his greeting.

"Nora, greet your uncle," the missus said.

"Hi, Uncle," she said in a barely audible voice.

"What, no proper greeting for your uncle?" He spread his arms wide and grinned at her.

"I don't feel well." Nora leaped to her feet and raced from the room.

Mr. Tremblay stared after her, and the missus patted his arm. "Don't worry about her. Come sit and tell me everything." She gripped his arm and said to me, "Girl, get the kettle on and fix us some coffee."

I hurried from the room. In the kitchen, I heated the kettle and busied myself tidying.

Joey waddled into the room and pulled on my dress. "Hold me."

"I can't right now." I patted the top of his head.

"I want up," he protested louder.

"Shh! Your mum will be angry with us both if you start to fuss."

Big tears plopped onto his rosy cheeks. I bent and gathered him into my arms. He cuddled into my neck, and I felt the hotness of his flesh.

"Are you not feeling well?" I touched his forehead and realized he was burning up. I carried him to the sitting room doorway, where Mr. Tremblay and the missus sat on the sofa, chatting. "Missus."

They looked in my direction, and she glared. "Didn't I give you an order? And for heaven sake's, put the boy down. He doesn't need to be lugged around. You spoil him, and it will be us left to tend to him when you're gone."

"He ain't feeling well. Must be his teeth again."

"Bring him here. Let me take a look." She waved a hand.

I hurried to her side, and she grabbed for Joey. He wailed and turned from her, clutching me tighter. His small fingers pulled at the collar of my dress. Fear gripped my chest at the look of outrage that flashed in the missus's eyes.

She leaped to her feet and pried him from me. Then she sat and laid him across her lap, resting an arm across the wailing child's upper chest. "Ahh, shut up, boy. Ain't no need for carrying on so."

Pinned down, Joey panicked and fought the missus, but she pushed her fat fingers into his mouth as she had done to me at the receiving home. I wished the boy would bite her and teach her once and for all about putting her sausage fingers in people's mouths. But as soon as I thought it, I withdrew the thought; son or not, if Joey clamped down, she would punish him just the same.

In her determination to pry the boy's mouth open as he flailed, her arm moved closer to his throat. My chest pounded as panic shone in his eyes and he wheezed. I glanced at Mr. Tremblay for his help, but he sat in the armchair with his hands steepled, taking in the situation, never coming to Joey's defense.

"Missus, you're choking 'im," I said. "It's 'is teeth. 'E's been chewing on 'is fingers all day."

Face reddening and her eyes flashing, she released her grip and pushed him from her lap. He landed on his feet and lunged for me. Too afraid to comfort him in front of the missus, I stood poker straight while he buried his face in the fabric of my dress and howled. His fingers dug into my flesh as he tried to climb me like a tree.

"Take him upstairs before I wallop him good, and put him to bed."

"But 'e won't stay there."

Her eyes widened dangerously. "Then you stay with him until he's asleep."

"But the kettle?"

I jumped when she leaped to her feet. "Oh, for God's sake. Go before I give you a beating you won't soon forget." She gave me a shove.

"Yes, Missus." I bent and scooped up Joey.

As I strode from the room, she said to Mr. Tremblay, "The street scum is lucky we took her in. Canadians do Britain a favor, the way I look at it. We relieve them of the garbage congesting their streets."

Her words bruised my soul and made me squirm in my own flesh. Tears of shame and self-loathing overcame me. She had tainted my internal monologue, and as I climbed the stairs, the insults she had flung at me over my time with the Gagnons reverberated in my mind. Whore. Street rat. Scum. Unfit to be loved. Despite my trying to protect the flame inside me, it flickered in the breeze of her insults. Some days, I felt like a ghost of the girl I once was.

Joey's cries had turned to whimpers by the time we reached the upstairs landing. "There, there, Joey. No more crying. I will take care of you." I rubbed his back.

"'Kay," he said with a snuffle and lifted his head from my shoulder to look at me. "Mommy's mad at Joey."

She is always mad, I said to myself. "It's okay." I kissed his forehead.

The sound of weeping drew my awareness, and although I tried to ignore it, I halted and looked at the opposite end of the hallway, in the direction of Nora's room. I shook off the distraction and swerved back to continue to the bedroom I shared with Joey and the twins, but the anguish-filled sobs stopped my retreat.

Why should I care that Nora was crying? She had been nothing but cruel and vindictive, and the cause of several punishments I'd received.

As though concerned about his sister's distress, Joey peeked over my shoulder before centering his blue eyes on me. "Nora?" He jabbed a finger.

I cursed and grudgingly turned and walked down the hallway to find Nora's door closed. I lifted my hand and hesitated, but gritted my teeth and knocked.

The weeping ceased, but no reply came. I knocked harder.

"Go away!" I heard panic in her voice.

I frowned at Joey, but against all common sense I opened the door.

There was a shuffle, and a red-faced Nora scurried into the far corner of her bed, shielding herself with a pillow. "I'll tell. I swear I…" She stopped mid-sentence as she caught sight of me. "You! What do you think you're doing, coming into my room without my permission?" Her bloodshot eyes narrowed.

I gulped but took a step closer. "I 'eard you crying. I know you don't like me, but—"

"Get out!" She threw the pillow at me. "I'll scream, and Mama will send you to the cellar."

I clenched my jaw. I loathed the very existence of the dreadful girl. "Have it your way." I turned, but not before I saw her press her trembling body tighter against the wall. Confused by her behavior, but not wishing to further agitate the girl, I walked from the room and closed the door. Outside, I stood staring at the barrier between us before pushing her from my thoughts. I marched back the way I'd come before I turned fool enough to show sympathy to the villain within.

Minutes later, I lay on the bed, my body spooning Joey's. I stroked the letters from the sign of the distribution house on his back, a habit that calmed both of us, but that day it failed to calm my concern. Why did Nora hate Mr. Tremblay? And what did his presence mean for us all?

CHAPTER 25

GRAHAM TRIED TO TEACH MR. TREMBLAY HOW TO MANAGE THE fields, and in passing, mentioned how the missus's brother warn't cut out for life on a farm. Not long after, I became aware of his illegal smuggling of alcohol. The evenings he didn't spend in town, he would sit on the back porch, smoking and drinking moonshine. He and the missus cussed and fought more than not, and tensions became higher than ever. Nora had made herself scarce, and I was glad for it.

Mr. Tremblay wasn't the chatty sort. No, he sat watching a person with an intense stare as though trying to figure them out. The kind of bloke that made your skin crawl, and I did my best to avoid him.

The day I came to know what manner of bloke Mr. Tremblay was, the missus had taken the twins to visit the neighbor lady, leaving Joey in Nora's care. She had left me with a list of tasks for the day. After weeding the garden, I returned to the house. In the kitchen, I set down the basket of cucumbers and green beans I had picked. I heard footsteps on the stairs, and Mr. Tremblay's whistle.

He strode by the kitchen and halted. "What are you doing here?" His voice hitched before something dark registered in his eyes.

I could have asked him the same question. Wasn't he supposed to be in the fields with the others? "I've finished the outside chores," I said.

He strode up to me, and I took a step back. Interest flickered in his eyes, and he lifted fingers to caress my throat. I cringed from his touch. "A bit old, you are, but pretty."

My heart struck faster as recognized a look similar to one I'd seen on the faces of Benji Cooper and his mates the night they cornered me in an alley in Liverpool. Only my cleverness had gotten me out of that predicament unscathed, and safely home.

Mr. Tremblay pressed himself against me and my fear surged, but I squared my shoulders and stared him straight in the eye. "I wouldn't be getting no funny ideas. I've been known to make men's fings shrivel."

Concern shadowed his face.

"That's right—got the disease, I do."

He jerked his hand away and stepped back as though I was plagued with leprosy.

"I ain't skeered of you." I jutted my chin, never letting my eyes leave his.

"We will see about that," he said before promptly exiting the room.

The screen door slammed, and through the window, I saw him pause in the yard and rub a hand over his face before hurrying off to the field.

I released the breath I'd been holding, and it was then I registered the soft noises coming from the sitting room.

I found Joey lying on his belly, quietly playing with the toy train set Mister had bought for his birthday. I recalled how Joey had squealed with delight, and how the missus chastised her husband for wasting money, going on to claim Joey would be underfoot.

I eyed the boy with longing, wishing I could play with him for a spell and bask in his sweetness. "Joey?"

His face brightened, and he scrambled up to rest on his knees. "Girl, you wanna play?" He pointed at the train.

"Not now. Where is Nora?" I asked.

"Don't know," he said. "You play?"

"Come." I urged him with a hand. Where had Nora run off to? And leaving Joey unattended—the missus would hear of it. I heaved a sigh. Who did I think I was fooling? Ratting her out to the missus would cause me harm, not her. Although I would revel in pure bliss to see her finally get what she deserved.

Joey followed me through the house to the stairs; applying patience I didn't have, I didn't pick him up and we slowly climbed to the second floor. We walked to Nora's room and found the door open.

"Nora, you in 'ere?" I stepped inside and found no sign of her. "Slacking off, I expect." Aggravated, I swung Joey up onto my hip and turned to leave the room.

A noise came from the corner by the chest of drawers. I frowned, but with no time to waste and chores still needing finishing before the missus returned, I stormed forward. "There's no time for mucking 'bout. Your mum..." My words faded. "Nora?" Her name drew out long and soft on my lips.

She sat huddled in the corner with legs drawn up to her chest, and I sensed something was amiss by the faint mewing coming from her. Placing Joey on the floor, I ordered him to stay before kneeling before her. "You all right?"

I recalled Mr. Tremblay coming downstairs after I'd entered the house, and then Nora's odd behavior since his arrival at the farm. A harrowing realization struck me, and I sank back on my heels.

Tears cascaded over Nora's pale cheeks.

"'E 'urt you," I said as though trying to convince myself that the madness in my head was real.

Nora craned her neck as if seeing me for the first time, and I saw the overwhelming fear in her eyes. "'E did," I said with certainty. The hairs stood up on the back of my neck.

She nodded.

I groaned as the terrible fact registered. "You 'ave to tell your mum. You must. She will send 'im away."

She shook her head and said, barely above a whisper, "She won't."

"'Ow can you be so certain?" I said as urgency gripped me.

"Because I've told her before. She don't care."

Why would I assume the missus would care about an act so heinous at her brother's hands? She had never shown her children the slightest warmth. I didn't know precisely what had transpired between Nora's uncle and her, but I knew it wasn't right. How could I have not understood how Nora had acted around him? Like a frightened kitten in need of shelter.

"Then we will go to the neighbors, or anyone," I said.

"You're a fool. She will kill you and me." Lip quivering, she lowered her head. "Leave. Please, just leave." Sobs racked her body, and helpless and unsure what to do, I left.

Later that night, after the younger children slept and I had finished in the kitchen, the missus marched into the sitting room from outside.

My fingers tightened on the broom, and my heart skipped a beat. Had Nora spoken to her about Mr. Tremblay's doings?

She rounded the corner and, like a demon possessed, charged at me, and I braced for her impact. "My brother says you made advances at him while I was away." Her fist connected with my right cheek and sent me reeling backward. My hip struck the corner of a stand next to the sofa, and I cried out in pain. "I knew you were nothing but a dirty little whore." She grabbed me by the bodice of my dress. The fabric ripped, pulling away at the seams. I put my hands up to shield myself from her madness.

"'E 'urt—"

Her next blow split my lip and silenced my plea.

You don't understand, I wept in silence. *He hurt her in unthinkable ways.*

"Mama, please." Nora appeared and tugged on her mother's arm. "She didn't do anything. He lies. I was next to her all day."

I gawked at Nora, tears of pain blurring my vision.

"You joining up with the likes of her, are ya?" The missus shook Nora's hand free and thrust her elbow backward, sending the girl sailing to the floor in a heap. Then the missus turned her attention back to me. "You will learn your place, or I'll rid us of your insufferable presence." She hauled me toward the back door. "You think you can talk back to me?"

"Stop. Let me go." Tears tattered my voice. I fought her like I'd never fought her before, but I was no match.

She stormed down the back steps and marched across the yard. I dug my heels into the dirt, trying to gain leverage. But it was no use.

At the storage cellar, she pulled open the wooden door and bellowed, "Get up here, and make it quick."

Scuffing footsteps came up the stairs, and soon Emory's head poked out as he ascended. He had spent more time in the cellar than before; without Mister to intervene, the missus had become ungovernable in her need to torture us all. Weak, Emory staggered on the last step and sprawled on the ground. With her grip chewing into the flesh of my neck, I was powerless to help him.

She swiveled to face me. "I won't have you—" The other field lads entered the yard at the sudden commotion, and she glared at them and rolled back her shoulders. "Or any of you defying me.

Mr. Gagnon is gone, and may God rest his soul, but he was too soft. I don't like weakness. I will govern this farm my way. This girl has proven herself a whore, and I won't tolerate it. She will be punished accordingly. Do you know what they did to harlots in the Bible?"

The lads never moved or spoke. Graham's eyes chiseled into her face, and I feared what she would do if she noticed.

"You!" She jabbed a finger at Farley. "Answer me."

"They stoned them?" His voice quavered.

After Mister's death, her delusion had taken on a new form, and on Sundays, when she returned from the service, she stood on the back step, preaching hell and damnation to the lost souls—us.

"That's right," she said with satisfaction. "The girl is my property and has committed a sin that needs amendment in the eyes of God. He has chosen me as the Redeemer to lead the lost souls in my care. He comes to me in visions and has given me His divine blessing. If I deem you unsalvageable, He asks that I smite you from the earth."

A gasp went through the lads. My knees knocking, I glanced at Graham. He stood with clenched fists and looked ready to pounce.

"But," her voice rose, "I will show forgiveness, and grant this poor wretched soul mercy one last time." The missus gave me a rough shake and centered her gaze at me. "In you go."

"Please, I didn't mean to." I grasped onto anything to stop her deranged behavior.

She grinned, a look that hollowed my stomach, and without warning, released me.

I gripped the fabric of her dress as I fell back, then my hands grabbed at empty air to stop my descent.

"No!" Graham shouted.

I hit the wooden stairs, and pain ricocheted through my body.

I screamed, hitting one hard surface after another. There was an audible snap, and a burning sensation ripped through my shoulder. My head cracked against something hard, and all went dark.

When consciousness returned, pain racked my body, and I felt the stiffness of the dried blood caking my face. I struggled to sit up and cried out at the agony coursing through my shoulder, and the intense throbbing in my head.

The moon shone through the plank doors overhead. Coddling my shoulder and dangling arm, I crawled to the stairs, as the space was only a few feet high. The stairway provided room to stand, and I climbed to the top and pushed against the doors with my right arm, but they wouldn't budge.

I sank onto the third step and rested my head back against the cold earthen wall. Silent tears fell as I peered at the full moon and clung despondently to visions of my brother. Would I ever see him again?

Mum entered my thoughts, and tears of hopelessness turned to anger. "Why did you do it? Why? You shouldn't 'ave left us. I can't bear it. I can't…" I pounded my lap with a fist, but pain swiftly stilled my movements, and rationality returned.

No one cared. No one. Miss Appleton had shown me the most kindness since I'd come to Canada, but where was she now? She'd promised to help me. She promised. Adults' words were nothing but empty lies. As soon as I thought ill of her, remorse settled in my chest. Why would she travel from the city to only watch from afar if humanity didn't thrive within her? The realization that she was as helpless as us defeated any hope of her getting me out.

"Hazel?"

The sound of my name and shuffling overhead silenced my sobs. "Is that you, Graham?"

"It's me." Fingers poked through a small gap between the planks.

Hope erupted within me, and I touched his fingers.

"You hurt bad?"

"My shoulder—I think it's broken."

"Why'd she lock you up?"

"I don't know for sure, but I fink Mr. Tremblay is the reason."

"Why? 'E cause trouble?"

"Yes…" I paused. The words turned my stomach. "'E is doing fings to Nora. Bad fings."

"I didn't like the bloke from the moment I saw him."

"I wish Mister was still alive. 'E was the only 'ope we 'ad 'ere."

"She got one thing right," he said.

I squinted through the slat to get a look at him and could only see an outline of his leg. "'Ow so?"

"The bastard was weak. She is like a rabid dog, and he should've done away with her like she did that poor dog. She is crazed in the head, I tell ya. Mark my words, another will die at her hands. Which one is the question." The deadness in his tone chilled my blood.

I pulled my legs to my chest and sat quietly, pondering on the horror of his statement. After some time I called his name, but no answer came.

"Graham," I said a little louder.

My melancholy intensified as I realized he'd abandoned me.

Days later, when the missus opened the cellar doors, I raised an arm to block the sun's glare.

"Have you learned your lesson?"

"Yes, Missus." My parched throat broke my words, and I ran a thickened tongue over cracked lips.

After that day, I no longer stayed in the house with the family. I bunked in the shed, and each night the missus bolted the door, keeping me in. But I found comfort that it also kept Mr. Tremblay out.

CHAPTER 26

M Y DUTIES INSIDE THE HOUSE CONTINUED, BUT NORA TOOK OVER my position in the children's bed at night. From time to time she offered me a tired smile, and her snitching ended. In passing, she told me that as exhausting as it was caring for baby Herbert, it kept her uncle away. She never strayed far from her mum's side, as though seeking protection in her company.

The missus cut the field lads' and my rations in half. Soon their eyes were hollow and their flesh pallid, and the weakness of hunger I had known in Liverpool returned. Mr. Tremblay delivered our allotments in a pail he tossed into the pigs' trough. As we scrambled to eat, he stood back, smoking and relishing the sight of the ravenous creatures that groveled before him.

The first few times, Graham had stood back, glaring and refusing to eat. "I ain't a sow," he said one autumn evening while hiding in the shadows as I pumped water from the well. Once muscled from hours in the fields, he was now thin and gaunt.

"I know, but you must stay alive. The 'arvest is done. It's time you left this place. You suffer for no reason." I kept my head turned, not wanting to reveal the panic brewing inside me. The thought of him leaving terrified me. Although I'd given up believing I'd be rescued, I clung to his and the lads' friendship.

We were all aware that what we had suffered before was only a foreshadowing of what was yet to come. Fear shone in all our eyes.

I lifted the pail. "You can't stay. If you wish to survive, you must go. You do us no good dead."

"But what about you and the lads? I can't just leave. How would I live with myself if something were to happen?"

"You aren't responsible for us," I said over my shoulder. "Besides, you can't stop them anyway." I hurried toward the house, with the water slopping over the sides of the pail and soaking my coat and wool stockings.

The missus and Mr. Tremblay had left for town some hours ago. On Monday nights, she attended prayer meeting while Mr. Tremblay tended to his illegal dealings. As I walked down the hallway, I considered the missus. No amount of prayer would save her soul. If there was a heaven or hell, hell had a ticket with her name on it.

Nora, dressed in a white cotton nightgown, sat at the table, hunched over a newspaper. Not tall enough to rest her feet on the floor, she let them dangle as she traced her finger down the pages. Her brow was puckered with concentration.

"Ain't you a bit young to care what that got to say?" I gestured at the paper.

She looked up. "Trying to find me a lawyer lady."

"What for?"

"I've been thinking about what you said about Uncle Roy's doings, and well…I'm fixing to hire me someone to make him pay. And this advertisement right here says there is a lady lawyer in the city."

"And how you fixing to pay?"

"I'll take every last penny Mama has if it means I can stop him," she said, misery alight in her face.

"I'd 'elp you if she didn't keep me locked up at night." I stood to my full height and shot her a cheeky grin. "I've been known to get in and out of places without anyone ever knowing I was there. And blokes like your uncle deserve to pay." As the bold statement left my lips, I wondered if I had made a mistake in making that claim to someone who had proven to be bent on causing me harm.

But she smiled—revealing a prettiness I'd never associated with her before. "No one has ever stood up for me." She grew quiet for a moment before continuing. "Why did you do it, anyhow?" She eyed the arm I still coddled.

"'Cause it ain't right, what 'e's doing."

"But I've been horrible to you."

I shrugged. "Dreadful, in fact."

Her shoulders slumped. "I'm not a good person, Hazel." Tears gathered in my throat at her use of my name. "I can't say I would've done the same for you." She eyed me as though seeing me for the first time.

The starkness of her honesty didn't jar me. "You stood up for me with your mum."

"And what good did that do?" She jumped down off her chair, pulled it up to the cupboard, and climbed onto the countertop. She opened the top door and pulled down Mister's candy jar.

I eyed the colorful, individually wrapped treats inside, and my mouth watered.

She removed the lid and held the jar out. "Take one."

I shook my head. "I ain't looking to go back in the cellar."

"No one is going to know." She reached into the jar and removed a candy and held it out for me.

I hesitated only a second before my stomach got the best of me. I grinned and unwrapped the treat and popped it into my mouth, and she did the same. We moaned and smiled at each other before she grew serious.

"I ain't got much, but if I could repay you, I would," she said.

A thought jumped into my head. "Maybe you can."

Her eyes widened. "How?"

I stroked the letters I had traced over and over since leaving the receiving home on the countertop. "Tell me what those letters say."

Confusion played across her face, and she moved closer to get a better look. "Do it again."

I did as she asked.

"Those ain't letters. Well, not all of them. It's an address. 1975 Hoover Boulevard."

As though she had breathed air into my lungs, I gasped. My body shook as I repeated the address in my head.

"Who or what is there that you know?" she asked.

"No one now." My mind drifted. I added the detail to the memories I kept in my head, the map that would one day lead me to my brother. I had left Liverpool and crossed the ocean, where the organization had registered me at a receiving home in Toronto with the address 1975 Hoover Boulevard.

Later I lay in the shed, shivering in the brisk evening temperature, when footsteps approached. My heart raced with anticipation over who might arrive, and I pulled my thin wool blanket up to my throat as someone fumbled at the door. Then the sound of the bolt sliding followed by fading footsteps eased my fear. I fell asleep and dreamed I was standing in a field, and in the distance, a tall blond bloke stood with his back to me. When I approached him, he spun, and smiled when he saw me, and I looked into familiar eyes. My stomach skipped—Brock.

CHAPTER 27

Charlotte

MONTHS AFTER MR. GAGNON'S PASSING, I HAD OVERHEARD THE news in town following a trip to the farm. Although the man had seemed ineffective against his wife when he was alive, his existence in Hazel's life had registered a sense of false hope, although one could not overlook how Annie had fared in their care. I was concerned for Hazel's safety, now that she was left solely in the hands of Mrs. Gagnon.

One evening I sat propped against the headboard of my bed, writing in the journal I kept of the comings and goings at the receiving home. Hazel weighed heavily on my mind, as she often did. The last two visits to the farm, I hadn't spotted the girl.

"What stills your pen?" Frederick lowered his newspaper. Part of our routine had become me recording the day's events while he read the business section of the paper. He kept a close watch on the rising and falling of stocks, and I, like his clients, admired his brilliance when it came to the stock market.

"It's Hazel."

"What about her?"

I had told him about Hazel and explained the connection I felt to the girl. "I want to pay Mrs. Gagnon a visit."

"You intend to speak to her?"

I closed my journal and placed it on the nightstand. "Yes.

It's a risk I must take. If something happened to her, I don't know if I could forgive myself."

"Forgive yourself for what? You have no control over what happens to them, and you cause yourself unnecessary stress and worry."

A kernel of anger kindled in me at his nonchalant response, but before I could speak he lifted his hand to stop me. "Now, no need to get upset. I understand and support your efforts, but I worry about the pressure you put on yourself. Each time a child is placed or a new shipment comes in, you become obsessed to the point I've wondered if you working at the home causes more harm than good."

I understood his rationale. But he came from a place of love, and as hard as he tried, he would never fully understand the ordeals a home child suffered. I'd spent every day trying to offer the children kindness and reassurance. They often arrived frightened, and as minuscule as it seemed, I had taken it upon myself to offer a sense of refuge in this new land far from home.

Agnes had changed my position, and my job no longer included overnights. Ellie had informed me she had hired another woman more to her liking. Agnes had acted as though she'd done me a favor, me being a married woman and all. But Ellie had said she'd heard mention of her cutting my hours.

In the extra time allotted me, I had written several articles under a secret name about the injustices endured by the British home children, claiming my experiences as a victim to the system. I had queried the local papers about publishing them, but they'd refused. As time went on, defeat had set in, and I wondered if my efforts were fruitless. But then I thought of the children and why I had taken the job at the receiving home. There had to be usefulness in that, right? Well, as long as Agnes didn't turn me out for good.

Heaving a sigh, I turned on my side to face Frederick. "I've wanted to speak to you on something I've been thinking about."

"Oh?" He traced the bare flesh of my shoulder, and goose pimples coursed up and down my spine.

"What if, when Hazel's contract is up within the year, we give her a home with us?"

His fingers paused, and he frowned.

"Hear me out."

He gave me a look that said *if you say so.*

Nerves jumped in my stomach. "I became part of the British home children scheme at a tender and impressionable age and lost all sense of self. Most days, I felt more like an animal than a human. The amount of shame a home child carries over their very existence is something I can never explain. I wonder, if someone had been there for me after I started out on my own, maybe I wouldn't have sought affection and attention in all the wrong places." I lowered my eyes. "And perhaps I wouldn't carry regrets of past transgressions. Finding you breathed hope into me, and now that no secrets stand between us, I want to be honest with what is in my heart."

"Tell me, Appleton: what is it that toys with your heart?"

"I want to give Hazel a home and help her find her brother."

"You speak the impossible. You have no access to the boy's records and no information on where he has been placed."

"I'm aware." The truth of his words shrouded me in despondency. Was I deceiving myself into believing I could help her? Providing Hazel with a home where she would be loved and cared for was achievable with my husband's approval. But extending the offer to help find her brother may be absurd and lead to more heartache.

"How can you be sure the girl would want to?" he said.

I lifted my eyes to search his.

"You mentioned how she doesn't trust you."

"I hope to change that," I said.

"How?"

"I'm not sure yet, but I will." I jutted my chin in determination.

He smiled and pulled me closer. "I admire your determination."

I laughed and melded my body into his, wrapping my arms around his neck. He scooped his arm under me and twisted me onto my back. I lay peering up at him, and the safety I felt in his presence and the love thumping in my chest filled me with desire. He eyed my lips before lowering his to meet mine, and kissed me with such passion it left me breathless.

When he pulled away, I smiled at him and said, "Mr. Taylor, I do say, you have a way of making me weak." My hands tangled in his hair, and he traced my body with longing, his fingers slipping the strap of my blue silk negligee off my shoulder, exposing my breast.

He drew me to him, and we surrendered to the desire burning within us.

The next afternoon I strode up the porch steps to the Gagnons' front door.

"You've lost your mind," I muttered before taking a deep breath and rapping on the door.

Soon the door creaked open, and I lifted a hand to stifle a gasp. "Hazel?" Rage exploded in my chest at the sight of her. Bruises yellowed with age marred her face, and her arm hung in an awkward position. What had the woman done to her?

She gawked back at me, and her lip quivered.

"Did she do this to you?" I said through clenched teeth.

Hazel lowered her head, and a tear plopped onto her cheek.

I realized the girl appeared paler than usual. "What does it matter," she said in a low voice, but cringed and pressed her lips together when Mrs. Gagnon's voice rang out.

"Who is it?" Mrs. Gagnon strode down the hallway, and somewhere glassware clattered with her arrival. She wiped her hands on an apron that appeared to have missed laundry day and braced when she recognized me. "You. What are you doing here again? I told you I have no need of you people here. I don't care what new policy you've put in place. What happens on my property is my business."

Hazel cowered as the woman came to tower over her.

"Go help Nora set the table," Mrs. Gagnon said.

Hazel hurried to obey, and once she was gone, I looked up at Mrs. Gagnon. "What happened to the girl?"

"Took a fall down the stairs. The clumsiest girl I ever saw."

"That arm needs tending. Has she not seen a doctor?"

"Samuel is dead," she said bluntly. "I had to ask my brother to help me manage the farm. Got no extra money to pay for a doctor."

"Yes, I've heard. I'm sorry for your loss, but that is no excuse." I squared my shoulders. "The girl appears to be in pain and requires a doctor's care. I will fetch the doctor myself."

"You will do no such thing." She threw open the screen door, barely missing my face. "I told you last time that I didn't want to see the likes of you or any of you folks from the institution out here poking your noses around in my business. Perhaps I'll call Miss Keene and give her a piece of my mind. I'm sure she ain't looking to lose the hefty bonus the government provides the home with."

"The girl needs help, and either you send for the doctor, or I will file a report and have all children, including your own, removed from this home," I said with more confidence than I felt.

Her eyes narrowed. She stepped closer in an attempt to intimidate me.

Instinct set in, and all common sense abandoned me when I lifted a hand and slapped her face.

She gasped and cradled her cheek, her eyes wide. Then her face darkened. "I'll have your job for this." She rocked on her heels.

"And I will tell your neighbors and the townsfolk about Annie."

She dropped her hand, and her flesh paled. "The girl died. It was none of my doing."

"I don't believe you. I will see you are flagged as an unfit family to govern children. Perhaps the CAS should be alerted."

Her face hardened. "She ain't the first home child to die around these parts, and she won't be the last."

My heart struck harder, but I rooted my feet. "Your intimidation may work on others, but it certainly won't work on me."

"Roy," she bellowed over her shoulder, never letting her eyes leave me. When no answer came, she let out another shout. "Roy! Get on out here."

Through the gap in the living room curtains, I saw a lanky man get up from the sofa and mosey to the door. As he strode toward us, I regarded his dirty denim overalls and plaid shirt, but overall the fellow seemed put together. Not a lock of hair was out of place, and he smiled with ease.

"What is it?" he said to her while eyeing me with interest. He was a quarter her size, but who wouldn't be? Mrs. Gagnon had more manly traits than woman, and her appearance left much to be desired. Summing her up, I again questioned what her late husband had seen in her.

"Get on in to town and fetch the doctor," she said.

"What for?" He finished inspecting me and looked at her.

"To fix the girl's arm. This here woman is from the organization."

He stood a little taller, as though that information made him uneasy. "I see," he said. "Let me grab my coat."

Soon the Gagnons' green car drove down the drive and out of view.

"Are ya happy?" She crossed her arms over her ample bosom.

"If you don't mind, I'll wait until he returns, and the girl is tended to."

"Fine, have it your way. But you will remain outside. Got it?"

"As you say," I said with a politeness that soured my stomach.

She walked back inside, and I settled down in the frost-covered rocker to wait. An hour later, the Gagnons' car came up the drive, and I stood. The passenger was an older gentleman with unruly hair that jutted in all directions. When the car pulled to a stop, the fellow struggled to get out. Roy hurried around to help him before retrieving his bag from the backseat. The doctor walked toward me with unsteady legs, and I questioned his ability to care for Hazel. As he drew near, I realized it wasn't only age I had to worry about, but the scent of liquor oozing from him.

"Good evening, Doctor." I stuck out my hand. "Are you well?"

He squinted at me before removing his spectacles from a shirt pocket. He gave the glasses a shake and put them on. They sat lopsided on his face. "Oh, there ya are. About as pretty as you sounded."

I blushed.

The screen door swung open and crashed against the exterior wall, and Mrs. Gagnon waddled out. "Afternoon, Doc. Got a girl needing tending."

"Well, let me have a look at her." He trudged inside.

I stepped forward to follow him, but Mrs. Gagnon put out her arm, catching me in the throat. "You stay out here."

I looked from her to Roy, who stood at the bottom of the stairs, grinning. I turned back to Mrs. Gagnon and leveled an unwavering gaze on her. "I will help the doc. He looks unfit to be caring for patients." And before she could stop me, I ducked under her arm and entered the house.

Hazel stood with a fussy toddler on her hip in the living room while a small boy clung to her side, looking at the doctor with leeriness.

"There ain't nofing to worry 'bout, Joey. You go on now and play." She urged the boy with a gentle push before her gaze settled on me.

I smiled and strode to her side. "Here, give me the child." I removed him from her arms and turned to Mrs. Gagnon, whose hot breath dampened my neck. I handed her the boy, who fussed all the harder, but I ignored him and turned to Hazel. "Come. This will hurt, but we can't leave it untreated." I removed my coat and gloves before guiding her to an armchair.

The doctor placed his bag on a stand beside the chair. "Get that baby out of here. My eyes may be failing me, but my ears have yet to," he growled.

Mrs. Gagnon's brow glistened, and her eyes twitched. She gave me a look of warning and strode from the room.

I clasped Hazel's sweaty hand in mine. "It will be over before you know it."

She chewed on her lip and cast a nervous glance at the doctor. He leaned forward to roll up Hazel's sleeve, and her nose twitched before she regarded me with uncertainty.

"How did this happen?" I said in a low voice.

Hazel stiffened and shot a glance at the window, where the

gap in the curtain revealed Mrs. Gagnon pacing the front porch with a feverish panic.

"Don't worry about that brute." The doctor surprised us both by speaking. "Go on and tell the pretty lady how you ended up in this shape. This isn't the first time I've come here to fix up the farmhands." He fumbled around in his bag as though searching for supplies.

Hazel swallowed hard as a shadow darkened the window, and Mrs. Gagnon pressed her forehead against the glass. "She threw me in the cellar," Hazel said through lips that barely moved.

I angled my back to the window and bent as if aiding the doctor. "Why?"

"'Cause I accused the new mister of 'urting Nora."

My brow furrowed. "How?"

A tear slid down her cheek. "In ways unspeakable."

I tensed, and I pondered what she could possibly mean. A daunting thought came. "You don't mean…"

"Yes," she said without hesitation.

"You saw him?"

"No, but she told me when I found 'er the first time…" Her voice drifted.

I felt physically ill. The doc and I exchanged a look, and his lips compressed, but he said nothing.

"And you? Or the other children that reside here? Has he harmed them in this way?"

"Not that I know."

"But what about you?" I pressed.

"No. 'E tried to scare me, but I told 'im I make men's fings shrivel 'cause I got the disease, and 'e's stayed clear of me since."

The doctor gasped, and I stifled a horrified laugh at an uncomfortable situation.

"'E treats the lads and me the same as the missus does," she said bitterly. "Like we're less than 'uman."

"Do not despair. Miss Scott and I are trying to do what we can to help."

"Miss Scott? What does that old coot care 'bout the likes of us?"

"She cares very much. You must trust me."

"Trust? 'Cause of you and the institution, I'm in this place. You ain't 'elping children. You've made us slaves." She leveled me with an accusatory glare. "Do you know a girl by the name of Annie died here?"

My pulse raced. "What do you know of her?"

"So you do know." Her eyes flashed. "I should 'ave figured as much. You're all the same." Like a flower tucks in its petals before a storm, she angled her body away from me, shoulders slumping.

"I am not like Miss Keene or Mrs. Gagnon. I want to help."

"Sure you do," she sneered.

"We can't dally any longer, or Peggy will grow suspicious and send me off before we tend the girl," the doctor said. "We need to set this arm." He eyed Hazel. "You ready?"

Tears of panic glistened in her eyes, but her jaw set. "Get it over wif." Her hand tightened on mine, and although she deemed me the enemy, in this moment of needing comfort, she clung to me.

"Hold her good." The doctor nudged his head at me. "Best you look away." He looked over the rims of his glasses at Hazel.

She turned her head and squeezed her eyes tight shut. The popping sound and the wail from her made me jump.

"There we go." He stood back with a surprised expression, as though he couldn't believe what he had accomplished. "Good as new."

I frowned at him, flabbergasted that he still practiced.

The screen door squeaked, and Mrs. Gagnon's heavy treads entered. "It's time for you to leave." She scowled at me.

"Perhaps I can get a ride back to town with the doctor?" I said

"Roy is waiting in the car. He will take you," she said.

"If you don't mind—"

She huffed with impatience. "What is it now, Miss Appleton?"

"Can I use your outhouse?"

"If you must. But be warned, I'm watching you. Don't you get it in your head to venture off."

"I will be out of your hair shortly."

"I relish the moment." Sarcasm ran like poison from her tongue.

"If you don't mind directing me, I'll go and be on my way."

"It's out back, next to the barn." She pointed through the kitchen.

I nodded and hurried in the direction she had pointed.

As I exited the outhouse afterward, a voice hissed, "Miss Appleton."

"How did you get out here without Mrs. Gagnon seeing?" I said without moving.

"Neighbor showed up," Hazel said.

I glanced back at the house before circling the outhouse to find Hazel.

"Are you serious 'bout helping us?" She searched my face for assurance.

"Yes."

"But why?"

"Because I too was a home child."

"You?" Tears pooled in her eyes. "Then 'ow can you work at the institution? 'Ow can you stomach what 'appens to us?"

"I can't." My voice broke. "That is why I took the position. I wanted to help. I can't stop an organization and government that is bigger than me. I resolved myself to that. But I must do what I can to help."

She gripped her arm. "I won't last 'ere. You got to get me out. All of us."

"I'm trying. I promise you, I am." I stepped forward and wrapped my arms around her. "Don't lose hope. Stay alive, and be careful."

Her body trembled. "I can't do this. I can't. All I can fink of is me brother and what 'e is suffering. What if…" She choked on the words. "W-what if 'e is dead?"

"You mustn't think like that. You can't. Or it will be the end of you. I searched a lifetime for my sister, and fate saw that we were returned to each other. If you can't hold on to anything else, hold on to that." I stepped back and lifted her chin, peering into her eyes. "I won't abandon you, Hazel Winters. Know someone is out there who cares."

"When will you come back?"

"As soon as I can."

"Promise?"

I crossed my heart with a finger. "Now I have to go or that horrible woman will come looking for us both." I left her and hurried to join the others.

The doctor sat in the front seat while Mr. Tremblay leaned against the front of the car, smoking a cigarette, and as I strode past him, he exhaled smoke into my face.

"It will do you good to keep your nose out of our affairs." The threat in his dark eyes hurried my steps past him.

I took one last look at the house and eyed Mrs. Gagnon, who stood on the front steps, chatting with a woman wearing an oversized brown wool coat. The woman shot me a look but paid me no mind and swiftly returned to her conversation. Mrs. Gagnon continued her discussion, but her eyes never left me. The drapes in the living room moved, and I wondered who peeked from beyond, but not wanting to draw attention to them, I turned and climbed in to the backseat.

During the drive to town, I kept quiet while the doc drowned himself in a flask of whiskey. Mr. Tremblay kept an eye on me from the rearview mirror. I considered what I could do about his crimes against his niece. The law would see him as the innocent, not the child. They would insist on a psychiatric examination of Nora because of the common belief that women and children tend to fabricate stories of abuse. Nora, a child not more than eleven or twelve, would be deemed the wrongdoer. But regardless of my lack of faith in the justice system, I couldn't in good conscience not report what Hazel had told me. Fear of what my reporting would mean for Hazel and Nora stood at the forefront of my mind.

When we reached the town, Mr. Tremblay stopped the car outside a quaint little white house dirtied from passing car exhaust. The doctor held out his hand, and with a grumble, Mr. Tremblay pulled out his wallet and slapped some cash into his hand.

"Now out with you both," he said.

From the sidewalk, I watched the car until it disappeared before turning back to the doctor.

"Come on, you wretched thing. Get out of there." He shooed away an orange tabby cat using a flowerbed to relieve itself. The cat darted past me, and the doc strode to the steps and placed a hand on the rail. He had made it one tread before I raced to him.

"Here, let me help you." I circled his waist and smiled at him.

He grunted. "Thank you kindly, little missy. These legs of mine aren't what they used to be."

At the door, I released him. "I can take it from here," he said.

"I must know," I started, and he laughed.

"How did I know you were going to put the questions to me?"

"I saw your reaction when Hazel mentioned Annie. You knew the girl?"

"I did." He lowered his head.

"What happened to her?"

He glanced at passersby and removed the whiskey flask from his bag and took a big swig before opening the door and standing back. "It's best you come inside."

My pulse raced as dread rushed through me.

Inside, we sat in the small kitchen decorated in green and red-tulip wallpaper, an older design featured in the Sears Roebuck catalog. The scent of freshly baked pie hung in the air, and I spotted one on the counter.

"Just finished baking that before the Gagnon fellow showed up. Do you care to join me for a slice? It's peach."

Usually the temptation would make my mouth water, but I didn't think my stomach could handle anything at the moment. However, I hoped to get information from him, and perhaps sharing a slice of pie would ease his tongue. "I'd love a piece."

He smiled with delight. "I will put the kettle on."

After we sat at the table with pie and a cup of tea before us, I asked again, "Please, tell me what you know."

He twisted the fork lying next to his plate, and after a long moment, he said, "I've been a doctor around these parts for most of my life. I've known the Gagnons just as long. Samuel was a decent man, but he never had the backbone to stand up to his wife. Since they started taking in home children over the years,

I've visited their farm on a few occasions. Usually to fix a broken bone or dislocated shoulder like young Hazel. One evening, Samuel showed up here in a panic, said one of the home children needed tending. I went with him. He was sweating real bad and drove like all hell chased at his heels. When we arrived at the farm, I was shown to the barn where a young girl lay on a bed of hay. I guessed her to be around eight or so, but later found out she was fourteen. The girl was emaciated, and the foul stench of feces and urine rising from her clothing had me racing from the barn to release my stomach."

His trembling hand rattled the fork, and as though overcome with emotion, he stood and shuffled to the cupboard and removed a whiskey bottle. He downed a gulp followed by another before returning. He plopped down on his chair with a grunt and laid his cane across the table. "I tended the girl the best I could and instructed Peggy to give her broth and something of substance."

I digested the heinous way Annie had died. We had failed her. I had failed her. Guilt stormed through me, and tears welled. "But why send for you at all?"

"It wasn't her that sent for me. Samuel did that on his own."

"Did you report your findings to the authorities?"

"I did," he said.

"And?"

He shrugged. "From the backlash I received from the townies, I suppose they sent someone."

"You never inquired?" Judgment rang strong in my tone.

He narrowed his eyes. "Why would I go to the effort to report it if I wasn't going to follow up?"

I bowed my head. "I'm sorry. I suppose I'm a little emotional about the whole situation and feel at a loss."

"I know folks around here see me as a washed-up drunk, but

I did what I could to help that girl. I returned to the Gagnon's farm a few days later, then again the next day, but Peggy met me on the front step with a shotgun and said I didn't need to come no more because the girl was dead." He lifted the whiskey bottle and chugged. "Each day, I'm haunted by that child. I should have carried her out of there that day. I failed her, you know." His voice broke, and his watery eyes held mine. "I was her one hope."

I gulped back the emotions clotting my throat. His hand trembled on the bottle, and I encased his with mine. "I'm sorry for judging you. It's obvious that you care."

"Just an old man's guilt, I suppose." He lifted a napkin and patted his eyes. "After that, Peggy never requested my services. Many bad people walk this world, and she and her brother are some of the worst. People are scared of her in this town." He focused his eyes on me. "Don't believe I ever saw anyone stand up to her like you did today." A gleam of admiration shone in his glazed eyes. "You are small but mighty in spirit."

"I don't feel so mighty, and when I report what Hazel said about Nora and Mr. Tremblay—"

"Report? Have you lost your mind?" he said.

"Pardon me?" I gawked at him.

"Some folks around here may believe what you have to say, but no one will help. You are a lone fish in a sea of denial. Folks prefer to turn a blind eye to the situation. You will be picked apart, and in the end, they will label you as crazy. Tell me, are you ready to face that?"

"I wouldn't be able to live with myself if I didn't."

"I didn't pin you as a fool. Well, maybe at first when you had the nerve to face off with Peggy, but you must know you'll put Hazel in danger if you report Mr. Tremblay. Peggy will know she said something."

"But, in good conscience, to walk away knowing what Mrs. Gagnon and Mr. Tremblay are capable of...I won't stand by and see injustice come to those children."

"Understandably admirable, but no amount of courage you may possess can withstand a government-run organization or the abuse young Nora endures. The law does not take these types of things seriously," he said.

My shoulders slumped with the truth of his statement. Could I risk Hazel's safety to protect Nora? Was one child's well-being more important than the next? I might have sealed my fate at the receiving home if Mrs. Gagnon decided to call Miss Keene and report my visit. Not to mention I had struck the woman. *What were you thinking?* I chastised myself for my idiocy. *Well done, Charlotte. You planned that out brilliantly.* My hands balled in my lap.

"I heard what you said to the girl. You were one of the poor bastards too?" the doc said.

"That's right."

He gestured at me. "I take it that is what drives you to help."

"Yes."

We continued to talk a while longer. I shared about Ellie and me and our arrival in Canada. He told me about the love of his life, who had died twenty years earlier. When I looked at the time some time later, I pushed back my chair and rose.

"I'd better get to the station. It was a pleasure to meet you, Doc." I held out a hand, and he regarded it before clasping it and giving it a vigorous and surprisingly firm shake.

"Name's Gilbert Wilson."

"Well, then, Dr. Wilson, I've enjoyed our time together, regardless of the situation that crossed our paths."

"Let's drop the formalities. We are basically friends after revealing our demons to each other." He chuckled pleasantly.

I smiled. "It does feel like it."

On the journey home, I thought of what had transpired and the information I carried. Defeat slumped my shoulders, and my heart felt heavy. I leaned my face against the train window, watching the countryside rush by. What was I to do? Tears came in floods. I wept for Ellie and me, for Hazel, William, Annie, and all the others that had been gathered from England's streets and shuffled around the world. The institutions had sold a vision to families of how their children would be better off, but it wasn't the case for most. We had suffered, and ingrained in us was an unimaginable shame, as if we were filthy and undeserving of a childhood or a life of substance.

Then Nora...what about her?

CHAPTER 28

Hazel

HOPE HAD BUOYED ME WITH MISS APPLETON'S PROMISE TO HELP, AND I felt guilt at my past treatment of her. I worried her pledge would fade like the seasons if she lost her job at the receiving home. After she'd left that day, the missus called Miss Keene, and guessing from the satisfied look on the sow's face afterward, I suspected it hadn't gone well for Miss Appleton.

"That's what I get for 'oping," I said to Herbert while changing his nappy. He looked at me oddly, as though trying to decipher what I said. The boy had grown on me. Unlike Joey, he was a solemn child with a demeanor like Nora. Where Joey had been chubby, Herbert was so ghastly thin, I could practically count his ribs. I often worried about him and mentioned his lack of weight gain, but the missus insisted he was fine. I had attempted a second time and told her the doctor who had fixed me up may have a solution for the boy. My concern for Herbert was genuine, but the doctor visiting was my one hope of finding out how Miss Appleton fared.

After I changed Herbert, I hoisted him on my hip and walked downstairs. In the sitting room, I put him on the floor to play with Joey. The missus and Mr. Tremblay had taken the twins into town with them to buy groceries and run errands. Nora had been extra sour that morning, and I wondered what troubled her. I would've asked her, but she had bundled up and gone for a walk.

At a rap on the back door, I ordered the boys to stay put and went to answer it. On the other side stood a red-faced Graham, with the collar of his threadbare coat rolled up to keep out the cold. Snow dusted his shoulders and hair, and I eyed the small sack he held in his hand.

"What ya got there?" I asked.

"My second set of clothes and a couple apples."

"What you be needing those for?" I looked past him to where the field lads stood in the yard with solemn faces.

He cleared his throat. "I'm leaving."

I snapped my gaze back to him. "Leaving? But..." My words faded. What had I thought would happen? Harvest season had come and gone, and Christmas was around the corner. He had stayed too long already.

He twisted to look at the lads, and agony played on his face. "Look out for them the best you can. All right?"

I nodded.

"But when your time comes, you got to leave."

I fought back the tears gathering in my throat.

"Well, I'll be off. Goodbye, Hazel." He leaned forward and planted a kiss on my cheek, then stepped back and offered a sad smile. "Who knows, maybe life will bring us together again someday."

"Maybe."

He crossed the porch and walked down the stairs. I pulled my cardigan tighter and followed after him, the cold biting through my stockings and thin cotton dress. The lads came forward to join us.

"Bye, Graham." Farley's expression revealed his struggle to stay composed, and emotions shook his voice, but he held out a hand. Graham clasped it and pulled the lad in for an embrace.

"You're the top lad now," he said. Farley acknowledged the title with a nod.

Graham moved on to Timmy and bent to regard the lad. "No tears, me mate. Everything will be all right."

"I wish you could take us with you."

"Come on, Timmy, it's hard enough for him. Don't place that on his shoulders too." Farley's tears surfaced and silently spilled.

"I wish I could too." Graham straightened and pulled the lad's head to his chest, placed a kiss on top of his hair, and gave his back a pat before walking to Emory. Timmy took to crying, and tears burned my eyes.

Emory had stood back, watching with his emotions tucked away. "Well?" Graham said with a half-smile. "You don't have anything for me? Not even a goodbye?" He jostled the lad's thin shoulders.

Emory snuck a peek at Timmy as Farley moved in to console the lad with an arm around his shoulders. He ducked his head and kicked at the dusting of snow with the tip of his boot. "I reckon it ain't gonna be easy around here without you. I suppose we're all gonna miss you."

"Come." Graham motioned to the other lads. They moved in, and he hugged them. "Stick together. And look out for each other. You're family."

"We will," Farley said, clearing the tears in his throat. He stepped back and squared his shoulders. "Now, you get going. I will see to the lads." Maturity governed Farley's every action that day, and I felt a keen sense of respect for him.

Graham released the lads. Tears glittered in his eyes as he turned, murmured one last goodbye, and strode across the yard.

The lads and I huddled together, regarding Graham as he walked down the drive. Timmy and Emory's sobs rose, and Farley looped his arms around their shoulders and pulled them close. I tucked my hand in the crook of Farley's arm, and he glanced at me. His jaw quivered, and I saw worry in his eyes. He stood firm and returned his gaze to the retreating back of the one who had been both older brother and friend.

As Graham's figure grew smaller in the distance, I considered the fear he had to have felt facing a world without a home or a family. What would happen to him? And what of the lads and me? What would life hold for us after we left the farm?

CHAPTER 29

Charlotte

"YOU MUST EAT SOMEFING." ELLIE LOWERED HERSELF INTO A chair across from me at the table. Frederick had gone to New York on business and left her in charge of looking out for me, but her days off had ended, and she had to return to the receiving home.

"I failed them." I stared into my mug of black coffee. "If only I hadn't been so impulsive."

"Nonsense. It wouldn't 'ave mattered. As soon as you involved yourself in 'azel's life outside of the 'ome, you jeopardized your job."

I looked her. "What would you have had me do?"

"I warned you what would 'appen if she found out," she said. "But I can't fault you. Your 'eart was in the right place." She scraped the last bite of scrambled eggs from her plate and popped it into her mouth.

I glanced at the untouched food on my plate. I'd lost my appetite, and each day I found it hard to get out of bed.

"I 'ave to catch my train." Ellie scraped back her chair and rose. "You going to be all right? Agnes 'as me scheduled to work through the weekend." Worry pleated her brow. "With Frederick not due back until Thursday, I don't like leaving you."

I waved a hand and forced a smile for her sake. "Don't worry about me. I will make do. I plan to tackle my Christmas shopping. Maybe we will have a proper Christmas this year, and make up for missed ones," I said with more cheeriness than I felt.

She smiled. "That sounds like a splendid idea, and it will be somefing to keep you busy."

"Yes." I stood and adjusted the tie of my pale pink silk robe. "There's no need to worry about me."

"All right, but unless you plan on catching your death in that when you drive me to the station, you better get dressed." She gestured at my robe. Ellie was the modest sort, never caring to own more than a couple interchangeable garments. She referred to my lingerie as impractical and fashioned for floozies.

After I dropped her off at the station, I drove to the department store that had displayed a beautiful cashmere cardigan that would look charming on Ellie. She would insist it was too grand, but I wanted more than anything to spoil her with the new addition to her wardrobe.

Leaving the store, I passed a girl and her mother and halted to take a second look. The girl bore a remarkable resemblance to Hazel. The mother frowned at my intense observation and hurried her daughter inside.

I returned to my car and sat behind the steering wheel, regarding the comings and goings of people. My mind pulled to Hazel and my promise to help her. I had also pledged to Frederick that I would stay away from the Gagnons' home until he returned. But nights of worrying undermined my commitment to my husband, and I started the engine and pulled out onto the street.

"I will observe from afar," I said as though trying to convince myself. I had spied on the Gagnons several times before and slipped away unnoticed. My mind made up, I turned the car around and drove toward the station.

Later that afternoon, I parked the rental car down the road

from the Gagnons' driveway. Overhead the sun blazed in the clear blue sky, appearing deceptively warm in the air's freezing temperature. The open countryside provided no protection from the wind whipping across the fields. By the time I reached the old maple tree that provided the best view of the home and backyard, cold nipped my toes through my winter boots.

I pulled my hat lower and hunkered down to watch the home. I counted three boys coming and going from the barn and yard. There was no sign of the older boy I had observed before. When the front door opened and Mr. Tremblay stepped onto the porch, I crouched back. He descended the stairs, walked to the car, and started it before clearing off the fresh layer of snow from the previous night. Soon he returned inside, and I watched the house's windows for movement, but most of the curtains hung closed. The living room drapes were open, but I was too far away to get a good look.

Fifteen minutes passed before Mr. Tremblay exited the house, and behind him, someone moved. I released a breath of relief when Hazel stepped into view and handed him a leather satchel. Was he going on a trip? Or leaving altogether? The bag wasn't large enough to hold all of one's belongings.

I waited until he drove down the drive before backtracking to the car. Once behind the wheel, I headed for town. Mr. Tremblay had a head start, and I didn't encounter him on the road. I returned the car and walked through town to the cafe to wait until the day's last train would arrive.

I sipped on a cup of rich black coffee and picked at a chicken sandwich, my thoughts occupied by the trip to the farm. Seeing Hazel and the boys had alleviated some of my concerns, but not seeing the older boy worried me. Frederick would be angry that I had broken my promise, but I had no choice. I couldn't go another day without knowing how the home children fared.

Lost in thought, I never noticed him come in until he placed an order with the cashier. My heart struck faster when I aligned the voice with the back of Mr. Tremblay. Glancing around for an escape but finding nowhere to go, I gathered my things and exited the cafe before he turned and spotted me. Avoiding the risk of walking by the front windows, I dashed down the alley, intending to circle around and return to the street.

Blood pumped in my ears as I hurried along. A black cat bolted in front of me, and I let out a yelp. After my heartbeat settled, I continued. I thought I heard footsteps behind me. I looked over my shoulder just as a hand covered my mouth, and someone gripped me from behind.

"Keep your mouth shut," my captor hissed in my ear. "What did we say about poking your nose in where it doesn't belong?"

I clawed at his hand and dug my heels into the ground as he hauled me backward.

No, no, no! my brain screamed as he dragged me behind a building where nothing but a field stretched beyond. Only then did he release me. He threw me to the ground, and I landed on my stomach, the wind knocked from me. I scrambled around to face my attacker as Mr. Tremblay lunged at me.

"No!" My cry reverberated across the fields. I put my hands up to block the first blow of his fist, but it caught my right cheek and reeled me backward. He landed another punch, followed by another, leaving me swaying and helpless. Warmth poured into my eyes and down my cheeks, and my senses faded in and out.

"You won't cause no more trouble. I'll see to it." Breathing heavily, again he lunged.

Pain racked my body as I tried to fight him off. He knelt over me, and the next blow stilled my struggles.

CHAPTER 30

Hazel

FROM WHAT I GATHERED, THE MISSUS WAS IN JEOPARDY OF LOSING THE farm. Mr. Tremblay's overnight journey to the city to speak to a fellow about a loan to help her keep the farm hadn't happened. He returned later that evening, and I hadn't been aware of his arrival until he strode downstairs, bathed and gleaming. The missus seemed distressed, but they never spoke about why he'd returned.

When I slipped back inside after taking the lads their meal, I overheard him talking to the missus in the kitchen as I continued toward the stairs.

"Good as dead, she is," he said.

His words stopped me at the bottom of the stairs. Who was dead?

"Did anyone see you?" The missus sounded nervous.

I ducked into the small landing at the bottom of the stairs and peeked around the corner. From that angle, I could see inside the kitchen. A grin plastered on his face, Mr. Tremblay sat at the table with his legs casually crossed. The missus sat with her back facing the doorway to the hallway.

"Don't think so. I grabbed her before she could let out a sound. They will find her if the crows don't first."

"You imbecile. Couldn't you have beaten her over the head and taken her away to let the beasts of the woods finish His will?"

"And risk being seen for sure?" he snapped. "I handled the

woman. And I ain't about to sit here and listen to your blabbering about how you've been chosen."

A shadow fell across the floor beside me from above, and my heart sprang into my throat as I whipped my head up to see Nora listening from the upstairs landing. She had gone to put the children to bed before I headed for the barn. She stood with her mouth open in disbelief. We exchanged a look of concern, then I returned my attention to the kitchen.

Missus thrust her hands toward the heavens. "May His Almighty hand protect us. May no more evildoers come."

"Oh, for God's sake, Peggy." Mr. Tremblay slammed a fist on the table, and the dishes clattered. "Enough."

"Tread carefully, brother." Her voice trembled with both warning and fear for his soul, as though he walked on sacred ground. He threw up a hand in exasperation, and the missus continued. "She should never have involved herself in the Lord's work. I failed Him." The missus's next words kicked me in the gut. "I guess being fired wasn't enough to stop her."

Miss Appleton. Horror washed through me. Dropping the pail, I gripped the banister to remain upright. Somewhere chairs scraped, but my head was spinning and I couldn't move. I heard thumping footsteps, and someone dashed by and shoved me back.

"Nora, what are you doing?"

The scent of the missus's rose perfume wafted ahead of her. From my position, I saw the two elongated shadows on the hallway linoleum.

"I've come to get a bite to eat," Nora said.

"But we've just eaten," her mum said.

"I'm extra hungry tonight."

One more step and the missus would spot me. I pressed farther into the landing's shadows.

"You will fatten up if you keep eating the way you've been lately. We can't afford another mouth to feed."

Nora snorted, and footsteps moved away.

I feared my legs would collapse as the previous conversation between the missus and her brother fully registered in my brain. They had to have been talking about Miss Appleton. Hot tears burned my eyes. She was dead, and it was all my fault. I bit down to stifle a wail.

"Where is that girl?"

I stiffened, grabbed the pail, and tiptoed to the back door.

"If I catch her whoring around with those field boys, she'll never leave that cellar."

"Mama," Nora gasped. "You're a churchgoing woman. Doesn't the Holy Book speak against killing?" Nora emphasized the last word, like a dagger making its mark.

"Watch your tongue, girl," the missus said. "The Lord put me here to help them. They are tarnished and beyond redemption with no place in heaven. They are to serve God's people. The girl is a fornicator. Did you not see how she tried to woo your daddy? I knew the devil's hold on her was strong from the day she stood before me at the receiving home. It's my duty to cleanse her of evil, so she can be pure and serve the righteous."

I opened the door and shut it firmly, and their voices turned to whispers. Taking a deep breath, I walked down the hallway and entered the kitchen. Avoiding their gazes, I marched to the counter and set the pail down. My hands shook more than usual as I gathered up the dirty dishes. My whole body felt tight with tension as I waited to be questioned. But no questions came.

The missus and her brother retired to the sitting room and chatted as though taking a life was no different than a normal trip to town. I washed the table and counters, forced to keep my emotions hidden while Mr. Tremblay observed me from his chair. Only after the missus had locked me up and I lay on my pallet of burlap sacks did I crumble.

CHAPTER 31

I FIGURED NORA'S DARK MOODS DERIVED FROM THE SICKNESS THAT seized her in the mornings. But as January came and went, then February, she continued to race to the outhouse. I noticed a change in her, but I couldn't grasp what. Then one day, clean clothes in hand, I climbed the stairs to her room and found the door open and her standing at the window with her back to me. When I knocked, she jumped and turned, her expression troubled.

"It's just me." Gesturing at the clothes, I entered and walked over to place them in the middle of the bed.

She peered at me, but as though looking through me.

Now I wouldn't have called us mates or anything, but we tolerated each other. "You all right?" I asked. "'E been keeping away from you?"

"Hazel," she said, ignoring my question about her uncle.

"Yeah?"

"If I tell you something, will you help me figure out how to tell Mama?"

"I'll try my best."

She gave a weary smile, then walked over and shut the door before turning to face me. Her eyes flitted around the room, and she wiped her palms on the fabric of her blue dress.

"What 'as you in such a reck?"

"I've seen it before."

"What?" I gawked at her with puzzlement.

"When the sickness came, I thought it would pass. But it's been months now. When Mama was pregnant with Joey…"

Her words faded, and bells went off in my head. I looked from her moving mouth to her stomach. She had put weight on and ate more often. Nausea roiled in my stomach. If she was pregnant, that meant her uncle was the father.

Nora's voice rose. "Are you listening?"

I gave my head a shake, saw the tears staining her cheeks and her panicked expression. "I'm listening. Maybe you're mistaken. Maybe it isn't what you fink." I didn't want it to be true. The horror of it all was…well…downright ghastly.

"I wish I was wrong, but there is no denying this." She lifted her dress, and I gasped at her protruding stomach. I felt the blood drain from my face, and the room began to spin.

A hand grabbed me. "I see you're shocked." Nora guided me to the bed, and we sat. I looked at her. My mouth opened, then snapped shut. She had turned thirteen last month. "I've had time to deal with the predicament I find myself in. But I fear what Mama will do. I need your help."

"Your mum got no use for me or anyfing I 'ave to say." I sat numb with my thoughts a jumbled mess. "Does 'e know?"

"No. I didn't want him to do away with me like he did that woman from the receiving home."

"Her name was Miss Appleton," I said. I had cried myself to sleep many nights over her death.

Nora flinched at the bite in my tone. "Yes, Miss Appleton. I meant no disrespect. Until you came here, I followed Mama like she was a prophet sent to Earth by God to show us the way. She had me believing it. And Annie…" she lowered her head "…her death didn't trouble me as it has this past year. Mama had me convinced she had the evil in her; that is why she took those fits."

"What kind of fits?"

"She would seize up and collapse to the ground, jerking all around with her eyes rolling back in her head. It was terribly frightening. Mama had the priest sprinkle her with holy water and attempted to cast her demons out, but it never worked. Then she took to thinking she would starve them out."

My hands knotted the quilt at the madness of the missus. I had seen attacks such as the ones Nora described, in a woman who lived in the slums. Mum had said she suffered from epilepsy.

"Your mum slips between reality and religious fanaticism. It sounds like Annie had epilepsy."

She swallowed hard. "Once my eyes opened to Mama's ways, I realized that."

"And this God of 'ers condones the raping of children?"

She winced and shrugged. "He makes sure he never comes to me when she is around. So it's my word against hers. My brothers and sisters are prisoners as much as you all are. But, unlike you all, we have no fond memories of a loving mother."

"But your daddy loved you."

She looked down at her hands folded in her lap, and sadness haloed her face. "Yes, and I miss him. But he was no match for her. I suppose he was under her conditioning too."

"What are you going to do 'bout the baby coming?"

"Mama may kill me—or the baby and me—when she finds out, and I can't hide it much longer. I have no one to help me, and I'm scared." She rubbed her stomach with affection, and I frowned. How could she love something created as the being inside her had been? She glanced at me; I saw vulnerability in her eyes. "Will you be there when I tell her? For support, I mean."

I nodded. She let out a yelp of glee and threw her arms around me, and we toppled backward.

"Thank you," she said.

I lay there awkwardly and patted her back once or twice before trying to sit up.

She pulled back and grinned sheepishly. "Sorry."

"It's all right." Aside from the hug Miss Appleton had given me behind the outhouse one day, it had been a long time since I had felt an affectionate touch.

Later that day, I stood in the kitchen peeling potatoes for the evening meal when Nora walked in and gave me a nervous look. I offered her a small smile of encouragement, and she nodded her appreciation. She looked at her mum, who had just returned from a neighboring farm.

The missus dropped into the rocker in the sitting room and bent to remove her shoes. She glanced at Nora as she walked into the room and straightened, chest heaving after the effort of bending over. "Come, girl—remove my shoes." She gestured.

Nora walked forward and knelt before her. I envisioned the gears in her brain turning as she chose how to approach the matter. "Mama, there is something I must speak to you about."

I held my breath.

The missus waved a hand of dismissal. "Not now, girl. I have a headache and need to lie down."

Nora glanced at the window behind the missus, where the lads and Mr. Tremblay were visible, out working the field. After a moment she regarded her mum and squared her shoulders. "What I have to say can't wait."

The missus arched a brow and regarded her daughter with annoyance. "Out with it then."

Nora rose and stood wringing her hands. "Well, you see—"

"No, I don't see. Get on with it." The missus eyed Joey and Herbert, who were sitting on the sofa, looking at picture books.

"I'm pregnant," Nora blurted.

The missus's head snapped back. "You're what?"

"I-I'm pregnant." Fear made Nora's voice tremble.

The missus looked dumbfounded. "H-how is that possible?"

"How do you think?" Nora's tone lacked all emotion.

"It's those field boys, isn't it?"

"Oh, for God's sake, Mama. You know very well who is responsible." Nora stomped her foot.

The missus bolted to her feet, and Nora took a step back. My heart pounded as I observed the missus's red face and her fingers flexing at her side. "No." The missus shook her head. "I won't listen to any more of your lies."

"Dammit, Mama!" Nora said, all her pain and anger surging forward. She glared at her mum with a look of pure disgust. "I'm sick of your denial. You claim to be a God-fearing woman, but you're a joke, and unfit to be a mother."

The missus lurched at her, and her hand's impact left an ugly red welt on Nora's face. She never cried out but cradled her cheek with her hand, and I suspected it was the ache in her heart, not pain, that brought forth tears. My throat thickened. Although I admired Nora's courage, I feared for her life at her mum's hands.

The missus turned away and paced the room, muttering under her breath. After a moment she stopped and regarded Nora, who stood trembling. Then her gaze dropped to the girl's stomach.

"How many months?"

Nora shrugged. "Maybe three or four. I'm not certain."

Hope expanded my chest. Maybe her mum would grant mercy.

The missus's jaw tightened. "You bring disgrace to this family. Frolicking with those heathens." She gestured toward the field. "This is what we get for trying to help them." Her lip curled with a snarl. "I won't give people something to talk about. No one can know."

"And how do you propose we hide it?" Nora threw her hands in the air.

"There are places for fallen women."

"Fallen women?" Nora said in disbelief.

"You heard me correctly. Tomorrow I will make arrangements to have you sent to a maternity home, where you will stay until the child is born. They will see the bastard is taken care of, then you will return home, and all will be well." She straightened to her full height, as though at ease with her decision.

Nora cradled her stomach. "But what if I don't want to give up the baby?"

The missus spun back to look at her, and again I feared for Nora's safety. "If it is true and a bastard grows within you, I will see it plucked from existence before I allow you to keep it. You are a wicked child, and I will see your sins are washed away, starting with Satan's seed within you."

"My sins?" Nora's laugh echoed loud and mocking. "Your brother raped me. Time and time again for years, and you knew but did nothing. Tell me, Mother, what line from the Good Book will you try to line up with your lunatic beliefs? If there is a God, I know one thing: He would disagree with your madness. It is this world that needs cleansing of *you*."

I gasped. Nora had gone too far.

The missus lunged at her, and she shielded herself from the blow, but her mum retracted her arm. Instead she grabbed Nora by the arm and hauled her toward the back door.

"The Bible says to obey your mother and father, and it's about time you learned it. Too high and mighty, you've been, and I ought to take the horsewhip to you. But as Mary Magdalene stood before her condemners and the Almighty showed mercy, I'm called to do the same."

The depths of the missus's derangement gripped me with fear for Nora's life.

"You're mad, I tell you. Mad!" Nora twisted and tried to reef her arm free. "Let go of me."

"You want to frolic with the help, then you will be treated no differently." They marched down the hall and out the back door.

From the kitchen window, I watched her storm across the yard, dragging Nora behind her. At the cellar, she opened the door and gestured for Nora to get in. Nora tried to pull away, but her mum pushed her forward. Nora's arms flailed, and my heart seized, but she caught herself.

"In, now!" The missus jabbed a finger at the opening.

Nora turned and walked down the steps and disappeared into the cellar. The missus slammed the door shut and padlocked it. Heart pounding and tears burning my eyes, I stepped away from the window.

Three days later, the missus drove Nora to the station and placed her on a train.

CHAPTER 32

ARCH BROUGHT A DEEP FREEZE, AND THE NIGHTS IN THE SHED became unbearable. The wind howled across the fields, blowing in drifts of snow. In the mornings, the field lads spent hours shoveling and picking away at ice build-up to open the barn and shed doors.

Early one Tuesday morning, while I waited for them to release me from the shed, I held the worn and cracked photograph of William. Since coming to the Gagnons, I had kept his image next to my heart to keep the one treasure I had in life from being discovered, and to hold him close. Between my shivering hands and numbed fingers, it took great concentration to stroke the image. I wondered how he had changed over the years, and if life had awarded him a good family, or if... My breathing caught. Did he still live? I pressed the photograph to my lips before tucking it between my binding and breasts.

One of the lads pounded at the door, trying to free it from winter's grasp. I stood and pulled my wool coat tighter, thankful for the extra warmth it provided. I turned to gather my hat and noticed the strands of blonde hair on the sacks of my makeshift bed. Instinctively I lifted a hand and touched my bald patches. Malnourishment had wreaked havoc on the lads and me, and I feared we would not last much longer. Rations had been limited before, but with the missus's money troubles, she hoarded food for the family. After learning of Miss Appleton's murder, I concluded no help would come. My contract was up in the summer, and worry about leaving the lads behind plagued me. But my survival and finding my brother depended on me going.

"We'll have you outta there soon," Farley said.

"All right." I pulled the hat over my head.

The scraping of shovels continued.

"Stand back, lads. I need to put some shoulder into it," Farley said.

Someone banged against the door, and it sprang open to reveal the reddened faces of Timmy, Emory, and Farley.

"Morning," I said. "'Ow did you all fare last night?"

"We're still alive, if that's what you're asking." Timmy pulled up the collar of his coat, seeking relief from the cold.

I glanced at Emory, who stood in the lads' shadows. We all looked a bit ragged and gaunt, but he seemed predominantly gray.

"We survived to live another day," Farley said. "Mighty glad to find the same with you."

I stepped into the daylight and turned to Emory. His auburn locks jutted out from beneath a dark wool cap. "You all right?" I placed a hand on his thin shoulder.

"Reckon as good as one can expect." He gave me a weary smile.

"Can't you sneak us some extra rations?" Timmy asked. "After us getting ill from eating the horses' grain and the missus locking it up, we can't hold up much longer. Take a gander at Emory. He's 'bout to drop where he stands."

The lads had taken to sneaking the grain in the barn, but mice droppings had caused them to become ill.

"I will try my best."

"You gotta do better than that," Farley said.

"I said I'll do my best." I turned and walked to the house.

Responsibility had been a burden I hadn't been able to shake most of my life. After Dad's death, I had become the sole care-giver for William while mum was away at the workhouse. And for the last years in the Gagnon household, I had also taken on the burden of ensuring nothing happened to the field lads. They had become like brothers to me. Worry had commanded my days since Graham left.

Graham's voice chanted in my head: *"When your time comes, you have to leave."* How would I find the strength to walk away? My heart was torn between the lads and the brother who had never strayed from my memories. How could I choose?

Later that morning, from the sitting room window, I watched Mr. Tremblay climb into the truck. He had mentioned heading to town to purchase some feed for the animals, but the missus had given him a disapproving look, and I knew he was off to his illegal doings. I frowned when Emory climbed in beside him.

When he returned before the evening meal, there was no sign of Emory, and my heart beat faster. Mr. Tremblay marched into the house and mopped his sweaty brow. His eyes flitted to the missus, who sat up from lazing on the sofa. "Get up."

Her brow puckered. "What is it?"

Panic or fear, I wasn't sure, gleamed in his eyes as he glanced at me. I looked away and continued sweeping the floors, but my ears were tuned to their conversation.

"Not in here. I need to show you something."

The missus scowled but heaved to her feet and followed him outside. I crept closer to the window, and through the webbing of frost, I spied on them from behind the drapes. They stood at the back of the truck, and Mr. Tremblay leaned forward and pulled back a tarp.

The missus's voice reached me. "What the hell happened?"

"It was an accident."

Panic seized my body, and I dropped the broom.

"An accident?" She sent a blow to the back of his head before turning her gaze toward the house. I ducked away from the window, my heart pounding in my ears. They spoke in hushed tones, and I strained to hear what they said.

"You imbecile!" She shoved him, and he tumbled back. "We don't need CAS out here again. If we don't have those boys to work our farmland, what will we do?"

"I'm sorry," he said.

"Sorry won't cut it this time." She paced and pressed her fingers to her forehead before coming to a stop. "Get him covered up and put the truck in the old barn, so none of the others discover what you've done. Later tonight, we'll bury the body after everyone is in bed."

He nodded and raced to the driver seat and climbed in.

I stood numb as the engine roared to life and the truck pulled away. *No.* I shook my head. *It can't be.*

At the sound of the screen door opening, I scurried from the window and gathered up the broom. I swept with steady, calm strokes while everything but calmness roiled within me.

The missus halted upon seeing me, as though she had forgotten I existed. She glanced back the way she'd come, and worry crossed her face before her permeant scowl returned. "Go on, girl—get out of my sight. The very sight of you makes me sick. And take them with you." She gestured at Joey and Herbert, who played in the room across the hall. The twins had bundled up and were in the backyard building a snow fort. When I hesitated a moment too long for her liking she swiped the air with a hand, looking to plow aside anyone in her path. "Now! Outside, all of you."

I placed the broom in a corner and raced from the room. "Come, lads." I held out my hands, and they scrambled to their feet. Joey sent a nervous glance at the sitting room where his mum paced, muttering to herself.

My hands shook more than usual as I dressed the lads in their warmer clothing. I tried to process what I had witnessed. Maybe Emory had stayed in town. But as I attempted to deceive myself into believing he was well and good, the daunting realization that the body under the tarp belonged to him dashed aside the thought. Why? Every part of me screamed at the madness, and horror enveloped me. Legs wobbling, I walked outside with Herbert perched on my hip and Joey's hand encased in mine. I gasped, releasing the breath I'd been holding, and the crisp air seized my lungs as I inhaled. Aimlessly I strode the yard, cursing the cold that nipped at my flesh and demonstrated that I did, in fact, breathe by clouding my exhalations. Tears blurred my vision, and I placed Herbert on the ground. He tottered to his sisters.

"Stay away," one of the girls said before leveling a cross look at me. "He'll ruin our fort."

Herbert stopped a few feet away from them, and they turned to continue building their fort. The lad stood watching with interest but never advancing.

"Joey, why don't you go play with 'erbert."

He firmly shook his head and clutched my hand tighter, as though sensing the turmoil inside me. I glanced back at the house before walking to the shed and ducking behind it, out of sight. Pressing my back against the wall, I slid to the ground. Nausea roiled my stomach, and it revolted. I straightened and used the back of my hand to wipe my mouth.

Joey knelt beside me with his big blue eyes observing me with concern. "You okay, girl?" He scooted closer.

His sweet face blurred in my endless tears, and I reached out, and without urging, he climbed into my lap. "Oh, Joey."

I buried my face into his neck, and he sat still, allowing me to soak up the comfort he had brought me in my time at the farm. "You're a good lad."

Against my chest, he bobbed his head in agreement.

"Hazel?" Farley's voice snapped my head up.

He crouched down and took Joey's small hand in his, and offered the lad a smile before turning his gaze on me.

"Somefing dreadful 'as 'appened," I said between hiccups.

He tensed. "What?"

"Em…" I couldn't say his name.

Farley's brow dipped. "Emory?"

I nodded.

"What about him?"

"I-I fink Mr. Tremblay killed 'im." Panicked sobs gathered as I spoke the truth aloud, and I removed Joey from my lap.

Farley staggered back, his face turned ashen. "No." He shook his head. "You're lying."

"Why would I lie 'bout somefing like that?" I leaned forward and punched him repeatedly on the shoulder.

He gasped and sat on the ground. No tears fell. He just sat there, stunned and unmoving for a dreadfully long time. Then he struck the ground with a fist. "Dammit!" Sobs racked his body, and a guttural sound came from the depths of his soul. "She will kill us all."

"That is why you need to be quiet." I scrambled to my feet and glanced around the corner of the shed, alert for prying eyes before turning back to him. "'E is in the back of the truck 'idden in the old barn. They plan to bury 'im tonight."

Farley composed himself and said, "The ground is like a block of ice. It would take days to dig a grave."

"I'm not sure what their intention is. When they set out, I will follow them."

"How do you intend to do that?"

"I'll need your help getting out of the shed."

"That's all well and good, but I'm going with you."

"No; it's too dangerous."

"He was my mate. We lay in that barn each night and dreamed of our life once we left this place. I will see his body is put to rest properly or die trying."

I looked at his determined face and realized I wouldn't convince him otherwise.

Later that night, after Timmy had fallen asleep, Farley slipped out and unlocked the shed.

"What took you so long?"

"Took forever for Timmy to drift off." Farley peered at me from behind the shield of hair that swept over his left eye.

I glanced at the sky, thankful for the clear night and the moon hanging like a lantern, spreading light across the farm.

At the sound of movement, I closed the shed door and we ducked out of sight. From our hiding place behind the woodpile, we spied on the house. Mr. Tremblay and the missus stepped outside, and we tensed.

Farley looked back at me as I tried to peek around his shoulder to get a better view, and through gritted teeth, said, "We should dig a hole and kick the two of them in it, for Annie and, if what you say is true, for Emory."

Footsteps crunched across the snow. Mr. Tremblay and the missus hurried to the dilapidated barn at the front of the property.

"Come on." Farley pulled me toward the house, and at the corner, we craned our necks to see what was going on. I squinted into the dark, but couldn't make out details, only the elongated shadows stretching across the ground. The beam of an electric torch shone, followed by the murmur of voices, but the barn sat too far away to catch what they were saying.

When they stepped inside, Farley grabbed my hand and we hurried across the yard. We hunkered down at the right side of the barn, and between the gaps of the exterior plank walls, we got an obstructed view inside.

"I've been thinking," Mr. Tremblay said. "We'll never get him in the ground until spring."

"What do you suppose we do, then?"

"Don't rightfully know."

"Well, it can't stay here," the missus growled. They fell silent, as though thinking of what to do. "I know. The old Carson farm has sat abandoned for years. We will dispose of the body in the well, and in the spring, you will fetch it and see that he is buried, so no one finds out."

"You've got to be joking! I'm not retrieving a decomposing corpse."

The missus strode forward and poked him hard in the chest. "You will so. It's because of you that we have to deal with this. If you hadn't frightened the boy, he wouldn't have fallen and cracked his head."

"Too timid, he was."

She waved a hand in annoyance. "I need all the help I can get around here. Now because of your carelessness we are down to two boys, and planting season is approaching. What do you expect me to do now?"

He shrugged. "We'll figure it out."

The missus balled her hands and anchored them on her meaty hips. "Like you intend to figure out your little mishap with the Appleton woman?"

At the mention of Miss Appleton, I froze. Then I leaned forward and pressed my face against the plank, as though a better look would enable better hearing.

"I'll figure that out too."

Figure out what? Miss Appleton was dead, and no bobbies had come for him. He'd gotten away with her murder like he would Emory's.

A sob caught in my throat, and a soft moan escaped. The pair whirled, and the missus shone the torch in our direction. Farley pulled my head to the ground, and we lay there, breathing in each other's air. Squeezing my eyes shut, I tried to quell the thrashing of my heart.

"Did you hear something?" the missus said.

"Probably just a critter."

The pair turned back to the task at hand.

"This had better be the last of your mishaps because I don't need anyone poking their noses around here. I've more important matters to deal with, like losing this farm."

"Yes, Peggy," he grumbled. "Get in the truck, and let's get this over with."

The missus waddled to the truck and climbed in to the passenger seat while her brother strode to the barn doors and pushed them open.

At the sound of advancing footsteps, Farley and I glanced behind us to find Timmy. Farley reached out and pulled him to the ground. "What are you doing 'ere?" he hissed.

Wide-eyed, the lad peered back at him. "I woke up to find you gone."

At the roar of an engine, Farley pulled Timmy closer. "Get down." We melded into the shadows of the barn as the truck came into sight and stopped. From her seat, the missus looked in our direction and squinted as though spotting us. Mr. Tremblay opened the truck door, jumped out, and hurried to seal the barn before darting back. The missus's gaze turned to him, and the truck started moving. After the vehicle turned down the drive and drove out of sight, we sat up, and Farley released his grip on Timmy.

Farley's eyes narrowed. "Murdering bastards."

I jabbed him in the ribs, and he let out a yelp. "What was..." His words trailed off when I nudged my head at Timmy. "What are you doing here?" he asked.

"Ain't your ears working? I told you. I awoke, and you were gone. Spotted a light coming from this old place and thought you and Emory were playing a trick on me after he didn't come back from town. Figured if Mrs. Gagnon caught you two messing around, we'd all be punished. And I ain't about to be punished 'cause of you two blokes. Never expected to find Hazel here." He looked from Farley to me. "What you doing here, anyway? And where is Emory?"

I peered past him to Farley.

Timmy's brow furrowed. "Come on, what you keeping from me?"

Farley pulled to his feet, and without speaking, started walking back in the direction of the barn.

"Are ya going to answer me?" Timmy jumped to his feet and chased on his heels, and I followed. "Where is Emory?" The lad tried again.

"I don't think we will be seeing him anymore," Farley said.

"Why not?"

"'Cause, well..." Farley glanced over Timmy's head at me.

"C-Cause Mr. Tremblay took 'im to the receiving 'ome," I rushed to say. Farley gawked at me. "You know the Gagnons are 'aving money trouble, and can't feed us all, so they returned 'im."

"But I never got to say goodbye." Timmy halted, and his lip quivered.

Farley draped an arm around the younger lad's shoulders. "I'm sorry 'bout that, mate. But at least now he has a fighting chance. Think of him as if he's in a better place."

Again Farley's and my gazes met.

Timmy's shoulders slumped. "Let's hope his next family is better." As though the news had sucked the life from him, the lad walked slowly to the barn and disappeared inside.

I stared after him, my thoughts turning to an eerie consideration. Had the Gagnons taken on home children before the lads and Annie? If so, how many unmarked graves lay on their property? How many young souls cried out for justice? I wrapped my arms around myself to rub away the chill racing up and down my spine.

"We won't survive to leave this place." Farley's haunting words jerked me from my thoughts. "We ought to kill them all while they sleep, before we also lie at the bottom of a well."

I gasped.

He scoffed at my horror and shrugged. "What?"

"Stop it. Don't speak like that. We ain't murderers."

"We could be gone before anyone found out," he said, as though giving it serious consideration.

I gripped his arm. "Farley, what you speak is madness. We ain't like them."

"Easy for you to say. You're leaving in a few months. Timmy and I got some years yet. Hope of a way out ain't looking so promising." He kicked at the ground. "If I could end them all, I would. Burn the house down while they sleep."

I gripped his arm tighter and gave him a rough shake. "And punish the children for the missus and Mr. Tremblay's crimes? No, I won't allow it."

He thrust his hands deep into his pockets, and the fields summoned his gaze. "It's what they deserve for what they did to Emory. He didn't deserve to die. He was just a kid." Tears cracked his voice. "Our country disposed of us as though we were nothing. We were dead before they placed us on the ships to travel across the ocean to a land of *promise*." He laughed bitterly. "A land of starvation and death is more like it." He heaved a sigh, and all the anger in his tone faded, replaced by defeat. "It's best you leave this place and never look back. Forget you were here. Perhaps, in that, you can find a way to erase the nightmares. Although no amount of distance will erase the years enslaved in this place and how they've claimed our souls. A person hardly feels human anymore."

His words resonated with me. The last time I felt like a living, breathing person, I stood outside the Liverpool home gates with Mum and William. "I understand. Too many nights I've wished to end it all, but dying inside makes them the victors. They can only make us nobodies if we allow it." My words sounded empty even to me. "I won't allow them to take my spirit. I won't."

"I'm not an animal. I'm not!" Farley's shoulders shook as he gave way to sobs.

I stepped forward and wrapped my arms around his middle. He towered over me, but regardless, he sought comfort and returned my embrace.

"We will survive to tell our story," I said. And he cried that much harder.

If I didn't believe in something, I feared what would happen. So I fought to protect the ember inside me. The light that would keep my memories alive, and me anchored in my truth.

I was Hazel Winters from Liverpool—the daughter of Colleen and Alfred, and sister to William. I was somebody!

CHAPTER 33

Charlotte

MY EYES FLUTTERED OPEN, AND I PEERED UP AT A WHITE CEILING. A funny, unpleasant odor tickled my nose, and confusion fogged my brain. I took in the sterile room with pale green walls. Looking sideways, I saw a bed next to mine, and in it a motionless, dark-haired woman. An open door showed a corridor, where a reedy blonde nurse glanced at her watch before jotting on a clipboard.

I was in the hospital. What had happened to me? I tried to search my memories. All that came was a winter scene stained with crimson and pain—bone-jarring, unbelievable pain. The impact of a blow to the face and my head snapping sideways. The cold of the snow-covered ground against my cheek and the tall grass of a field that stretched out before me. A shadow hovering over me and a man's heavy breathing as he said, "You won't cause no trouble again. I'll see to it."

It all came rushing back. The Gagnons. My trip to the farm. I tried to sit up, but weakness pinned my body against the bed.

"Nurse," I said, but my words didn't lift above a whisper. My tongue felt thick, and my lips and mouth dry. "Nurse." I tried again, and heard only a croak. Still she didn't turn. Tears of frustration bloomed, and I looked at my hand, lying by my side on top of the white linens. I looked at the metal tray on a stand inches from the bed, then focused again on my hand. It felt like a foreign object attached to me. I willed it to move, but it lay motionless. Tears cascaded down my cheeks and tickled the curve of my neck. Concentrating on my fingers, I strained to move my index, and when there was a slight movement, hope buoyed. A flash at the door caught my attention, and my heart thudded. But the nurse turned and walked down the corridor, the clicking of her shoes echoing in her retreat. *No!* my brain screamed.

I returned my attention to my hand. Hours passed, and I thought of how worried Fredrick and Ellie must have been. How long had I been in the hospital? And what of Hazel? She would think I'd turned my back on her.

The nurse returned and pressed a hand to her chest when she found me staring back at her. "Oh, you're awake." A pleased smile split her long face. "I will be right back. I must fetch the doctor."

Before I could speak, she raced away and returned shortly, following behind a balding fellow who walked with a strange gait, as though stepping on the tips of his toes.

"Mrs. Taylor, I'm delighted you've decided to join us." His gray eyes gleamed as he strode to my bedside.

I opened my mouth to speak, but my voice came out as a squeak.

"Nurse, get her some water," he said.

Again she raced away and returned with a glass of water. She propped me up with pillows while the doctor checked my vitals. After several sips, I tried to speak.

"How long..." My eyes widened at the sound of my voice.

"It's been six months since you arrived," the nurse said.

"Who brought me?"

"We were told a farmer found you and took you to the town doctor. He and the farmer drove you to the city."

"My husband?"

"Upon his return from out of town, he and your sister visited every day for weeks, but you didn't show any sign of regaining consciousness, so they had to return to work. I told them I would inform them of any changes. Your sister visits on her days off, and your husband comes on Friday nights and Sunday mornings. I will have someone call him and inform him of your progress."

"Thank you," I said. "My hands—they don't work."

"After the brutal beating you received, you're lucky to be alive," the doctor said. "The local authorities will want to question you. But, for right now, I must check your muscles' response."

After a complete check over, he stood back with a troubled look. "It's as I feared. The nerve damage is severe. Perhaps I should wait until your husband arrives to give you the prognosis together."

Fear thumped in my chest. "No," I said with more firmness than intended, and he frowned. "I want to know now."

"Very well." He scratched his temple and regarded me cautiously. My heart hammered faster. "I'm afraid you may never walk again."

I stared at him, and all sounds around me blurred. The doctor's mouth moved, but his words were muffled. Tears clotted my throat. Never walk again? Had I heard him correctly? I looked to my legs and willed them to move. My head ached from my concentration, and when they refused to budge, tears of frustration fell.

"I wish I could give you better news." The doctor placed a hand on my shoulder, and I looked into eyes radiating sympathy.

It was then I cried. The nurse tried to soothe me.

"Please, leave me," I said.

"Certainly. Nurse Burns won't be far." The doctor bowed

his head and walked from the room with shoulders slumped forward in defeat.

After they were gone, I lay staring at the ceiling, allowing a ribbon of paint that had run and dried to seize my attention. Numbness, in the literal sense, controlled my mind and body. *I'm afraid you may never walk again.* The doctor's words repeated in my head. Life as I'd known it was over. The daunting realization of what that meant terrified me. How could Frederick love a cripple? I reflected on our lovemaking before he left, the last morning I'd seen him. I thought of our plans to have children. His desire to travel. All our dreams had vanished with my decision to visit the Gagnon farm. Tears of self-pity carried me away for a spell.

Then I thought of Annie and what she had suffered. Since Dr. Wilson had informed me of how she had died, I'd been tormented. I wanted to scream the injustice from every corner, but in doing so, I'd put Hazel's life in danger. I had fantasized about walking up to the farm and removing the children, but I had no authority. No amount of protest would save them. Behind prison bars, I would do no one any good. Were the past years all for nothing? I wanted to scoop up all the children and take them home, but another shipment would come, and another.

Exhaustion carried me into a restless sleep where I dreamed of Frederick in the arms of another.

Later, when I awoke, the sun had set, and light from the hallway spilled into the darkened room. I tuned in to the warmth gripping my hand, and it was then that I noticed him.

Frederick sat by my bed, holding my hand, his forehead pressed against my thigh as though praying. I tried to move my fingers in the hand he held and gasped when they responded.

Frederick stirred, and his gaze shot to me. He released my hand and stood, a look of relief and uncertainty on his face. He moved closer and leaned down and kissed my forehead before pressing his to mine. "I've missed you," he whispered.

I wanted to say the same, but the words caught in my throat. At my lack of response, he pulled back slightly and gazed into my eyes. "Appleton, you all right?"

I frowned at him. "What do you think?" I looked at my legs. A mixture of anger and frustration stirred in me. "I'm a cripple."

He winced. "Don't say it like that."

"What; for your sake or mine?" My voice sounded lifeless and hollow.

"I know this is hard. We will figure it out."

"And how do you suppose we do that?"

He straightened, laid his hand on my arm, and gently stroked it. "Our love will see us through."

I laughed, spewing all the hopelessness churning inside me. "Love won't heal my legs. Love won't return fading dreams." Tears shook my voice. I balled the bedsheet in my hand and pulled. "What good am I as a cripple? I can't be a wife or a mother."

"Sure you can. Others have. Together we will figure it out and learn to deal with what comes."

"Together." I turned my eyes on him. "You plan to be strapped to a cripple all your life? No, I won't do that to you."

The good-natured man I'd always known vanished, and his eyes flashed. "You are talking about my wife. Crippled or not, she is my wife and the woman I promised to spend a lifetime loving, come what may. Am I to think that if it were I in that bed, you would abandon me?"

I gasped, taken aback by his response. "No, of course not. How could you think that? I would never—"

"Then why would you accuse me? Am I less of a person, that I would walk away?"

"No." My body trembled. "It's not fair to you."

"Like it's fair to you." He swiped a hand through his hair.

"I brought this on myself. I didn't listen to you, and I involved—"

"Stop it." I jerked at his reply, and he softened his next words. "Your heart wouldn't allow you to forget the girl. There is no crime in that. More than legs that work, or a body more perfect than any I've ever seen, it is your heart I love. And only you can change that."

I shut my eyes to squeeze off tears. He was right, but guilt weighed heavily on me. He deserved more.

"Charlotte?" he said.

At his use of my first name, I opened my eyes. Misery twisted at my very soul.

He lowered himself onto the edge of the bed and lifted his fingers to tuck a piece of hair behind my ear. "I love you. You must know that."

"I do, but I fear your loyalty will keep you by my side."

"My parents taught me that loyalty was admirable. Now you seek to punish me for it," he said with amusement.

I smiled, appreciating his attempt to make light of the cloud of doom and uncertainty that overshadowed us. "No, it's just—"

He placed a finger to my lips. "Don't push me away. We will get through this. And we will seek justice for the ones responsible."

I shuddered as I recalled the dangerous glint in Mr. Tremblay's eyes and the pain of his first blow. "He wanted me dead. He said so himself."

"Who was it?"

"Mr. Tremblay. I was in a cafe when he came in, and I slipped out before he could see me. Or so I thought. But he caught up with me in the alley. The doctor said a farmer and the country doctor brought me in."

"We figured the Gagnons were responsible."

"We?"

"Dr. Wilson. He informed the staff to have me call him when I arrived. It appears you have made quite the impression on the doc."

The mention of the doctor who had set Hazel's arm and shared his story over a slice of pie made my eyes tear up.

Uncontrollable shaking rattled my jaw as the whole nightmare unraveled before me. Frederick removed his coat and lay down beside me, his arm resting on the bed above my head. The warmth of his body provided much-needed comfort.

"I love you, Appleton."

"I love you too." I turned my face into his chest and inhaled, pulling on his love and strength to face what lay ahead.

CHAPTER 34

S PRING ARRIVED, AND NEW LIFE SPROUTED FROM EVERY CORNER OF the farm while death hung heavy in the minds of the field lads and me. The bobbies came for Mr. Tremblay one Sunday morning in late May while the missus attended service. I wasn't sure which of his crimes caught up with him, but a sense of justice for Emory and Miss Appleton dampened my eyes as I stood on the front porch staring into the cloud of dust from the retreating paddy wagon.

The changes looming in the weeks and months to come stood at the forefront of everyone's thoughts. The bank had foreclosed on the farm. At summer's end, the missus and her children would move to an apartment in town. The missus had no choice but to breach her contract on the field lads and contacted the receiving home where she had gotten them. They had arranged to send someone to retrieve the lads and were scheduled to arrive in the next few weeks.

As my eighteenth birthday approached, I worried about where I would go once I ventured out on my own.

"Should be the missus in there too," I said to Farley, who stood at the corner of the house watching the paddy wagon until it disappeared.

"No justice can undo what they've done. It won't bring back the dead," he said.

I glanced at him. The slightest breeze could topple him over, but it wasn't his gauntness that troubled me, but the fragility of his mind. He had changed after Emory's death. All life had left his eyes, and I believed he existed only because life had not granted him mercy by taking him.

My attention went to the weight of the brown paper bag I clutched in my hand. The blue-eyed bobby's brow had wrinkled with concern when he spotted me, a look he had turned on Farley, too. The man had walked back to his vehicle before returning with the bag. "Take this," he had said. "My wife makes the best chicken salad sandwiches you ever put your lips on." I had snatched the bag from his hand without hesitation before mumbling my gratitude.

When the vehicle had driven down the drive, he cast one last look back before I assumed he pushed us from his mind, like all visitors who had come before him. No one had shown concern for the fate that would certainly befall us. Each day that passed was detrimental to our survival. Were we so dispensable? Those who had come and gone throughout the years had viewed us as no more than machines to work their fields or slaves to run their homes. It had been close to three years since I had seen farther than the property line. How many children worked in the fields and attended the families of the surrounding farms? Had the mentality of those in the Canadian and British governments extended to the minds of all citizens in the blasted country? I concluded that was why no one had bothered to inquire about the condition of the children enslaved to the Gagnons.

I descended the steps. "Come. The missus won't be 'ome for another 'our. Let's find Timmy and sit for a spell."

In the barn, we found Timmy mucking out the stalls. He was almost thirteen, but malnourishment made him look closer to ten.

"What ya got there?" He nodded toward the brown paper bag.

"Come and let's see," I said with a small smile.

We exited the barn and sat under one of the maple trees to keep an eye on the drive and the missus's arrival. I opened the bag and removed the parchment-wrapped sandwich and an apple.

Timmy's eyes widened. "Who did you nick that from?"

"One of the bizzies who came for Mr. Tremblay gave it to her," Farley said.

"He's really gone?" Timmy asked.

I divided the sandwich into equal parts and handed them each a piece. "It's the last we'll be seeing of 'im."

"Don't matter none anyway," Farley said. "Our days here are numbered. And I'm mighty glad about it."

Timmy grabbed his portion, and without pause, gnawed off a hunk. He moaned with pleasure, and between chews, said, "Blimey. It's the bes' thing I've eaten in years."

I relished the delight on his face. I thought of William and wondered about the state of his existence. Did hunger gnaw at his belly too?

Farley's harsh expression softened with the same pleasure as he took his first bite.

I sank my teeth into the sandwich. The airiness of the fresh bread, the creaminess of the mayonnaise, and the peppery flavor of tarragon delighted my taste buds, conjuring memories of the decadent Sunday dinners Mum had prepared before life had taken a turn for the worse. Tears of gratitude gathered. The lads and I would live to see another sunrise, only to anticipate what lay beyond the horizon of tomorrow. The richness and heaviness of the sandwich stirred my gut with nausea, and I clenched my teeth to keep it down.

Timmy had eaten his last bite when he moaned and rubbed at his middle. "I ain't feeling so good."

"Try to..." I forced back a gag "...keep it down."

But our hollow stomachs revolted against the food, and I turned as it erupted, and the lads followed.

"Well, that's a bloody shame." Timmy wiped his mouth with a sleeve.

"Is it?" Farley said. "Food will only prolong the inevitable."

Timmy kicked him in the shin, and he let out a yelp. "What the hell did you do that for?" Farley looked as though he wanted to pummel the lad.

"Nothing you didn't deserve," Timmy said with a scowl. "You'd think sour-faced Nora had returned, with how you been carrying on lately."

As quick as Farley's anger had surfaced, it vanished. "Forgive me, mate. This here life ain't easy. I reckon it's gonna get that much harder once they return us to the home. I want you to prepare for what's coming."

Timmy picked at a blade of grass. "You're worried they'll separate us."

Farley nodded.

"I expect it," Timmy said as though he had already given it much consideration and had resigned himself to the outcome.

Silence fell until Farley directed a question at me. "What you planning on doing once you leave this place?"

"Probably fixing to run off and find Graham, ain't ya." Timmy gave me a cheeky grin.

I pulled my knees to my chest and wrapped my arms around them. "Don't suppose I'll ever see 'im again."

"Probably forgot all 'bout us, he did," Timmy said sadly.

"I doubt that. You two ain't easy to forget." I gave him a gentle jab.

He grinned, then it faded. "I wonder what Emory is doing 'bout now?"

Farley and I exchanged a glance. "I'll tell ya one thing he

ain't doing, and that is starving to death. No, I reckon life ain't cruel enough to get him another home as merciless as the last. Probably a fat lad by now, he is. Lying in some field, twirling his thumbs and slacking off."

I laughed at the image and allowed myself to daydream of him alive and well-fed.

"Maybe he found himself a family to care for him, proper like." Yearning glistened in Timmy's eyes.

"I 'ope so," I said.

"I hope where we're headed next, they are better than the Gagnons." Timmy's shoulders drooped. "I'm happy to be leaving this place, but what if the next is worse than here? We will be alone, without our mates to watch out for us."

"You will make new mates." I tried my best to project hope, but what lay ahead for us all held so much uncertainty. The likelihood of me seeing them again after they left was slim. The world seemed like a place void of happiness, and the thought of treading through life alone seemed dreary and empty. But I had a plan, and that was to find William. The daunting task seemed implausible, but I would not stop until I held my brother again.

It took everything in me not to crumble the day the gentleman from the distributing home came for Farley and Timmy. Not wanting the lads to appear too gaunt, the missus masked their condition by upping their rations a couple of weeks prior. Bathed, heads shorn, and dressed in newer second-hand clothing, they gleamed on that day.

I walked to the barn and informed them that the gentleman had arrived.

"Reckon this is it." Farley dipped his head to hide gathering tears.

I tried to smile, but I couldn't find joy amidst the melancholy shrouding my soul. I would miss them terribly and worried my-self sick over what would happen to them.

Timmy stepped forward and embraced me. "I reckon if I had me a sister, I would want her to be like you."

Tears caught in my throat, and I wrapped my arms around him, craving the tenderness of human touch. *You must be strong*, I told myself. *Don't let them see you cry.* I patted his back and stepped back, gripping his narrow shoulders. "Mighty kind of you. You will always be me brothers." I looked from him to Farley, who stood aloof and at a distance. My gaze lingered as I wondered what ran through his mind.

"Don't worry 'bout him. He ain't much for emotions," Timmy said with a snort. He strode to the clean stall the lads slept in and retrieved a small sack, which he slung over his shoulder.

"Well, I suppose we bes' get going," Farley said, avoiding eye contact.

We walked to the house where the gentlemen and the mis-sus waited on the front porch.

The dark-haired bloke pushed to his feet from the rocker. "Good day, gentlemen." He eyed the boys with a warm smile.

"Good day, sir," Timmy said with a hint of cheerfulness. I suppose any place seemed brighter than what we had endured at the Gagnons'. When Farley didn't greet the man, Timmy jabbed him in the ribs, and Farley groaned before mumbling a hello.

He descended the stairs. "We have a train to catch. Let's be on our way." He capped Timmy's shoulder with a hand, and the lad flinched from his touch. The man's brow furrowed, but he re-moved his hand and took a few steps back, and Timmy's tension eased. He gestured toward the car. "Shall we?" Timmy nodded.

The fellow seemed pleasant enough, and I glanced at the missus as she stepped inside the house. Before she could return, I approached the man.

"Sir?"

He halted and turned to face me. "Yes?"

"Where are you taking the lads?"

He looked puzzled at my question, but he said, "They will go to the Fegan Distributing Home in the city."

"Is that where all lads go?" My heart raced.

"One of them." The groove between his brows deepened. "You are an inquisitive one, aren't you?"

I glanced over my shoulder, expecting the missus any minute, and urgency pushed me forward. "Do you know a lad named William? William Winters. 'E would be nine or so."

"Is he a relative of yours?"

"Yes, sir. Me brother. We were separated 'bout three years ago now."

He looked deep in thought before shaking his head. "Sorry, young lady. I don't recognize the name."

His reply sucked the life out of me.

"A boy that young wouldn't last long at the receiving home. But put your mind at ease. My guess is a nice family probably adopted him," he said with a dashing smile. "Living a fine life, I bet."

"Let the fellow be on his way," the missus snapped, and I jumped and took a step back.

"Come," the man said to the lads.

"Bye, Hazel," Timmy said.

"Bye." I offered a small wave. Emotions erupted in my chest.

The man walked to the car and opened the door. Timmy and Farley trailed behind him. As Timmy climbed in, Farley turned to look at me. I lifted a hand to wave, but my chest tightened at the silent tears staining his cheeks.

"I won't forget you," he said.

"Nor I, you," I said.

He nodded and, sadness haloing his face, he climbed into the car.

I felt as if my heart fractured into a million pieces as the vehicle drove down the lane and out of sight. "May we meet again," I whispered.

CHAPTER 35

Charlotte

THE SMOLDERING AUGUST DAY STUCK THE FABRIC OF MY FRENCH blue batiste dress to my flesh. Frederick turned the car up the Gagnons' driveway, and nerves churned in my stomach. My release from the hospital had taken far too long. I had no idea about the conditions waiting for me. Dr. Wilson had informed me that the bank had foreclosed on the Gagnon farm, and in a few weeks the family would be forced to leave. He also told me that the field lads had been taken to a distributing home in the city. To set my mind at ease, he had inquired about Hazel's whereabouts, and a neighbor stated Mrs. Gagnon had one girl in her possession. Hazel's contract had ended yesterday. I worried we would be too late, and Mrs. Gagnon had sent her on her way.

I tapped my fingers on the door as though I could move us faster.

"For the love of God, Charlotte, stop." Ellie gave my shoulder a jab from the backseat.

"I'm sorry, but I've waited for so long to remove Hazel from the Gagnons."

"You don't know if the girl will accept your offer," Ellie said. "She may want to put as much distance between 'erself and all reminders of life after she landed in Canada."

"Maybe, but it's a chance I'm willing to take." I glanced down at my lifeless legs. Mr. Tremblay had been arrested for attempted murder while his sister remained free. Once Hazel was free of her grasp, I would report Annie's death and Mr. Tremblay's crimes against the Gagnon girl. I held little hope justice would be served, but I was resolute in my duty to the innocent.

Ellie had informed me last week of the upcoming closure of the receiving home and her need to secure a new job. She inquired about a position at Dr. Barnardo's Home in the city and had yet to receive word if they had chosen her.

As Frederick pulled to a stop in front of the house, Mrs. Gagnon stepped onto the porch and stood with her arms crossed. She appeared ready for a fight, and I squared my shoulders. I would take her on with or without the use of my legs. Her children filed out after her. Two identical girls stood to her left and two smaller boys to her right. Then a taller girl I recognized as Nora stood in the shadow of her mother's bulk.

Frederick exited the car and retrieved my wheelchair before opening my door and scooping me into his arms. "I'm right beside you," he said, and I figured he felt my trembling.

I smiled at him. How had I gotten so lucky, to have caught the eye of a man as fine as him?

He placed me in the wheelchair and pushed me toward the Gagnon woman and her brood.

"We meet again." Mrs. Gagnon's gaze roved over me, and her nostrils flared with disgust. "I wasn't expecting company."

I folded my hands in my lap, trying to conceal the tremors. "I've come for Hazel."

"Have ya now? Well, you're too late. She left here about two hours ago." She nudged her head at the driveway.

Someone gasped, and I looked at the faces before me, but no one revealed otherwise.

What? It can't be so. Tears burned my eyes. "We didn't see her on the road," I said.

A satisfied smirk registered on her face, and she widened her stance. "That's because she caught a ride with a neighbor. Probably on a train by now."

"With no money?"

"Oh, I'm sure she secured money one way or another. The girl can be quite persuasive with the menfolk. I've had my troubles with her always sneaking off to visit the field boys."

"That doesn't sound like Hazel."

"Satan disguises himself in many ways. It's up to the righteous to sniff out the wolves in sheep's clothing."

"Ain't that the truth," Frederick said under his breath.

"It's best that you get in your car and head back to town." Mrs. Gagnon dropped her arms and took a step forward, providing a clear view of Nora, who appeared to have been crying.

"Nora, are you all right?" I said.

She tensed and looked from her mother to me.

Mrs. Gagnon swung to look at the girl, who flinched and took a step back into the shadows of the porch. "Wipe your tears, girl. I ain't fixing to hear no more of your blatting."

The girl burst into weeping, and Mrs. Gagnon lifted her hand to swat her. Nora ducked, and her mother's hand missed her.

"That is quite enough." Frederick stepped from behind the wheelchair.

We tensed, and all eyes turned to him.

Mrs. Gagnon descended the stairs with more swiftness than I'd have thought possible. "I don't take kindly to people involving themselves in my business. For a few more weeks, this farm is my property. I'm giving you two minutes to remove yourselves, or I'll remove you myself."

"Is that so?" Frederick stretched to his full six feet and rolled back his shoulders, planting his feet. At that moment, I loved him more than ever, and gratitude for his support washed over me.

"I ain't scared of you or any other man." Mrs. Gagnon's upper lip curled, and she eyed him, from his mahogany brown Oxfords to his straw Panama hat. "You rich folk sure have an uppity air about ya. Thinking you can come out here and threaten poor folk."

"No one is threatening anyone," I said.

"And I don't intend to inflict fear. That is best left to you, ma'am." Frederick tipped the brim of his hat.

She flinched at his remark.

Frederick stepped closer to me and placed a hand on my shoulder. "You're lucky I don't take it out of your flesh for what you did to my wife, but I pride myself in being a gentleman, and I don't find pleasure in harming women and children."

Mrs. Gagnon opened her mouth to protest, but thinking better of it she pressed her lips together.

"Now if you will excuse us, we will be on our way," he said.

"Then off with you." Mrs. Gagnon brightened with triumph before her scowl returned.

Despair blanketed my shoulders as Frederick turned the wheelchair around, and tears raced over my cheeks. I was too late. How would I ever find Hazel now?

"Wait!"

I jerked at the cry, and Frederick swung my chair around as Nora bounded down the stairs.

Mrs. Gagnon spun and stood staring at the girl, who cast her an edgy look but advanced with determination. Nora clasped her hands in front of her. "She is here."

"Here?" I said, my heart thumping faster. "But…" I glanced at Mrs. Gagnon. Why would she lie about Hazel's whereabouts?

"Yes, in the shed. Mama told her to be gone within the hour."

"You good-for-nothing slut." Mrs. Gagnon lurched forward, and Nora bobbed under her arm and raced to my side.

Mrs. Gagnon stood for a dumbfounded second, staring after her, before turning and marching inside the house.

"We thought you were dead," Nora said urgently. "Hazel gave up all hope that anyone would come for her."

My heart soared, and I gripped Nora's arm. "Take us to her." She nodded.

"Charlotte!" Ellie called. I hadn't heard her get out of the car.

"Take another step, and you will wish you hadn't." Mrs. Gagnon's voice rang out.

My heart jumped when I looked beyond Nora to her mother, standing on the porch with a shotgun anchored against her shoulder.

"I warned you. This is my property."

Her sons began to cry, and the twins eyed her uneasily.

"We don't want any trouble," Frederick said. "Fetch the girl, and we will be on our way."

"I will not."

"Mama, please. What does it matter? She is leaving today," Nora said.

"And the sooner, the better," Mrs. Gagnon said.

"Please, ma'am, you are frightening the children." Frederick lifted a placating hand, trying to ease the tension of the situation.

She glanced at the boys as though sensing their distress for the first time. "Quiet!"

The boys jerked at her bellow, and the older of the two gripped his younger brother.

Mrs. Gagnon's attention returned to us.

"We are not leaving without Hazel," I said. "Do us both a favor and get her, and then we will leave."

She aimed the gun in the middle of my forehead, and a look of pleasure passed over her face. Frederick flinched, ready to step in to protect me.

"It's quite all right, darling." I lightly patted his hand on my shoulder, never letting my gaze leave Mrs. Gagnon's face. I worked to conceal the fear coursing through me.

After a moment, she said, "Brave or plain stupid, I haven't yet figured that out." She shook her head and lowered the gun. "I have no patience for this. Nora, go and fetch the girl."

"Yes, Mama." Nora darted around the side of the house and disappeared.

Relief charged through me, and with much anticipation I awaited the Hazel's arrival.

CHAPTER 36

SAT ON THE MAKESHIFT BED IN THE SHED. YESTERDAY I'D TURNED eighteen, and one would think I'd have raced away at the chance of making the Gagnons a distant memory. After all, hadn't I longed for the very day? Then why, when the missus told me to be gone by noon, had panic seized my chest? I had no money. No one to count on but myself. What waited for me beyond the barriers of the farm?

I stood and opened the suitcase I had arrived with and removed William's photo from its secure place next to my heart. I laid it on top of the threadbare navy dress from the home in the city. I closed the suitcase and buckled the leather straps.

The approach of racing footsteps turned my gaze toward the door, and I braced myself. When Nora's face appeared in the doorway, my tension eased. To think the sight of her had caused me great distress not two years prior. "Come to see me off, 'ave ya?" I lifted the suitcase.

Nora had given birth to a baby boy and returned a week after. Again she had changed. Giving birth had matured her. Perhaps it was the heartbreak of giving up the baby. She never spoke of it, but I often found her crying, and other times, staring at nothing, as if caught up in a painful memory.

"You've gotta come quick!" She clutched the doorframe, trying to catch her breath.

My heart jumped. "What's the problem? Are Joey and 'erbert all right?"

She waved a hand for me to hurry, and confused, I dashed forward. She gripped my arm and I stumbled into a run, trying to keep up with her.

"You're frightening me." My suitcase thumped against my hip as we charged across the yard. Weakness slowed my pace. "Please, slow down or I shall collapse right 'ere."

Nora slowed, but wrapped an arm around my waist for support and walked onward. "You must see for yourself, or you will never believe me."

We rounded the house, and when I saw her, I froze in my tracks. A gasp caught in my throat, and I dropped my suitcase. "Miss Appleton," I whispered. It couldn't be. She was dead. That was what Mr. Tremblay had said. I gawked at the pretty blonde woman in the fancy blue dress sitting in a wheelchair. Stationed at her side was a handsome, dark-haired bloke who took off his hat and dipped his head in greeting when I looked to him. Behind him by a black car stood a sour-faced Miss Scott. What were they doing here? Had they found William? What if they had come to give me news I didn't want to hear? What if...no, I couldn't think about it. I shook my head, dislodging troubling thoughts.

"Hello, Hazel." A smile gleamed on Miss Appleton's face— or the ghost of her, come to haunt me for causing her death.

In a fog, I looked to Joey, sitting quietly on the front steps with a solemn face. Next to him sat Herbert. On the porch, the missus stood holding a shotgun. What was happening? The twins positioned next to their mum eyed her and the people in the yard with uncertainty and fear.

"Hazel," the woman who sounded very much like Miss Appleton said, and I jerked when I realized the bloke had moved her closer, and she sat but a few feet away.

Leery, I eyed the ghost of Miss Appleton.

"This is my husband, Frederick Taylor. We have come for you."

So that was it. I took a step back. The dead had come for me. My mind spun to the graveyard in Liverpool and the golden trinket I had stolen so William might live. The dead showed no mercy, taunting me by sending Miss Appleton.

"Please, I have to find me brother. I can't—" I took a few steps back.

"And we will help you. Frederick and I would like to offer you a home."

A home? I studied the ghost before me. She seemed so real. Had the hallucinations that had come and gone over the last weeks returned?

Miss Appleton reached out a hand to touch me, and I lurched back. "Don't touch me." Shivers chased up and down my spine.

The ghost's brow puckered, and a look of hurt or rejection spread across its face. "Ellie warned me you may reject our offer, but I fooled myself into believing you would be happy."

Nora gripped my arm and spun me around. I gawked at her, my mind in a fog. She shook me hard enough to rattle my brain, and said, with a clenched jaw, "What has gotten into you? I thought you'd be delighted to see her. This is your chance to have a better life."

I stood there staring at her. Then a hard pinch to my forearm made me howl, and I rubbed the spot. "What was that for?" I glowered at Nora before looking past her to the woman and man.

"Are you okay?" Nora said for my ears only.

"I don't want to die."

"What are you talking about?"

I had eaten the meal Nora had snuck me earlier that morning. Sustenance for the road, she had said with a sad smile.

I cast another leery look at the man and woman, then leaned closer to Nora and whispered, "Miss Appleton's ghost has come for me."

Nora's mouth dropped open, and then she belted out laughter. "You fool. They aren't ghosts. I assure you they are very real. Living, breathing people. Watch." She strode past me and swiped a hand at the couple. Each lifted a hand to block her blow.

"But your uncle said she was dead."

"He left me for dead," the woman said. "But I survived and have been in a coma for several months. Then I spent the last while recovering."

I took a step closer. Miss Appleton held out a hand and turned it over for my inspection. I touched her palm and jerked my hand back when it felt real. I closed my fingers over her hand, and the warmth radiating from it summoned my gaze to hers. "You're real."

"As real as can be," she said with a warm smile, and clasped my hand between both of hers.

Tears of relief cascaded down my cheeks.

"As I said, we want to give you a home. I know we can never replace your real family, but we want to help. I know what it's like to wish someone cared. I recall the fear and panic about facing the world alone. It doesn't have to be the same for you."

"But me brother."

"I can't promise we will find him, but I promise you we will not rest until we've turned over every stone."

Hope soared, and I dared to believe her words. "But why? Why help me?"

"Because something was stolen from you. Your home, your youth, your family. I know I can never repair the wrongs inflicted on you, but I want to help in whatever way I can."

"Thank you," I said.

"So you agree?" She brightened. "You will accept my offer of a home where you will be loved and care for?"

"But me mum and brother."

"The door is always open for you to leave." She looked up at the man. "We have the means to search for your mother and brother. We will hire the best private investigator."

"But why me?" I asked between building sobs, overwhelmed and humbled by her offer.

"Because," she said, and looked to Miss Scott. "From the day I laid eyes on you at the receiving home, there was something about you that reminded me of my sister." Her watery gaze returned to me. "I felt a kindred spirit in you. It took me years to find my sister, but I believe life returned her to me for a reason. We won't stand by and do nothing. We feel called to help children like us. And you could be part of that. We could help reunite children with family. If we can save but a few, we would find justice. What do you say?"

I bobbed my head.

She clapped her hands in delight. "Splendid. Now, why don't you say your goodbyes and let's leave this place."

I looked at Nora, and she smiled through tears. "I'm happy for you," she said. "I will miss you, and for what it's worth, I'm sorry for the trouble I caused you."

"I know. Perhaps we will see each other again."

"I would like that." She gestured at Joey and Herbert. "My brothers will miss you terribly."

I gulped, sent a cautious look at Mrs. Gagnon, and moved to the front steps. Before the lads, I bent and clasped their hands.

"Do you got to leave?" Joey asked.

"I must." My heart broke. The Gagnon children were no better off than me, with the mum they had been cursed with.

"But why?" Herbert said.

"'Cause I need to find me brother."

"Take us with you." Tears gathered in Joey's eyes. "Please; we'll be good." He leaped forward and threw his arms around my neck, and I stumbled backward. "Don't leave us here."

"Joey, get off of her this instant," Mrs. Gagnon said.

"You the only mama I got," he whispered in my ear.

I swallowed hard, tears clutching at my chest. He would forget me. Time would see to that. "I'm sorry, but I 'ave to leave."

Mrs. Gagnon thundered down the stairs, and with one quick swipe, she reeled him back by the collar and held him dangling in the air.

"Let me go!" he wailed, kicking his legs. "I want to go with her. She's the only one that ever loved me."

Herbert cried, muffing his ears with his hands to block out what was happening around him.

I bit down hard to stifle a cry. My legs felt as though they would give out. Arms captured me and kept me upright. "It's best we leave now," the bloke's gentle voice strummed in my ear.

I glanced up at him and nodded, allowing him to guide me to the car where the stern-faced Miss Scott still stood.

"'Ello, 'azel." She tried a smile, an expression that never came easy to her.

"'Ello," I said.

"Hazel," Miss Appleton said, "I'd like you to meet my sister, Ellie."

I gawked from Miss Scott to Miss Appleton. Well, bloody hell! Who would have known? Their impossible reunion filled me with hope.

"You best get in before she turns crazy again." Miss Scott gestured at Mrs. Gagnon, who had descended from the porch. Miss Scott stepped back from the open door and motioned for me to climb into the backseat. I did, and she climbed in after me and shut the door. I sat clutching my suitcase and observing her hesitantly before my gaze returned to the Gagnons. I lowered my head at the lads' distress and picked at invisible lint on my dress, attempting to ease the sadness tightening my chest.

The chap opened the front door and placed Miss Appleton on the passenger seat. She looked at me and smiled, looking like she would burst with happiness. You would think she was the one who had spent the last years enslaved to the Gagnons.

Her husband placed the wheelchair in the trunk of the car before climbing in behind the steering wheel and closing his door.

"Hazel?" a soft voice said.

I glanced up to find Nora standing at my window. "Yeah?"

Her eyes pooled with tears. "Even if you couldn't stop him, thank you for trying."

"I wish I could have."

A sob escaped her. "I know."

I reached out, and she quickly clasped my hand. "You take care of yourself. And please, be kinder to the children. They need someone to love them. You're all they got."

Shamed painted her flesh red. "I will."

I took one last look at Joey and Herbert. They had been what had gotten me through the days. I wondered if the emotions twisting my heart were similar to what my mum had felt the day she left William and me. Guilt rose at the anger I had carried for her.

I released Nora's hand. Looking straight ahead, I said, "Sir, can we leave now?"

The bloke turned the car, and I rode down the drive and toward the life Miss Appleton had promised.

ABOUT THE AUTHOR

Naomi is a bestselling and award-winning author living in Northern Alberta. She loves to travel and her suitcase is always on standby awaiting her next adventure. Naomi's affinity for the Deep South and its history was cultivated during her childhood living in a Tennessee plantation house with six sisters. Her fascination with history and the resiliency of the human spirit to overcome obstacles are major inspirations for her writing and she is passionately devoted to creativity. In addition to writing fiction, her interests include interior design, cooking new recipes, and hosting dinner parties. Naomi is married to her high school sweetheart and she has two teenage children and two dogs named Ginger and Snaps.

Sign up for my newsletter: authornaomifinley.com/contact

Manufactured by Amazon.ca
Bolton, ON

19404307R00178